L … ATCHET

CW01648941

"With *Die Do* … ritten one of my favorite books of the ye … of my favorites. If novellas are the format of kings (and Kings), then this collection is a royal smorgasbord. Stories that are tight, toned, and genre-confounding . . . Love this goddamn book and hate it at the same time. How is a British dude a better observer and hybridizer of junk Americana than most American writers?" —Adam Cesare, author of *Tribesmen* and *Mercy House*

"The recipe for Adam Howe's *Die Dog or Eat the Hatchet* is:
Two parts Joe Lansdale
One part *Justified*
and a heavy dose of WTF
The result is a swampy cocktail darker than any backwoods hayride, stronger than the meanest Sasquatch, and crazier than anything you'll find chicken-fried at your local state fair."—Eryk Pruitt, author of *Hashtag* and *Dirtbags*

"Whether you call it Splatterpulp or Punk-Noir, *Die Dog* is an out-of-control '46 Mercury coupe heading hell-bent for Dead Man's Curve without brakes; a velvet-swathed lead slapjack to the base of the skull; a hard kick in the balls from a twisted, homicidal clown with giant shoes wrapped in razor-wire. It's an explicit, hard-hitting, twisted funhouse ride into pulpish horror wrapped loosely in a tattered skein of irreverent, jet black humor. In short, it's a freakin' blast."—Walt Hicks, author of *Dirge of the Forgotten.*

"Adam Howe's skill with hilarious dialogue makes reading *Damn Dirty Apes* a laugh-out-loud experience, keeping you turning pages until the end and eliciting snickers from memory long after the story's over. Filled with brutality, atmosphere, and surprising depth, it's an absurd tale that explores not just the American south's backwoods in all its sticky, smelly grandeur, but also the all-too human yearning for stardom, even greatness. Don't let the Society for the Preservation of the North American Skunk Ape (SPNASA) prevent you from reading it! . . . There's no safe place to hide in *Die Dog or Eat the Hatchet.* Once it gets started, the story sticks to you like flypaper, keeping you right there with shaking hands and widened eyes. Every page ratchets up the tension another notch even as it descends deeper and deeper into terrible darkness." —David Dubrow, author of *The Blessed Man and the Witch*

"Hilarious, repulsive, caustic and downright rad, these yarns run the gauntlet of a true reading experience. The only common thread amongst these tales is an overwhelming air of menace and the genuine threat that anything can happen, nobody is safe. Least of all you, the reader. Adam Howe is not for prudes or the faint of heart."—Zachary Walters @ *The Mouths of Madness Podcast*

"*Die Dog Or Eat The Hatchet* is like James M. Cain on a bender with Spinal Tap. One louder and then some."—Kent Gowran, founding editor *Shotgun Honey*

"A nasty little cracklin of Louisiana noir with a great classic pulp vibe." —Thomas Pluck, author of *Blade of Dishonor*

"Adam Howe has done it again—I've neglected my family, forgotten to eat, lost track of time in my quest to devour each word & nuance of *Die Dog or Eat The Hatchet.* He's delighted me at every turn while making the darkest recesses of my mind feel both alive & sullied all at the same time. Whatever you're reading at the moment, stop it immediately and read this RIGHT BLOODY NOW" —Zombie Rob @ *The Slaughtered Bird*

"A rancid broth of gross distortions, misrepresentations and half-truths, played for shock value and scatological humor . . . I cannot, in all good conscience, endorse this work." —Lambert Pogue, General Secretary, Society for the Preservation of the North American Skunk Ape (on *Damn Dirty Apes*)

"A nasty little cracklin of Louisiana noir with a great classic pulp vibe." —Thomas Pluck, author of *Blade of Dishonor* (on *Gator Bait*)

"From its brilliant opening Adam Howe's short n sharp novella *Gator Bait* grabs you by the throat and drags you through the down and dirty world of 1930s Louisiana. A sleazy piano player makes one mistake after another in this atmospheric, brutal and darkly comic noir tale. I loved it." —Paul D. Brazill, author of *Guns of Brixton*

"Adam Howe writes dirty stories populated with characters working like hell to leave a scum ring around the tub while they circle the drain. *Gator Bait* starts with mutilation and murder then shoves a rocket up its ass and goes south from there. Sticky, icky, pure pulp fun." —Jedidiah Ayres, author of *Peckerwood*

die dog or eat the HATCHET

ADAM HOWE

COMETPRESS
WWW.COMETPRESS.US

First Comet Press Trade Paperback Edition
November 2015

Die Dog or Eat the Hatchet copyright © 2015
by Adam Howe
All Rights Reserved.

This book is a work of fiction. People, places, events, and situations are the product of the author's imagination. Any resemblance to actual persons, living or dead, is purely coincidental.

No part of this book may be reproduced or transmitted in any form or by any electronic or mechanical means, including photocopying, recording or by any information storage and retrieval system, without the written permission of the publisher, except in the case of brief quotations embodied in critical articles and reviews.

ISBN 13: 978-1-936964-25-3

Visit Comet Press on the web at: www.cometpress.us
facebook.com/cometpress
twitter.com/cometpress

COMETPRESS
WWW.COMETPRESS.US

CONTENTS

FOREWORD

BY RANDY CHANDLER

My introduction to Adam Howe came by way of a porn-star dwarf with a humongous member. The well-endowed munchkin was named Rummy Rumsfeld, and his misadventures as portrayed in "Of Badgers & Porn Dwarfs" struck me with revelatory illumination in much the same way a Zen master smacks his student upside the head to impart nonverbal enlightenment. Rummy, of course, is a fictional character (though perhaps a doppelganger of a real-life diminutive porn star), whereas his creator is the real deal: a wily wizard of a storyteller we now know as Adam Howe.

But Adam Howe hasn't always gone by his given name. For reasons known only to himself, he used the pseudonym Garrett Addams when he won the *On Writing* contest judged by none other than Stephen King and was awarded the prize of having his winning short story "Jumper" included in later editions of King's slim nonfiction tome.

Writing under his own name since then, Adam Howe has crafted a handful of astonishingly eccentric stories and novellas, some of which were collected in *Black Cat Mojo,* including the aforementioned porn dwarf with the legendary talent—one of the most affecting tales I have ever had the pleasure of reading. For all its cringe-worthy explicitness, delivered with razor-sharp humor of blackest hue, the story ends with a surprising twist that tugs at the heart. Who knew such hardcore stuff could be so heartwarming? Not I, genital reader. But Adam Howe pulled it off (pun admittedly intended). And that was when I knew I was in the hands of a uniquely talented storyteller.

The other two novellas and bonus short story in *Black Cat Mojo* (Comet Press, 2015) took me deeper into Adam Howe Land, inhabited by would-be play-yahs, half-assed criminals, delusional losers and a ragtag menagerie of dumb animals that are nevertheless generally smarter than their homo sapien counterparts. If you haven't read it, add it to your Read Me Next stack/cue/

cache. Speaking of animals, Adam says he has plotted out a novel featuring a chimp in a prominent role, adding "I think that might have to be my last animal story for the foreseeable future. Be weird to get typecast as a writer of lurid animal-themed pulp books." Yes, but it is a wonderful weirdness.

Which brings us to the book in your immediate possession.

A quick look at the titles tells you that animals also play key roles in these new tales. This time we get primates, a hungry man-eating gator, a dog-eat-dog serial killer duel, and what may be an Arkansas Bigfoot known locally as a skunk ape. And who could forget the simian descendants of Neanderthals bumping against lowlifes, rogues and brawlers in bizarre scenarios Hunter S. Thompson might've dreamed up on a weeklong binge of acid/booze/laughing gas.

Adam describes the stories in *Die Dog Or Eat The Hatchet* as "straight horror/crime," much darker than the first collection. And while that may be true, his trademark black humor (or *humour*, as Adam would say) is nonetheless present—in spades. The man can't help himself. He turns people and situations sideways, ass over teakettle (*ass over tit* if you're a Brit) and upside-down to expose the absurd follies of man, and he does it in a voice echoing the hollow laughter of the gods as they look down upon the capering human circus from a crumbling Olympus.

As these stories you are about to read will prove, Adam Howe has a natural flair for making sentences sing and images dance, sometimes to bluesy jazz, sometimes to good old rock 'n' roll. The dude turns phrases that stick with you the way catchy song lyrics do. Like this grab-you-by-the-balls description of a man tithing a pole dancer in a Louisiana swamp dive: "He waggled a buck beneath her butt like a corner man rousing his boxer with smelling salts." Trust me, it works perfectly in the context of the scene. It's not easy to write original neo-noir that doesn't suck but Adam clearly knows how. And he *kills* it.

Another lyrical example of the author's gritty eloquence: "He was a little gray sadsack with bloodhound eyes, a drooping mustache and worry lines corrugating his forehead. He wore a funeral-black suit. Cobwebs of hair were pasted across his sweat-beaded baldpate." And then the expositive kicker: "He was the kind of guy you don't give a second glance—especially when looming beside him was a rent-a-thug with a mug like a Universal monster."

I needn't give more examples. I've kept you long enough from the stories within.

But before you proceed, a word of warning. And that word is suspense. Adam will ratchet the tension to nearly unbearable heights but by that time you're so deeply involved in the story that there is no stopping. You must go on! The diabolical brew of humor and horror is the alchemical elixir that will fuel your journey to the climax of the tales, even as you're not sure whether you should laugh aloud or cry out in horror. These stories are intended only for those with strong stomachs and sturdy hearts.

To put it in laconic vernacular: NO WIMPS BEYOND THIS POINT!

And please . . . *don't feed the animals.*

—Randy Chandler, author of *Dime Detective, Bad Juju & HELLz BELLz*

ACKNOWLEDGEMENTS

My partner Suzie.

Ladies, pop quiz: Your fella tells you he has a 'good idea' about a randy skunk ape abducting a porn performer wearing a baboon costume . . .
Do you
a) Change the locks?
b) Have him committed?
c) Ask, what's a skunk ape?
d) Support him wholeheartedly?
I'm very lucky . . . for a guy currently residing in a lunatic asylum.

'Bloody' Bill Chaney: Helped me edit these stories, often under sufferance.

Clans Howe and Cooper: I apologise in advance.

Paul Cook (massively talented singer/songwriter—check him out @ Paul Cook & the Chronicles), Dave Head, Paul Usher, Alexis Liosatos (whose first short story *The Man Who Collected Dali* you should read in Verto Publishing's *Into the Trenches* anthology . . .)

Gino: For enduring the book's title with the plucky good grace of his breed. (His preferred title was *Live Dog and Bite the Axeman*.)

Also:
Chris Barnes @ The Slaughtered Bird
Jim @ GingerNuts of Horror
Col @ Col's Criminal Library
Paul D. Brazill @ Brit Grit & International Noir
Paul Nelson @ From Dark Places
Gef Fox @ Wag the Fox
Matt Craig @ Reader Dad
And Thomas Pluck

My e-buddies: Randy 'Big Dawg' Chandler & David Dubrow
One of these men survived a close encounter with a Floridian skunk ape.

For the *Gator Bait* early release, I assembled a crack-team of blurbers:

Jedidiah Ayres (follow his Hardboiled Wonderland blog)
Dave Dubrow
Walt Hicks
Zombie Rob @ The Slaughtered Bird
And they didn't leave this man behind.

For the *Die Dog* collection, these guys had my back:
Eryk Pruitt
Adam Cesare (we'll put our little misunderstanding down to cultural differences)
Kent Gowran
Zach @ The Mouths of Madness Podcast
And Dave Dubrow, Walt Hicks, and Zombie Rob served a second tour of duty: I salute you.

Thanks also to Cheryl Mullenax at Comet Press for weathering the skunk ape storm.

And indeed: Lambert Pogue, General Secretary of the Society for the Preservation of the North American Skunk Ape, and the late Gerard Hauser.

If you like my book covers, check out Inkubus design.

Thank you to my new friends and readers on Twitter and Goodreads. I genuinely enjoy interacting with you crazy bastards, and appreciate your support. Hope you like the book!

Last, but by no means least: Thank you to Champion Mojo Storyteller Joe R. Lansdale, who gave me the title for this book. Joe, you were crazy giving up a title this badass. But then, your next book's called *Honky Tonk Samurai.* Badass titles clearly aren't something you struggle with. Discovering your work—quite recently, I'm ashamed to admit—has reenergized my own. *Muchas gracias.*

Alright . . .

Now let's blow the roof off this bitch!

"All right, let's get it on. I promise to do my little number.
But I'm not going to talk about violence."
—Sam Peckinpah, 1972 *Playboy* interview

DAMN DIRTY APES

The Society for the Preservation of the North American Skunk Ape wishes to remind readers that the following is a work of fiction. Although the study of these remarkable hominids in their natural habitat is a rich and rewarding activity, the capture of skunk apes should only ever be attempted by trained professionals.
—Lambert Pogue, General Secretary, S.P.N.A.S.A.

1.

They arrived in a thunder of bike engines, hitched their hogs in the parking lot and swaggered inside the bar with their leathers creaking, shaking the road dust from their long lank hair. They wore weathered denim vests, sporting arm sleeve tattoos that would've made a Ku Kluxer blush. The patch on the back of the vests was a snarling ape skull wearing a Kraut soldier's helmet, the kind with a spike on the crown. DAMN DIRTY APES was spelled out in silver studs across the shoulders. The four bikers muscled their way through the Friday night crowd to the slab of oak bar. They demanded pitchers of beer and bottles of firewater and I knew it was going to be one of those nights.

The Henhouse was a titty tonk on the outskirts of town. The joint wasn't much to write home about, and why the hell would you? *Dear Mom, Getting a lap dance and thought of you* . . . Lit by neon beer signs, fairy lights, and a gaudy glitter ball above the T-shaped stage, the place had a seedy Pleasure Island ambience. A shrine of dusty bottles was shelved behind the bar. Butcher-block tables corralled the strippers' stage. Lurking in the shadows at the back of the room were a few horseshoe booths with slashed vinyl seats, a cigarette-scarred pool table, a rotary dial phone kiosk with an OUT OF ORDER sign, a jukebox that played both kinds of music—country *and* western—and a *Smokey and the Bandit* pinball machine on which I held the high score with damn fool pride.

As far as strip clubs go, the girls who danced there—the usual waifs and strays on the low road to nowhere—could've done a whole lot worse. The owner, Walt Wiley, doted like a daddy on his dancers, Fagin to their gang of lipsticked pickpockets. Hell, I could've done worse myself, though not by much. I was head bouncer at The Henhouse. That's not as grand as it sounds. I was also the only bouncer. Walt gave me the trumped-up title in lieu of a raise. There wasn't much to the job apart from taking out the trash—sometimes literally—and making sure the girls got home safe each night. For that I could pay the rent on my room above the thrift store in town, and keep that *Smokey and the Bandit* pinball machine fed with quarters. And gals love a tough guy, so I even got laid now and then.

Sensing trouble from the Damn Dirty Apes, I closed the *Ring* magazine I'd been reading. Not moving from my regular perch at the end of the bar slab, I sized them up. The biggest of the bikers was a blubbery giant with a head like an Easter Island statue. His vest looked tiny on him, like a midriff top that had shrunk in the wash. Not that it looked like it had been washed—*ever*. Next to Blubberguts was a grinning idiot with rotten brown teeth like shit-smeared punji sticks. The face of the guy next to him was shrapneled with metal piercings. The last guy was the ugliest of them all, and on second glance, not even a guy. She was a flat-chested, hatchet-faced hag wearing a necklace of plastic doll heads.

Blubberguts, Smiley, Shitface and Baby Doll; it helped me to depersonalize the people whose asses I kicked.

Walt gave them their first round on the house. A mistake, I thought. A crowd like this mistook kindness for weakness. Walt's appearance didn't help matters. With his shiny bald dome and exaggerated sad sack features, big doleful eyes and a red pickle nose, Walt looked like a Muppet with alopecia. As he fixed the Apes their drinks, he said: "Welcome to The Henhouse, fellas." Then he glanced at Baby Doll a second time, realized his mistake and said: "Ma'am."

Smiley saw me eyeing them from my spot at the end of the slab. He nodded at me, and then squinted to read the news cutting Walt displayed in a frame behind the bar.

I kept begging Walt to take that cutting down, but he claimed it made people think twice before starting trouble. It hadn't so far and it wasn't about to now. The headline read BIGELOW BOY BRUTALIZED IN PRIZE FIGHT and there was a grainy photo of yours truly—albeit younger, trimmer, mulleted—with a mug like ripe roadkill and swollen eyes bulging from a bloody mask. I was trapped on the ring ropes. The ref was diving between my opponent and me to stop the big bastard from decapitating me.

I swear Walt kept that cutting on the wall just to bust my chops.

"What's that word say?" Smiley asked me.

I don't think he was being ironic.

"Brutalized," I edified him.

Smiley snickered, and then the Apes took their drinks and commandeered the end of the runway stage, the regulars who were sitting there scattering like vultures when the lions arrive to feast on the carcass.

Eliza was working the stage that way she did, making every man in the room believe she was dancing just for him. I admit I used to have a hankering for her myself, but I knew a classy gal like Eliza wouldn't be interested in a pug-ugly bum like me. Buck Owens was playing on the juke as she danced. As Eliza snaked her hips to *Who's Gonna Mow Your Grass?* I saw a lot of would-be gardeners who would've lopped off their left nut to give her a trim. Not that it looked like she needed one. Her G-string was leaving little to the imagination.

I saw the way the Apes were leering at Eliza, even Baby Doll, and I knew right away a shitstorm was brewing. The Henhouse runs a strictly hands-off policy. There's a big printed sign above the stage, replete with a red-circled symbol of a hand with a cross for it, for when the grab-assers get too shitfaced to read. Despite the sign, before the Buckaroos had reached Buck's guitar solo, Eliza's lithe body was tattooed with the Apes' grubby paw prints.

Eliza's boyfriend, Lester, who never missed one of her shows, wasn't doing shit to stop them. He clearly wasn't happy about the situation, but if the Apes had climbed on the stage and started running a train on poor Eliza, Lester would've stood back making choo-choo noises. (Lester's buddy, Ned, wasn't with him at The Henhouse that night. At least, I hadn't spotted him. And a guy wearing a baboon costume is kind of hard to miss. But we'll come back to that.)

Walt gave me the nod, but I was already heading over to the Apes' table; if Walt's like a daddy to his dancing girls, albeit an incestuous one, then I'm like their big brother, albeit ditto. I cleared my throat to get the Apes' attention. They must've mistook me for the waiter because they just demanded another round of drinks. "You folks can't keep your hands to yourself," I said, "I'm gonna have to ask you to leave."

Third rule of bouncing: Be nice. Sure, I've seen *Roadhouse*—only about a hundred times—even used to wear my hair long at the back, just like Dalton, till I got tired of people yanking my mullet when we were brawling. Now I keep my hair short, like my patience was getting with the Apes.

Smiley afforded me a lazy glance. "Ask away, Palooka," he said. "Now fuck outta here, or we'll do more than just 'brutalize' your punchy ass."

To hell with nice.

I fixed his smile with a straight right that snapped his head back. Rotten teeth sprayed like dirty Scrabble tiles. He crashed off his chair to the floor. The other Apes lurched to their feet. Blubberguts swung a haymaker at my head. I ducked the shot and sprang back up, torpedoing the top of my skull into his chin; heard a muffled curse as his teeth snapped shut like a guillotine on the tip of his tongue. The next Ape got ready to pounce, and I booted him in the nuts like I was kicking a field goal, really put my laces through it, only realizing it was Baby Doll when she sank to her knees, clutching her cooter and hissing like a slashed tire. Now I respect the fairer sex—even the butt-ugly gals—I don't hit 'em as a rule and I'd never knowingly kick 'em in the privates. I had half a mind to apologize, when glass shattered behind me, and I turned in time to see Shitface lunging at me with the jagged end of a broken beer bottle. I whipped my head to the side and the bottleneck whistled past my face by a pussy hair. Snatching his wrist, I twisted his arm hard, like I was wringing a wet towel. Shitface dropped the weapon and yowled. Then I hip-tossed him, and he smashed through the table in an explosion of beer and broken glass and lay crumpled on the floor.

I did a little Ali shuffle, looking down at the Apes, waiting to see if they wanted any more.

Then I saw it in their eyes: There was someone behind me.

I suddenly remembered there'd been *five* bikes outside.

I had time to think, *Shit*—

Then whoever it was wrapped a pool stick over the back of my head, I went down like a sack of cement, and then next thing I knew, the whole colony of Apes were stomping me like they were trampling out a campfire. The only thing stopped them from killing me was when Walt fired a blast from the shotgun he kept under the bar. Plaster rained down from the ceiling, dusting Walt's head like a sugared donut. He masked his embarrassment by racking the shotgun and suggesting the Apes leave before he Swiss-cheesed their ugly asses.

The Apes glanced at the guy who'd sapped me with the pool stick. Built like a silverback, he was clearly in charge. He wore a Confederate flag do-rag, and a hoop toss of rusted iron chains around his neck, like a skid row Mr. T.

Chains eyed Walt's shotgun. "No need for that, old-timer."

Walt was outraged. I saw him mouth: *Old-timer?!*

"We were just leaving." Chains snapped his fingers at the other Apes.

They didn't like it, but they started filing out, clutching their war wounds and griping. Baby Doll evened the score as she hobbled past me, giving me a sly dig in the nuts with the steel-capped toe of her biker boot. Before I'd stopped rolling on the floor, whimpering, the Apes were outside and clambering onto their bikes.

Chains straddled his hog. A shadowy figure was slouched in the sidecar attached to his bike. The figure flipped Walt the bird as the Apes roared from the lot.

"Did you see that?" Walt said, as he helped me to my feet.

"See it?" I wheezed, not yet fully recovered from that kick in the balls. "I *felt* it."

"Sonofabitch flipped me the bird."

"Oh," I said, or maybe it was "Ow," I'm not sure, I was banged up pretty good.

Walt helped me back to my perch at the end of the bar slab. I sank down on my stool with a groan. He wrapped some ice in a bar towel, which I clamped on my pounding head like a Frenchman's beret, then he poured me a stingy shot of Wild Turkey. Instead I took the bottle from his hand and swigged straight from that. He looked like he was about to object, but instead, he necked the shot he'd poured me, and knowing Walt, made a mental note to dock the bottle of Wild Turkey from my next paycheck. I heard him mutter, "Old-timer, my ass."

Eliza sauntered over, swaddled in Lester's old Letterman jacket, and thanked me for defending her honor. She cut an accusing glance at Lester and he fidgeted from foot to foot and muttered something about being a lover, not a fighter.

"*De nada*," I said to Eliza, tipping her a weary salute.

Still glaring at Lester, she stood on tiptoes to kiss my cheek.

"Walt," Lester said, "put Reggie's bottle on my tab."

Walt said, "You ever planning on paying that thing?"

But Lester was already walking away with his arm wrapped protectively around Eliza's shoulders. I had to settle for the cold consolation of the bourbon.

The regulars were watching me with interest.

Walt clapped his hands, shooing them. "Mind your business. Carry on with your carryin' on." He fetched the bullhorn from under the bar and with a squawk of static, announced the next dancing girl to the stage.

Out of earshot of anyone else, Walt asked me, "What happened, Reggie?"

How'd I leave my back exposed and allow Chains to sucker me like that? I was wondering the same damn thing myself. There comes a time in every bouncer's career when he stops being Dalton and starts being Wade Garrett; maybe I was getting too long in the tooth for this shit? 'Course, I didn't say as much to Walt.

Dragging myself up off my stool, I steadied myself against the bar slab like a nervous swimmer clinging to the pool edge, and waited for my head to stop spinning. It slowed down enough that I tucked the bottle under my arm and then hobbled behind the bar towards the stockroom, where Walt kept an old army surplus rack. "Gonna take my break," I said to Walt. Before I shuffled off into the stockroom, I pointed at the news cutting on the wall. "And would you please take that damn thing down?" He called out behind me, "But Reggie—you oughta be proud!"

Heeling the stockroom door shut behind me, I collapsed facedown on the cot like I'd been smacked with the pool stick again. Too tired to even kick off my boots, I sank down into deep sleep, and the same old bitter dream.

2

'The Bigelow Bleeder' Reggie Levine versus 'Boar Hog' Brannon for the light heavyweight state title. Brannon's ring name was well deserved; he looked like the bastard offspring of The Thing from *Fantastic Four* and a razorback. At the weigh-in, I vowed to the boxing press I'd be leaving it all in the ring. "They're gonna have to carry me out there!" And I was true to my word. For seven hellish rounds, Boar Hog busted me up like he was breaking rocks on a chain gang. The eighth was my best round—I finally hurt him—when Brannon broke his fist on my skull. Sensing a change in the tide, I went in for the kill, forgetting he still had one good hand and walking straight onto a mule-kick uppercut that put me down again for a record ninth trip to the canvas. At the count of six, I dragged myself up onto legs like stilts, chicken-danced around the ring, and then stumbled into the ref. My bloody mug printed a deformed smiley face on the front of his shirt.

"How many fingers d'you see?" the ref asked me.

Fingers? The ref had three heads and more arms than a Hindu god.

"Two," I guessed, and he waved it off.

As he helped me to my corner, I glanced back across the ring, and before my swollen eyes pinched shut, I saw Boar Hog Brannon with his arms raised in victory, and I choked back a sob of shame.

The ref consoled me with a slap on the shoulder that almost put me down again. "Son," he said, "we ever go to war, you're the sonofabitch I want in the foxhole beside me."

It was my first pro loss, and the last time I'd fight in the prize ring.

Brannon went onto bigger, better things.

I got a one-way ticket to Palookaville, via the emergency ward.

The first face I saw in the hospital was Walt Wiley's. He told me he'd lost a good chunk of change betting on me, and if I was interested in working off the debt, there'd be a job waiting for me at The Henhouse. I tried saying, "Who the hell are you, mister?" 'Cause I'd never seen the guy before. But I was higher than God on the dope they'd given me, not to mention my jaw was wired shut, and all I could manage was a pitiful mewling sound. Walt left his business card on the nightstand and told me to think it over. Except it wasn't a business card, it was a flyer for The Henhouse with a cartoon picture of a busty redhead on it. I'd heard of the place; the context was, "Stay away from that place." But I appreciated the flyer Walt had left me. The picture of ole Red kept me company while I convalesced. 'Course, I would've preferred my fiancée, Cheryl-Ann, kept me company, fetching in candy and kisses. But it turned out she and my trainer had eloped while the doctors were patching me up. Mad as I was about that, I was even madder they'd run off with my loser's purse, because without it I couldn't pay my hospital bill. So I took the job at The Henhouse.

When I started working the door for Walt, I told myself it was just until something better came along, but something better never did, and I guess somewhere along the line I stopped even looking. Bouncing at The Henhouse wasn't exactly where I'd pictured myself at age thirty-five. But my childhood dream of being a prizefighter was shattered, along with my jaw, that night I stepped in the ring with Boar Hog Brannon. Turns out I wasn't the contender I'd always thought I was; I was just another bum, and I didn't have no brother Charlie to blame it on.

* * *

I snorted awake on the cot in the stockroom, with little idea of how I'd got there, until I tried to move and my whole body screamed, and memories of the previous night started flashing back like the Apes were still sticking the boot in.

I managed to sit up, swung my legs off the edge of the rack, and sucked deep breaths until the nausea passed. I swigged the dregs from my bottle of Wild Turkey, gargled with it, then spat bloody booze into the mop bucket next to the cot. Teetering to my feet, I tightrope-walked out to the bar.

Walt was behind the slab. He was aiming a TV remote at the idiot box behind the bar. Stabbing buttons and cursing when the picture didn't change. He grunted a greeting as I shuffled past him to fetch a bottle of breakfast from the beer cooler. "Why didn't you wake me?" I said, secretly glad he hadn't.

"Don't think I didn't try," Walt said.

I slumped down on my stool, bit off the bottle cap, guzzled my Coors, belched heartily, and then glanced up at the TV. *Scooby Doo* was playing in Spanish. Scooby and Shaggy sounded like Cheech and Chong. Walt shook the remote control in his fist, gesticulating furiously. "Goddamn piece-of-shit batteries!"

"Here's a wild idea," I said. "Try changing the channel by hand?"

But Walt was a stubborn sonofabitch, and I knew he'd sooner blast the TV with his shotgun than lose this battle with the remote control.

"Just mind your business and drink your breakfast," he said.

I glanced across the room.

It was noon in The Henhouse. The only customer was old Lou, parked at the end of the stage with a beer and a stack of rumpled singles on the table in front of him. Marlene was giving Lou her matinee performance. Clutching the dance pole like a Sumo who's thrown her back, Marlene gyrated her chunky caboose above Lou's leering face. He waggled a buck beneath her butt like a corner man rousing his boxer with smelling salts. Marlene squatted over the buck, her butt cheeks snatching at the bill in Lou's hand like a flabby arcade claw groping for a plush toy.

Used to be, Marlene could part a fool from his money with her tight little tush quicker than Mr. Miyagi catching flies with chopsticks. But that was before her car accident and she was still a mite unsteady on her feet, on account of all the pain medication and the weight she'd piled on—a few dozen pounds, give or take, mostly give.

Still, you couldn't fault her for trying. She could've taken a knee and allowed Lou to slip the buck in her G-string. After everything she'd been through, there was no shame in it, no one would've blamed her. But nope, she had her pride. No car accident was going to deprive Marlene of her trademark move.

On the fifth attempt, her buttocks snatched the buck from Lou and nearly took his hand at the wrist along with it. Lou's eyes welled with proud tears. He applauded like the coach of an Olympic gold winner. From my perch at the end of the slab, I raised my bottle of Coors to show my appreciation. Marlene tore the buck from her ass crack and dabbed the sweat from her face with it. She did a little curtsy and then limped backstage.

"She's back," I said to Walt, still farting around with the TV remote.

"Who's back?"

"Marlene."

His face brightened. "She did her move?"

I seesawed my hand. "Little rusty, but she got there in the end."

Walt chuckled paternally. "Good for her. I was afraid I'd have to let her go."

"Shame on you for even thinking it," I chided him, but I didn't think he really meant it.

Walt looked about ready to hurl the remote at the TV; I took pity on him.

"You mind?" I said. "I'm watching that."

"Zoinks!" the Mexican Shaggy exclaimed.

Visibly relieved, but too stubborn to thank me, Walt tossed the remote away and started searching for something else to piss him off. He wet a rag and began scouring the slab like someone had Sharpied it with innuendo about his momma. As he scrubbed around where I was sitting, I knew he was working towards asking me something, and I had an idea what it was. "You think those boys will come back for seconds?" he said at last.

Apart from Marlene, what happened last night was the *other* elephant in the room.

I glanced at my reflection in the back-bar mirror.

It looked like someone had broken a branch off the ugly tree and beat my ass black and blue with it. I wish I could've said: *You should see the other guys.* But I was barely conscious when the Apes left, and I couldn't say for sure how they'd looked. I know I got a few good licks in, but those boys, plus Baby Doll, would have to resemble the Elephant Man's nut sack to look worse than I did now.

"Christ, I hope not," I said, and shuddered down another swig of Coors.

Not the kind of thing a bar owner wants to hear from his bouncer, but what the hell, it was my ass they kicked.

"You ever seen 'em before?" Walt asked.

I shook my head. "Probably just passing through." Here's hoping, I thought.

Walt nodded, but he looked about as convinced as I'd sounded.

That's when we heard the roar of an engine approaching The Henhouse at speed. And what happened next, and what it led to, the whole sorry business, reminded me what they say about hoping in one hand and shitting in the other and seeing which hand fills up first.

3.

Walt grabbed the shotgun from under the slab and then joined me at the window. "Is it them?" He racked the shotgun.

"I don't think so . . ." I said, watching through the tinted glass as a pickup truck careened wildly about the parking lot.

A thicket of tree branches were tangled in the grill and the mudguards and under the windshield wipers, like the truck was wearing a sniper suit. The truck tore donuts around the lot, leaves billowing in its wake, tires screeching on the asphalt and spewing smoke. It looked vaguely familiar: A rattletrap, rust-red Sierra Classic. Walt pointed out the Bigelow Baboons pennant flapping on the flagpole attached to the bumper. "Ain't that Lester's truck?"

"Yeah," I said, sighing with relief that it wasn't the Apes.

Walt relaxed his grip on the shotgun. "The hell is that jackass doing?"

I was curious about that myself.

We continued to watch as the truck roared about the lot.

Then it swerved suddenly; started rocketing towards the bar like a missile.

"I'll tell you what he ain't doing . . ." I said.

Walt said, "Yeah?"

I said, "Stopping!"

I threw myself on Walt like a Secret Serviceman, tackling him to the floor as Lester's truck crashed through the window where we'd been standing in an explosion of glass. The truck bulldozed through the room, smashing tables and chairs to splinters before it slammed to a stop against the bar slab, and the horn honked like it was demanding service. A shower of leaves and dust rained down over the room. It went quiet real sudden.

I staggered to my feet and helped Walt to his. Choking on tire smoke, fanning falling leaves from the air, we gaped at the truck, the hood crumpled against the bar. Then the driver's-side door clattered open and Lester spilled from the cab. He thudded to the floor and started kissing it like he couldn't believe he was alive, though the way Walt was staring at him, that wouldn't be for much longer.

Sometimes, and this was one of those times, it was hard to remember that Lester Swash used to be something like a local sports star. Back in the day he'd played reserve quarterback for the Baboons, before he turned his throwing arm into a drinking arm, and pissed away whatever God-given talent he'd had. He was a lanky dude with a mop of blonde hair and a mustache he mistakenly believed made him look dashing, and not like a South-East Asian sex tourist.

Cradled to his chest was a video camera, but I didn't give that much thought right away, on account of the truck being embedded where the bar used to be. Lester wobbled to his feet, but Walt seemed to prefer him where he was, because he slugged Lester in the mouth and put him back down again. I decided it was prudent to take the shotgun from Walt. He relinquished it reluctantly.

"Shit-for-brains peckerwood!" Walt barked at him. "Look what you done to my place!"

But Lester just started hollering, "It took him! It took Ned!"

Walt glanced at me—I shrugged—he frowned at Lester.

"The hell are you yammerin' about?"

"The skunk ape!"

The look on Walt's face, I was glad I'd taken the gun from him.

According to legend, the Bigelow Skunk Ape stalks the great sprawl of woods beyond town that locals call the Sticks. He's Bigfoot with body odor, I guess. Our town's very own Fouke Monster, Scape Ore Swamp Lizard Man, or the Goat Man who stalks the East Texas Bottoms.

My momma described him to me once. A shaggy-furred beast with devil-red eyes, standing tall enough to block out the sun; he could crush a man in his fist like Popeye opening a can of spinach. Momma warned me, if I lollygagged home from fishing the river, and was late back for supper, I might meet him myself.

Now in the cold light of day, I reckon I knew she was pulling my leg. But as dusk started creeping in, it was harder to convince myself. The sun retreated over the horizon like it was telling me: *Kid, if you're damn fool enough to walk home at night with a skunk ape on the loose, you can do it alone.* Before full dark, I packed up my fishing pole and my tackle box, and then hauled ass home in time to set the supper table, ignoring Momma's smug smile.

Years later, I learned the legend was started by moonshiners to spook folks away from the woods and their hidden whiskey stills. But even now people still sometimes talk about the Bigelow Skunk Ape as if he really is living out there in the Sticks someplace. Parents use him to keep their rug-rats in line. And maybe a guy in a bar will spin you a yarn about his encounter with the skunk ape, and if it's a good one, you might shout him a beer for a tall tale well told.

Unfortunately for Lester, Walt was not in the fucking mood.

"Skunk ape?" Walt sputtered. "I'll give you skunk ape!" But he gave Lester another punch in the mouth instead. "That goddamn skunk ape could prob'ly drive a truck better than you can!" I wrestled Walt into a bear hug before he could pop Lester again, and that's when I noticed someone else in the truck.

"Eliza?"

I helped her from the truck cab. She was shivering, deathly pale and glassy eyed; leaves were tangled in her long blonde hair, and her arms and legs were viciously scratched as if she'd scrambled for her life through a briar patch. Of course, I noticed all that after I'd taken a moment to appreciate the fact that she was wearing a fuzzy brassiere and britches like Raquel Welch in *100 Million Years B.C.* And the cavewoman costume looked as fetching on Eliza as it did on Raquel. She really was quite a gal, even all scratched-up and upset like this.

I managed to unglue my eyes and told Walt to fetch some brandy.

He didn't move; he didn't blink.

"*Walt*!" I said, for the third time. "*Brandy*."

He dragged himself away to get the brandy. I sat Eliza down at the end of the bar slab. Thank god for small miracles, Lester's truck hadn't demolished my spot. Walt returned with the brandy and poured Eliza a shot. She gulped it down and then reached for the rest of the bottle. Walt poured her another shot instead. It went the way of the first. "That's enough for now," I told Walt.

To Eliza, I said, "What happened, girl?"

"I told y'all what happened!" Lester cried. He was pacing the bar with the video camera cradled to his chest like a babe in arms. "The skunk ape took Ned!"

Walt reached under the slab for his shotgun, before remembering he'd given it to me. The best he could do was shoot Lester with a glare.

Ignoring Lester, I asked Eliza again. "What happened?"

She looked at me with teary eyes, her whole body trembling.

"Sk-sk-sk-skuh-skuh-skuh—"

"Skunk ape?" I suggested.

She nodded, started blubbering.

I glanced at Walt and saw him sigh.

We watched as Lester continued pacing the bar.

"Alright, Lester," I said, "exactly what the fuck happened?"

4.

The greatest moment of Ned Pratt's life was when he was picked as mascot for the high school football team, and got to wear the Boogaloo Baboon costume.

Ned was no athlete, not like his buddy, Lester Swash. But with his hunched back, long dragging arms, and his strange waddling gait, Ned was only a tail short of being simian himself. So when it came time for the Baboons to cast a new Boogaloo—after the previous team mascot graduated—Ned was a dead cert to be the man in the monkey suit. And credit where it's due, he did the costume proud. Clad in the shag-furred bodysuit, the long stiff tail swishing about the red cushion of his ass, the heavy baboon mask bobbling on his shoulders like a dashboard dog, Ned would caper up and down the sideline, firing up the crowd and imagining all the cheers were just for him.

Ten years later, and it remained hard for Ned to let go of those glory days.

Ned's Boogaloo suit was retired when Ned left high school, out of respect for the best team mascot the Baboons ever had; not to mention Ned had sweated inside the costume something fierce—it reeked like a real baboon, or one of King Kong's jerk-off socks—it was unlikely the next Boogaloo would consent to wear it. So Ned got to keep his old outfit, the coach of the Baboons presenting it to him like a retiree's gold watch.

Ever since then, Ned had worn that damn costume more than he did regular clothes, mask and all. You'd often see him doing odd jobs around town—a giant baboon mowing grass astride a Lawnboy was a common sight—or he'd come to The Henhouse with Lester, scuttling alongside him like he was Clyde to Lester's Clint in *Every Which Way But Loose*.

After awhile, it gets so you can see something weird-as-shit and not bat an eye. It hardly registers. It's just Ned.

But until Lester started talking, it had never occurred to me that Ned did his screwing while wearing the monkey suit. Never mind that there were guys who would actually *pay* good money to watch Boogaloo Baboon banging a gal.

"Porno movies?" I said, with a nervous glance at the video camera Lester was clutching.

"Yessir," Lester nodded. He was perched on his truck like a hood ornament.

"Call me old-fashioned," I said, "but who in their right mind's gonna pay to watch a guy in a monkey suit banging a gal?"

"Oh-ho," Lester said, "you'd be surprised, Reggie."

"No shit," I said.

Lester went on to explain, in more detail than I would've liked, that 'gonzo' porn was a flourishing subgenre of the adult entertainment industry.

"What's wrong with *Juggs* magazine?" I protested.

"Nothing," Walt said, with the righteousness of a longtime subscriber.

Lester shrugged. "Some guys like a little wackiness while they're whacking it."

I just shook my head in despair. It takes all sorts, I guess.

"It was my Uncle Hank gave me the idea," Lester said. "You know Hank?"

"By reputation," I said, and Lester puffed up with pride.

Hank Sanderson was another grade-A fucking moron like his nephew.

I'd once heard a story about Hank that damn near beggared belief; the short version was he'd nearly killed his wife's Jack Russell terrier with an overdose of industrial strength laxative.

"Uncle Hank's the one who sold me the camera for just fifty bucks." Lester smiled at the outdated camera in his hands like he'd got a sweet deal on a magic lamp. "Hank says there's good money to be made in porno, you just gotta find the right angle. Any damn fool can make a fuck-flick, he says. What you need is a hook to stand out from the crowd.

"So Ned and me," Lester said, "we rent us a bunch of stag movies to watch for research. Taking it serious, you know. We're doing our homework in Ned's trailer. Ned's wearing his Boogaloo suit, like *there's* a surprise. The trailer's hotter than hell and Ned's Boogaloo suit is stinking like the devil wiped his ass with it. Smells so bad, I can hardly concentrate on the movie. And the movie's one of them ones with a plot—*Rump Pumpers*—I need to concentrate. So I say to Ned, 'Open a damn window! You smell worse than the Bigelow Skunk Ape!'

"And that's when it hit me." Lester mimed a lightning bolt striking down from the sky. "When it comes to 'gonzo' porn," he said, "the Bigfoot porn market's already pretty much cornered. But skunk ape porn? Well, that's like an untapped oil field."

Lester grinned.

"So now we got us our hook," he said, "a leading man with his own 'skunk ape' costume." I knew he meant Ned's Boogaloo outfit, but Lester finger-quoted 'skunk ape' just the same. "All that was left was for us to find an actress."

With a sinking feeling in my stomach, I looked across at Eliza.

She'd shrunk like a turtle tucking into its shell.

"Don't judge me, Mr. Levine," she said.

"I'm not," I lied. Shit, and this was the girl I'd thought was out of my league. Bumping uglies with the village idiot. Mating with a moron in a monkey suit.

"It was just a foot in the door."

"Of what? Hell?" I shook my head.

She looked at me like I was looking at Lester, which is to say, like *I* was the idiot. "Showbiz," she said. "Lester was gonna edit me a showreel to audition for *Tryout Tramps*."

"Christ, Eliza . . . You might've aimed just a little higher."

"Hey!" Lester said.

"With all due respect to your talent as a pornographer, Lester."

He seemed satisfied with that.

Walt was shaking his head gravely. "Moonlighting as a porn starlet," he said. "I don't like it. That's the kinda thing that could give The Henhouse a bad name."

A little late for that, I thought. "Let's let that lie for now, Walt."

I turned back to Lester. "So," I said, trying to wrap my head around it, "you two jackasses took Eliza out to the Sticks to make a stag movie?"

Lester nodded. "That's pretty much the size of it."

"What happened next?"

Eliza started trembling again.

Lester held out the video camera towards me, shaking in his hands.

"Maybe it's best if you see for yourself."

I took the camera reluctantly, flipped out the viewing panel, pressed the play button, the contraption whirred, and then an image blinked starkly to life on the screen. Now I'm no prude. As a bachelor, I was even on nodding terms with some earlier volumes of *Tryout Tramps*. But skunk ape porn was a new one on me, and I might've liked a little foreplay to ease me into the idea. I didn't get it.

Eliza was splayed over a log with her butt high up in the air, her fuzzy cavewoman britches teased down to reveal her bare ass. That would've been something to admire under normal circumstances. Unfortunately the aesthetic was ruined by Ned as Boogaloo Baboon, hunched behind her with his paws clamped to her hips, thrusting away with his tail swishing merrily and his red cushion ass jiggling like a big plate of jelly. Lester's shaky camerawork was giving me motion sickness, like one of those found footage horror flicks;

the image itself was just making me plain sick.

"Oh yeah, that's it," I heard Lester say off-camera. "Now slap her butt with your tail."

Boogaloo did as directed—Ned seemed happier than he'd been since his mascot days—and Eliza gave a shrill squeal of pleasure.

Back in the bar, Lester had climbed down from the hood of the truck and was now peering over my shoulder to watch, smiling proudly at his handiwork.

"Back off, Lester," I warned him, and he had the good sense to wipe the leering grin off his mug. I couldn't help being pissed off that a goddamn football mascot had gotten friendlier with Eliza than I ever had. A fucking monkey, no less.

Meanwhile, old Lou had crept up on my blindside and was getting an eager eyeful. "How much did you say these videos'd be going for?" he asked Lester.

Before Lester could start haggling, Walt pushed him away. "Go home, Lou. Bar's closed." Looking like a scolded dog, Lou left the bar, crabbing carefully through the hole in the wall where the window used to be.

I snapped at Lester, "How much more of this shit do I gotta watch?"

"Coming right up," Lester assured me.

Walt said, "So's Ned, by the looks it."

The performance was reaching its crescendo. Boogaloo was pounding away at Eliza like a giant clockwork monkey bashing an exotic drum kit. Ned was grunting and gasping for breath under the heavy baboon mask. Eliza was squealing with pleasure and adlibbing dirty talk that would've made a sailor blush.

"I think I know how this one ends," I said.

"Keep watching!" Lester said.

But I'd seen more than enough to scar me for life, and I was about to shut off the camera, when suddenly Eliza gave a cry of disgust. She pushed Ned away and squirmed out from under him. "Cut, cut!" she said, hoisting up her fuzzy britches.

Lester said off-camera, "What the hell, Lizzie? This is the money shot!"

Eliza punched Boogaloo's arm; Ned gave a little yelp of pain.

"It's bad enough you two bozos couldn't wash the suit before we started shooting," she complained, "without this big dumb baboon dropping ass!"

Boogaloo held up his paws to plead his innocence. "Wasn't me—"

Then Lester must've caught a whiff of it.

"Christ almighty," he wheezed, "that smells bad enough to gag a gut-wagon dog."

"It wasn't me," Boogaloo insisted.

But Lester wasn't listening to his leading man.

"We'll take five till the air clears," he said. "Ned: Don't lose that wood."

That's when something burst from the brush in an explosion of leaves and a bellowing roar. Lester's camera whipped around for a split-second glimpse of a shadowy giant standing silhouetted against the sun. It had devil-red eyes, a matted shag of ruddy brown fur, a boulder-sized head and knuckle-dragging arms. With long, lunging strides that quaked the ground—Lester's camera seemed to be attached to a paint-shaker—the giant stamped across the clearing straight at Boogaloo Baboon. Ned gave a muffled shriek as the beast picked him up like a plush toy and tossed him over its shoulder in a fireman's lift. Then whatever-it-was turned and thundered back into the brush, bushes shaking wildly in its wake.

The camera zoomed in on the bushes. "Nuh-Ned?" Lester said.

"The hell was that?" Eliza said. "Where's Ned?"

"The fuh—the fuck should I know, girl?"

The camera began tracking into the brush where the creature had vanished with Ned. Lester's arm made a cameo appearance, raking branches aside.

"Ned?" Lester cried, in a panicked voice. "Talk to me, bud! Ned?"

"Slow down, Les!" Eliza called behind him. "Don't leave me by myself!"

A hellish roar stopped them in their tracks—

And then they were running in the opposite direction.

I didn't blame them; even on the recording, that roar chilled my blood and prickled the hairs on the nape of my neck.

The camera was still rolling. All you could see was their feet crashing through the undergrowth; all you could hear was their gasping breath and Eliza sobbing and Lester yelling at her to run faster—

Then another blood-freezing roar behind them, and Lester must have bashed the camera against something, because the image suddenly exploded in a Hiroshima of static, and I jerked my head back from the viewing screen.

"We—we made it back to the truck," Lester said, "and hauled ass out of there . . ."

"And then crashed through my fucking window," Walt said.

Lester glanced around the bar as if noticing the devastation for the first time.

"Yeah. Sorry, Walt. I was pretty shook up, I guess."

"It didn't occur to you to go see the law before coming here?"

Lester shrugged. "I needed to take the edge off."

"Oh, smart thinking," Walt told him. "A good skunk ape yarn's that much more plausible from a fella stinking like a whiskey still."

"But—" Lester said with a frown, "but it ain't no yarn, Walt. Hell, you saw the video. You saw the damn thing for yourself."

Walt folded his arms across his chest. "I don't know what I saw."

Lester looked at me pleadingly. "Reggie?"

"Play it again," I said.

"From the top?"

"Just the skunk ape part," I qualified, with a sheepish glance at Eliza.

I watched the footage again. Between the dim lighting, Lester's piss-poor camerawork, and the speed of the creature, if was impossible to say for sure what the damn thing was. Even freezing the film and playing it in slow motion didn't help. The one thing I knew for sure . . . ? Whatever it was, it had taken Ned.

5.

Constable Randy-Ray Gooch entered The Henhouse through the hole in the window, ducking his head beneath the hanging shards of plate glass. The town lawman was a wiry little guy with the drooping red mustache and fiery temperament of Yosemite Sam. Inordinately proud of his uniform, he seemed to believe it made him not only a foot taller, but also righteous and bulletproof. His Sam Browne belt and boots were polished to a shine that would have been the envy of an Italian fascist. "Happened here?" Gooch said, when he saw Lester's truck. "You open a drive-through service, Walt?"

Walt clenched his teeth. "You're a real riot, Randy-Ray. Let me jot that one down so I don't forget to laugh later."

Gooch waited, seemed to realize Walt wasn't actually going to memorialize his wit, and then hung his uniform hat on the wing mirror of Lester's truck, like it was some kind of art deco hat stand. He hooked his thumbs into his belt.

"Heard you boys had a little trouble with some bikers last night?" he said.

"Nothing we couldn't handle," Walt said.

Gooch noted my fucked-up face. "Looks like they handled Reggie here pretty good."

"There were five of them," I told him.

"You counting the girl?" Lester said.

"Shut up, Lester."

Gooch was unimpressed. "Only five?" Like some short men, Gooch prided himself on being a giant-killer.

"One of 'em suckered me," I said.

"Six including the one in the sidecar," Walt chipped in. "Sonofabitch flipped me the bird." He just couldn't let that go.

"So this truck-through-the-window bidness," Gooch said, "it's blowback from what happened last night?"

Walt glared at Lester. "No, that was *this* fucking idiot."

"Son," Gooch said to Lester, hitching up his pants in a sawing motion, "did you drive your truck through Mr. Wiley's window?"

"Yessir," Lester said.

Gooch frowned, like he'd been expecting Lester to at least *try* and lie.

"You been drinking?"

Lester put down his drink. "Not when I done it, no-sir."

"So what happened?"

No one said anything; funny thing, but none of us wanted to be the one to tell the constable that the Bigelow Skunk Ape had kidnapped Ned.

"Tell him, Lester," Walt said. "This is *your* damn mess."

Lester gave a heavy sigh. Then he told Gooch the whole sorry story. From skin flick to skunk ape. To his credit, Gooch let Lester finish. Then he said, "Skunk ape, huh?" Nodding solemnly, as if he'd expected today would herald something like this from the moment he awoke. Then he snatched his hat off the wing mirror and swatted Lester over the head with it. "I ought to charge y'all for wasting po-lice time! You think I don't have a hundred other better things to do than to come down here and have my peter pulled? Where's Ned? Hiding out back, I suppose? Ned! Get your ass out here, boy! I ain't buying it!" He shook his head in disgust at Walt and me. "I expected better from you two boys. *This* jackass," he swatted Lester once more with his hat, "not so much."

Gooch clamped his hat back on his head and prepared to leave.

I said, "Randy-Ray, wait."

He turned on his heels. "What now, Reggie? I suppose next you're gonna tell me Mothman and maybe the Loch Ness fucking Monster was in on it, too? They stole Ned away in a flying saucer?"

I said to Lester, "Show him the video."

Gooch's eyebrows raised sharply when the video started.

He glanced up from the camera at Eliza, who, to her credit, blushed.

When the skunk ape appeared, and snatched Ned, Gooch damn near dropped the camera in surprise.

"Well?" I said, when the film ended. Gooch just shook his head in disbelief and played back the film again. From the top, I noted. I gave him the benefit of the doubt that he believed the key to solving this mystery was contained somewhere within the footage of Boogaloo Baboon screwing Eliza. He shut off the camera and stood in silence a moment. Then he said, "First of all, I'm gonna need a copy of that there film." Lester gulped and nodded. "Second of all," Gooch said, "take me out to where this happened."

* * *

While Lester and Eliza took Gooch to the scene of the crime, Walt and me towed Lester's truck from the bar to the parking lot. Walt tried to even the score by giving the truck a few kicks, but it was already so beat-to-shit, the extra dents hardly showed. We swept up the broken glass and fixed sheets of plywood and cardboard over the bar's broken window. Walt spray-painted STILL OPEN across the front of the new facade. When we were done, we sat outside in the sun, sipping bottles of suds and reflecting over what had happened.

"So what do you think?" Walt asked me.

I raked my palm across my stubble, still struggling to reconcile myself with the image of Boogaloo Baboon clamped like a giant tick to Eliza's butt. "Hell, I don't know," I said. "I wouldn't put it past Lester that this is all some kind of half-assed publicity stunt for his stupid movie."

"That's crediting the boy with more brains than he's due," Walt said. "Lester's hardly P.T. Barnum." He sloshed the dregs of his beer around his bottle, clearly troubled. "You ever seen the like of it, Reggie?"

"The skunk ape?"

"Well, yeah, that too. I meant skunk ape *porn.* You'd told me there was a market for that kinda thing, I'd have said you was crazy and then kept my eye on you around the girls." Walt shook his head. "But did you see the way Randy-Ray and Old Lou were rubbernecking that film?"

"I'm trying to forget it."

"Hell, I remember a time when the lingerie catalogue was all the eye-candy a fella ever needed," Walt wistfully recalled.

"Not to point fingers," I said, "but you *do* run a titty bar."

"This is a respectable gentlemen's club," Walt protested, "not some damn Tijuana donkey show! I take care of my girls. I mean, how in the hell did Lester ever talk Eliza into doing something like that?"

"Ask me," I said, "she wouldn't have needed much convincing."

Walt looked at me.

"Eliza's pretty as you please, but she's got talent like Lester's got brains," I told him. "She's so desperate to be a movie star, she'd do anything to get noticed."

"Movie star?" Walt exclaimed. "You think Meryl fucking Streep's got skunk ape porn on her resume?"

"Once she hit it big, she probably took her early work off there," I said, "but I see your point."

"I'll tell you one thing, Reggie. I'm never gonna be able to look at Boogaloo Baboon the same way again. If nothing else, Lester and Ned have ruined high school football for me. Both of those jackasses are eighty-sixed."

"What if Ned never comes back?"

"Then I'll settle for Lester and send the skunk ape a thank you note."

* * *

Shortly before dark, Constable Gooch returned from the Sticks with Lester and Eliza and no Ned. "Find anything?" I asked.

"Just a whole bunch of nothing," Gooch said. "It smells like King Kong took a crap out there, but that could be on account of Ned's Boogaloo suit, and not no skunk ape. Come first light tomorrow, I'll send some boys back there with the coonhounds to beat the brush. Maybe Ned'll turn up before then? Here's hoping. Cuz I'll tell you, I'm in no kinda rush to file an official report reads 'Skunk Ape Attack.'"

Gooch turned to Lester and prodded his chest with a finger.

"Last chance, Swash. This is some kinda prank, 'fess up now and I won't whup you too bad for wasting my time. Cuz I find out later this is yours and Ned's idea of a joke, believe me, I'll be taking the last laugh outta your ass."

Lester whined, "I don't know what more to tell you, Constable."

"Eliza?" Gooch said.

"The skunk ape took Ned," she said firmly.

Gooch sighed. "Fuck."

He took a drink for the road and prepared to leave. "Don't forget," he told Lester, but eyeing Eliza, "I want a copy of that video on my desk first thing tomorrow." He tipped the brim of his hat to Eliza and then left.

Lester looked at Walt. "So," he said, "I guess I'm eighty-sixed, huh?"

Walt gave an exasperated bark of laughter. "You think? I got *more* good news for you, dumbass. I want your bar tab paid within the week."

Lester started saying, "Let's be reasonable here, Walt—"

"What about me, Mr. Walt?" Eliza said.

Walt tried to scowl at her, but couldn't quite manage it. "What about you?"

"Am I fired?"

"So help me, I ought to." He shook his head and sighed. "I'll expect you back at work just as soon as those scratches are healed. Make sure you wash 'em out and disinfect 'em." Eliza gave him a hug and a kiss on the cheek. Blushing, Walt said, "And no more skunk ape porn." Glaring at Lester, he added, "Or any other kind, for that matter."

Walt and me watched through the window that wasn't covered in plywood and cardboard as they trudged outside to Lester's truck. They climbed in the cab and Lester gunned the engine and the truck growled to life. Lester honked the horn and waved at Walt. "Can you believe it?" he shouted over the engine noise. "Crashes through a bar and she still runs like a dream!" I doubt Lester heard Walt cursing him over the roar of the engine as they pulled away.

6.

It was four days before the glass fitter came to The Henhouse and replaced the broken window. For those four days, my ears took the brunt of Walt's bitching.

"How can a glass fitter run a glass fitting business when it takes him four fucking days to fit glass!"

Other stuff happened, too.

My bruises faded to a rich mahogany color, making me look tan; on the peanuts Walt paid me, a solid beating was as close as I got to looking like I'd enjoyed a vacation in the sun.

Gooch's searchers found no trace of Ned Pratt, or the skunk ape.

When the story first broke in the *Bigelow Bugle*, Ned's abduction by the skunk ape was reported as gospel truth. The front-page story included a photo of Lester and Eliza, looking traumatized by their brush with death, and a file photo of Boogaloo Baboon, which I guess Ned would've approved of. The article coyly described the trio as "keen amateur filmmakers" who'd been filming a "nature documentary" in the Sticks when the skunk ape attacked. There was also an artist's impression of the skunk ape, apparently drawn by the news editor's six-year old, which resembled a rabid Cousin It.

Eliza was delighted to get her picture in the paper. She even asked Walt if he'd have it framed and put it on the wall next to mine. Eliza was convinced this was the exposure she needed to jumpstart her career as an actress. And compared to a starring role in a skunk ape porno, maybe she was onto something.

By the second news day, the *Bugle* had shifted their focus from the skunk ape to Lester. The dumb bastard had put his neck on the chopping block, and now here came the hatchet job. With very little effort, the *Bugle* dug up an Everest of dirt on Lester Swash, accurately describing the "local sports star turned village idiot" as a natural born fuck-up, and an unreliable witness in his poor friend's mysterious disappearance.

As for Ned, incredibly, he was martyred. The *Bugle* tugged at readers' heartstrings by recounting Ned's glory days as our beloved Boogaloo Baboon. He was described as a "lovable local eccentric" and a "simple soul with a sunny disposition," and not the dim-witted star of a bestiality porno. Funny how the press works. Anyway, it wasn't long before people in town began to wonder if maybe Lester had a hand in Ned's disappearance. By the end of the week, I started seeing T-shirts that read, THE SKUNK APE DIDN'T DO IT!

To help clear his name, Lester posted his video footage on YouTube. The blurred image of the skunk ape—or whatever it was; even I was having doubts by now—not to mention Lester's shitty camerawork, failed to convert the skeptics, and the video was roundly condemned as a hoax.

From the riot of Internet haters, only one man came forward in Lester's defense.

His name was Jameson T. Salisbury: Skunk Ape Hunter.

And hell followed with him.

7.

The proud owner of a shiny new window, Walt wore a big sappy grin as he polished the glass with Windex. I was watching him from my spot at the end of the slab, happy for Walt, but mostly relieved he didn't have a broken window to complain about anymore. We both glanced up when we heard the tubercular growl of a clapped-out engine approaching The Henhouse.

A hell-and-back Dodge Minnie Winnebago, it looked more like a derelict ice cream van than a recreational vehicle, apart from the fact it was painted in jungle fatigue, and fitted with a monstrous grill guard like something from a *Mad Max* movie. An oversize loudspeaker was strapped to the roof, like the one on the Blues Brothers' Bluesmobile. On the roof behind the loudspeaker was a lawn chair shrouded with a sheet of tarpaulin. Even for Bigelow, the vehicle was strange; then I saw the Florida license plate, and it made a little more sense.

As the Minnie Winnie roared towards the bar, a look of horror filled Walt's face. He must have thought lightning was about to strike twice, that the camper would come crashing through his new window. He looked about ready to throw himself in front of it as a human shield. I started mentally composing my resignation letter; I didn't think I could stand another week of Walt's bitching.

But mother of mercy, the driver hit the brakes in time, and the Minnie Winnie shuddered to a stop in a twister of tire-smoke. Walt breathed a sigh of relief.

The tire-smoke and exhaust fumes cleared. The driver's-side door cranked open with a squeal of rusted hinges. A leg wearing khaki breeches, flared at the thigh, tucked into a knee-high leather hunting-boot, extended from the cab and slammed down onto the asphalt. The big bearded man who climbed from the cab looked like a department store Santa who'd turned Injun. Apart from his hunting boots and breeches, and the machete-sized knife sheathed on his hip, he wore a safari shirt with all the pockets a man could ever want, plus a few more for luck, and a fringe buckskin jacket. His shirt collar was open to reveal a thicket of chest hair, like he was wearing an animal pelt undershirt. His beard looked like it was wearing him. A long scar curved from his left temple to his lower-right jaw, carving a line through his shaggy gray whiskers, as if the Grim Reaper had slashed him with his scythe before thinking better of it and letting him live awhile longer. A wide-brimmed slouch hat was tamped down on his graying mane of hair. One side of the brim was rolled up to the crown. The sharp fangs of some kind of critter were tucked around the hatband like shotgun shells in a bandolier.

"Who the fuck is this guy?" Walt muttered.

The stranger came inside like a bad man in a Western movie. The only reason the music didn't stop was because there wasn't any playing. He gazed around the room, before considering Walt and me.

"Gentlemen," the stranger declared in a boomingly mellifluous voice, "I have traveled many miles, day and night, without respite for refreshment or comfort stops." He shifted from foot to foot. "I now require the use of your facilities," he said, "and right quick."

Walt blinked, jerked a thumb over his shoulder, said, "Crapper's out back."

The stranger waddled to the men's room, returning moments later with something more like a swagger about him. "Much obliged to you," he said. "I really ought to fix the commode in the camper." He prized the slouch hat from his head, raked his fingers through his mane, and then tossed the hat down on the bar, a cloud of dust coughing up when it landed. He lowered himself onto a stool with a grateful moan. Then he just sat there in silence, his keen eyes darting between Walt and me like a tennis spectator.

"Uh..." Walt said, "Get you something to drink, mister?"

"Ginger ale, if you have it," the stranger said. "I no longer imbibe. In my line of work, it's imperative I keep my wits about me. Learned that the hard way."

He gestured to his scar with a rueful smile.

Walt poured the stranger a ginger ale.

The man took a sip and then smacked his lips at Walt as if he'd tasted none sweeter.

"Exactly what is your line of work?" Walt asked him.

Then he frowned, "Wait— You're not selling nothing, are you?"

The stranger smiled enigmatically. "Peace of mind, friend. Only peace of mind."

He took another sip of ginger ale and then put his glass down on the bar.

"Permit me to introduce myself," he said. "My name is Jameson T. Salisbury."

He seemed to be waiting for that to mean something to us.

When it didn't, Jameson T. Salisbury added, "Skunk ape hunter."

Walt snatched the man's ginger ale off the bar.

"Alright, bud. Get the hell out of here before I fetch the scattergun—"

Salisbury held up his palm and Walt instantly fell silent, like he'd been mesmerized. A helluva trick; I wondered if maybe Salisbury could teach it to me.

"As I understand it," Salisbury said, "a man is missing, presumed abducted by a skunk ape. If I know anything about skunk apes—and believe me, I know everything there is to know, more than any man could ever want to—then more than likely the victim is already dead. That said, it is breeding season for skunk apes, and it's possible he is being kept alive to feed the litter, which means time is of the essence. Now I implore you to tell me what I need to know. For if you hinder me in my work, this man's blood will be on your hands!"

Salisbury slammed his fist on the bar for emphasis.

Walt and me exchanged a look.

"Uh, right . . . What exactly do you wanna know?" Walt asked him.

Salisbury produced a rumpled copy of the *Bugle* and smoothed the newspaper across the slab. It was the edition with the front-page story about Ned's abduction by the skunk ape, and the photo of Lester and Eliza; not the later story dragging Lester's name through the mud, and all but accusing him of murdering Ned.

"The two witnesses," Salisbury said. "Lester Swash and Eliza Tuttle; I must speak with them as a matter of urgency.

"You won't find Lester here," Walt said.

Salisbury scanned the article. "But I understand Miss Tuttle is in your employ?"

"She dances here," Walt said, "if that's what you mean."

"Then perhaps you might tell me where I can find her?"

"Perhaps I might not?"

Salisbury arched an eyebrow, bushy as a foxtail. "If it's a question of money—?"

"It's a matter of Eliza being a sweet young gal," Walt said, "and I don't wanna see her in no more trouble."

I was proud of Walt for not taking the money, not to mention surprised.

Salisbury narrowed his eyes at Walt, but trying to stare down Walt was like playing don't-blink against a guy with no eyelids. Salisbury must have realized this, because he stood up abruptly and swept his slouch hat from the bar with a flourish. "Very well," he said. "No doubt I can find the information I need elsewhere." He clamped his hat on his head, tucked the newspaper under his arm, and began striding out. He paused at the door, looking back at us. "Make no mistake, gentlemen. I have come to Bigelow to bag me a skunk ape, and I will not leave town without one. On that, you have the word of Jameson T. Salisbury."

Then he tipped the brim of his hat and left.

We watched as Salisbury made his way back to the Minnie Winnie.

Walt shook his head and sighed.

"Well," he said, "what are you waiting for?"

I said, "Huh?"

"Go with him," Walt said. "Make sure he doesn't make trouble for Eliza."

"I'm a bouncer," I protested, "not a damn babysitter—"

"Would you just go before he leaves?"

I wasn't happy about it, and as I went outside after Salisbury, I let Walt know it by leaving a big grubby handprint on his new window.

8.

I hailed down the Minnie Winnie before it pulled from the parking lot.

"You want to speak to Lester and Eliza," I said to Salisbury when he wound down his window, "I'll take you out to the trailer park where they live."

He ushered me inside the cab, sweeping clutter off the passenger seat. I took a pew, my feet sinking ankle-deep in wheel well trash. As we pulled away, I glanced in the back of the camper and saw it was pack-ratted with animal traps and cages, rifles and bows and other weapons and accoutrements of what I guessed was the skunk ape hunting trade. Everything clattered about like pots and pans on a prospector's mule wagon as the Minnie Winnie rumbled along.

On the wall above the rumpled single bed were yellowed news cuttings of nationwide skunk ape sightings—most of them concentrated around the southern states—and maps with various spots marked with thumbtacks. I recognized the Bigelow Sticks on one of these maps. A single red thumbtack marked the spot where Ned had been abducted. Salisbury must not have known about all the other local skunk ape sightings over the years, and I was in no fit state to fill him in, because the stench inside the camper could no longer be ignored. "Mind if I roll the window down?" I gasped.

Salisbury glanced at me and saw I was fighting the urge to puke.

With a chuckle, he said, "It takes some getting used to."

"No shit," I said. It just smelled like it.

Eagerly unwinding my window, I thrust my head outside and gulped the clean air. I dragged my head back inside the cab, glanced in the back of the camper once more, and saw a tower of ice cream buckets, filled with Christ knows what. Flies were crawling over the bucket lids and dropping to the floor like they were drunk or stone dead. "What the hell *is* that?"

"Bait, Mr. Levine," Salisbury said. "Everything a growing skunk ape needs."

He started giving me the recipe. Maybe he thought I'd like to cook up my own batch some day? My stomach churned as he listed the ingredients. "Coyote urine, skunk pheromones, swine excrement; ripe slaughterhouse offal; a few pieces of roadkill I scraped up on the drive to town—"

I shoved my head out the window again, breathing deeply. "I think I get the idea," I said, "if it smells nasty as shit, these skunk apes can't get enough of it."

Salisbury nodded.

"You been doing this long?" I asked him.

"Skunk apeing?" Salisbury said. "All my life."

Maybe it was just the smell of the bait, but my head was spinning, like I'd been bagging glue. "I always thought it was make-believe," I muttered in disbelief. "What about Bigfoot? Sasquatch? Whatever the term is?"

Salisbury shook his head. "Couldn't tell you," he said. "I'm a specialist. A skunk aper. No more, no less. Insofar as 'make-believe' goes—the greatest trick the skunk ape ever pulled was convincing the world that he doesn't exist."

I frowned. "I thought that was the devil?"

"Same difference," Salisbury said.

And then he crunched the camper into higher gear, I stuck my head out the window like a dog on a road trip, and we rode the rest of the way to the trailer park in silence.

* * *

Whenever I was feeling blue about life, all I had to do was drive out to the Sunnyside Mobile Home Park, and remind myself how the other half lived. By the time I returned home to my flophouse in town, and showered the Sunnyside off me, I'd feel like Donald Trump luxuriating in his Trump Tower penthouse. My chipped and faded bathroom suite would seem like Italian marble trimmed with gold.

The Minnie Winnie wended its way through a warzone of rusted trailers and burned-out vehicle chasses. Kids with faces like Depression-era Okies shadowed us through the park on BMX bikes. Chained dogs barked outside trailers from which TVs blared and couples squabbled drunkenly for the remote. We pulled up outside Lester's trailer. Salisbury seemed reluctant to leave the sanctuary of the Minnie Winnie. I had to remind him this was *his* idea.

Outside Lester's trailer was a postage stamp of lawn corralled within the rotted ruins of a picket fence. The grass was brown and urine-scorched where Lester must have pissed off the stoop in preference to using the commode. Next to the door was a mildewed plaque that read IF THE TRAILER'S A-ROCKING, DON'T COME A-KNOCKING! The trailer wasn't A-ROCKING, so I knocked.

A scared voice said, "Who's that?"

"Lester," I said through the door. "It's me."

"Me, who?"

"Reggie," I said. "Reggie Levine."

"Reggie Levine from The Henhouse Reggie Levine?"

"No, the other one."

A silhouette appeared at the window beside the door. I glimpsed Lester peeking out through the ragged net curtain before he scuttled back into the shadows. "Who's that with you, Reggie? I don't know him."

"Someone who says he can find Ned."

Lester barked bitter laughter. "Haven't you heard, Reggie? Ned's dead. Everyone's saying I killed him!"

"I know that's not true, Lester. Now open the door."

Another voice inside: A girl's hushed tones, pleading with Lester.

I said, "Open the door, Eliza."

The door cracked open and a big baby blue eye peeped out from under long lashes. The eye darted from me to Salisbury back to me again.

"Who is he, Mr. Levine?" Eliza said.

Salisbury snatched his slouch hat from his head and started bowing like an old English dandy. "Permit me to introduce myself, madam—"

I cut him off before he got going.

"Better leave this to me, chief. They're spooked enough already."

I turned back to Eliza. "This, ah, colorful-looking gentleman . . ." How the hell to put it? "He's someone with experience in these matters. Now can we come in?"

"No, Lizzie!" I heard Lester cry. "It's a trap! Don't let 'em in!"

"Damn it, Lester. We're here to help."

I lowered my voice and said to Eliza, "How long's he been like this?"

"Since the rumors started."

She opened the door and let us inside.

"Careful, Mr. Levine," Eliza said, as she closed the door behind us, "he's got a gun."

I stopped in my tracks.

"You might've told us that before we came inside."

"I prob'ly should've," she agreed, "you're right, Mr. Levine, my bad."

Lester was pacing the end of the trailer like a caged animal. A revolver shook in his fist, in his other hand he clutched a can of Keystone. He aimed the beer at Salisbury and me, realized what he was doing, and raised the gun instead.

"No funny business," he warned us. "I ain't afraid to use this."

He looked like he hadn't changed his clothes or slept in days; he definitely hadn't bathed, I could smell him from the other end of the trailer. His eyes were bleary red, bugging from his skull. He slurped from his beer can; shit, maybe we'd get lucky, he'd take a sip from the revolver and blow his damn fool head off?

I showed him my palms. "Take it easy with that thing, Lester."

He thrust the gun at Salisbury. Had to hand it to the skunk aper. He didn't so much as flinch. Just stared steadily back at Lester.

"Who's he?" Lester demanded. "You bring a hitman to my crib, Reggie?"

"Lester," I said, "what the fuck are you talking about?"

"I've had death threats."

He waved the gun at Eliza. "Show 'em the letters, Lizzie."

"Lester—"

"Show 'em!"

Eliza upended a tin cookie jar over the kitchen table. Hate mail spilled out in a jaggedly scrawled, profane rain. BURN IN HELL, MUDRER. JUDAS SHITBIRD. GOD WILL PUNISH YOU FOR WHAT YOU DONE TO BOOGALOO. My favorite read, simply: FUCKEN ASS.

"They're all saying I killed Ned . . ." Lester said, choking back tears. "He was my best friend. My only friend. And it ain't even Ned those bastards care about. It's Boogaloo fuckin' Baboon!" He fired a shot at the cookie jar, deafening in the enclosed space of the trailer. With a flash of sparks, the jar leapt off the counter like a scatted cat. Even Lester looked a little surprised.

"Christ almighty, Lester!" I said. "Would you put that gun down?"

I noticed Salisbury was inching slowly towards Lester. He had his hands in the air, showing his palms to Lester, that he meant him no harm. I recalled the magic trick, maybe the miracle, which Salisbury had performed on Walt to shut him up.

Lester swept the gun towards him. "Mister," he said, "get back." He thrust the barrel in Salisbury's face and thumbed back the hammer. "Think I'm funning you? I said, get back!" But Salisbury kept inching forwards. The gun trembled in Lester's hand. A river of sweat flooded down his face. His finger teased the trigger—

Quick as a snake, Salisbury struck the gun from Lester's hand. It clattered to the floor and Salisbury kicked it across the trailer. Lester let out a yelp as Salisbury snatched the front of his shirt, slammed him back against the wall and stared him dead in the eye. He whimpered as he saw his own haunted reflection peering back at him in the coal-black pits of Salisbury's eyes. Lester tried to wriggle free, but the older man had a firm grip on him, and he could only moan as Salisbury stared into his eyes, his heart, his very soul.

"He's seen it," Salisbury declared, "he's seen the skunk ape."

Then he released his grip on Lester and Lester slid down the wall and crumpled to the floor, buried his face in his hands, and started sobbing.

* * *

A little later, we were crowded around the trailer's kitchen table. Lester was working through yet another can of Keystone, not fully recovered from his glimpse into the Nietzschean abyss of Salisbury's eyes. Eliza was playing hostess: Picking up around the trailer as best she could, even fixing Salisbury a plate of scrambled eggs. Salisbury wolfed down the eggs like he hadn't eaten in months. Once he'd finished eating, he asked to see the original video of the skunk ape.

Salisbury seemed startled by the unedited footage.

As Eliza's squeals and Ned's grunts echoed through the trailer, he said: "The newspaper said you were filming a nature documentary?"

Eliza pouted, as if he'd criticized her performance.

"In a manner of speaking," Lester said, "we was."

"No wonder the creature was riled," Salisbury said, "you were rutting on its patch. You might as well have been ringing a dinner gong."

Salisbury watched the footage several times, prudishly fast-forwarding through the prelude to the skunk ape attack.

"Well?" I said, when he finally shut off the camera.

"Hard to say for sure," Salisbury said. "The video is very poor."

"C'mon now," Lester protested, "it ain't that bad."

Salisbury ignored him. "It's hardly surprising the so-called 'experts' dismissed it as a hoax. For me to be one-hundred percent certain," he said, "I'll need to visit the attack site." He looked at Lester and Eliza. "Will you take me there?"

Lester lurched back from the table. "Are you outta your mind? Mister, I ain't never going back in them Sticks again. Point of fact, just as soon as I rustle up enough money, I'm moving to the city, someplace where the biggest tree is a potted plant. 'Take you there.' Sheeeeeit." He took a hearty slug of Keystone.

"I'll take you," Eliza said, softly.

Lester gaped at her. "The hell you will."

Eliza warned him, "You're not the boss of me, Lester." Lester was about to retort, but chose the safer course of action and took another pull of his beer instead.

Salisbury gave a throaty chuckle. "I admire your sand, missy. But skunk apeing's no place for a lady."

Eliza bared her teeth. "I ain't no lady," she said. "Tell him, Mr. Levine."

I said, "What she means is she's tougher than she looks."

Eliza nodded fiercely. "Damn straight I am."

And she looked about ready to punch Lester's lights out to prove it.

"But Salisbury's right," I told her. "You don't want to get mixed up in this any more than you already are." She didn't look convinced. "Hell, the only reason I'm here is 'cause Walt asked me to keep an eye on you."

"Then you'll be coming too," Eliza said, "'cause I'm going."

"Eliza—"

"No, Mr. Levine. Talk to the hand, 'cause no. It's my career on the line here."

"But Walt said you could come back to work when your scratches healed."

"You think I plan on dancing at The Henhouse all my life?" She raised her chin proudly and fluffed the bottom of her hair. "It just so happens," she said, "that a nice man from Austin, Texas saw Lester's video on YouTube and he's offered me a starring role in a movie."

"What kind of movie?" I asked, with that familiar sinking feeling.

"A real movie. With a real fella. Not Ned in his stinky-ass baboon costume."

"Another stag movie, you mean?"

"Another step up the ladder, Mr. Levine."

It was hard to argue it wasn't an improvement on skunk ape porn.

Lester looked like he'd been slapped.

"You . . . you never told me 'bout this, Lizzie. I thought I was your manager?"

She dismissed him with a flap of her hand.

"Well, it mightn't ever happen now," she said. "Everything's all hanging in the balance. 'Cause ever since people started saying Lester killed Ned, they been looking at me all fishy-eyed too. Now the nice man from Austin, Texas says he won't sign me till after everything's straightened out. And if that means I've gotta catch me a skunk ape, then by God damn it, that's what I'm gonna do."

I held up my hands in surrender.

Salisbury preened his beard, chewing things over. "I suppose I could use some extra hands," he decided. "Judging by the footage, we're looking at a seven-footer . . . That's a whole lot of hominid."

Lester realized everyone was looking at him and lowered the beer can from his lips. "What?" Then he cottoned on and glared at Eliza. "Well, thank you very much, girl. I'm gonna look like some kinda pussy I don't tag along too!" He angrily chugged the rest of his beer. "Alright . . . Fuck it, let's go."

9.

"Has the world gone batshit crazy?" Walt said, watching from behind the slab as I inventoried my camping gear on the barroom floor.

"You told me to keep an eye on Eliza," I said.

"That was before I knew she planned on leaving me in the lurch to go make another stag movie."

"She's hardly leaving you in the lurch. You've got plenty other girls."

"She broke her word to me, Reggie. She promised me she wasn't going to make those movies anymore."

"The way I see it, she can do what she wants. You're not her daddy, Walt."

He looked away.

"Shit," I said, "are you?"

Walt gave a burdened sigh. "Can't say for sure. But I got my suspicions. Let's just say I once knew Eliza's momma. You know . . . *intimately*. And more than once, come to think of it." Walt drifted away. "Henrietta-Sue . . ." he murmured wistfully. "Goddamn, she could dance . . . Just like little Eliza."

I knew where this was leading, and now wasn't the time for one of Walt's Penthouse Forum stories; Salisbury was waiting with the others in the Minnie Winnie.

I slung the strap of my camping bag over my shoulder.

"Walt," I said, "I've gotta get."

"It should be me going with her," Walt said, suddenly looking very old.

"I'll make sure nothing happens to her," I promised him.

"You're a good man, Reggie."

"I reckon I have my moments. But I'm not doing this just for you and your maybe-daughter." Walt cocked an eyebrow. "Think about it. All this time we've thought the Bigelow Skunk Ape was just a myth. And who the hell knows, maybe it is. But what if it isn't? Then that's a whole new species we've discovered."

"Maybe you can name it after Lester? *Swashus Retardus*."

"This could be history in the making, Walt!"

"Just what the world needs," Walt said, "a man-eating monster that smells like a septic tank. You just watch your ass out there, son."

He'd never called me that before; I choked down a lump in my throat.

Then I said, "You, uh . . . you didn't know *my* momma, did you, Walt?"

He waggled his eyebrows. "Just a turn of phrase."

I breathed a sigh of relief, we shook hands, and then I headed for the door.

"Reggie, wait—"

Walt fetched the shotgun from under the slab. I took it with a grim nod of thanks. "Mind yourself around Salisbury," he said. "I don't trust him."

Of course, Walt didn't trust his own mother.

"I'll see you, Walt."

"How long will you be gone?"

"Can't speak for Salisbury," I said, "but Lester and Eliza? One night in those Sticks and they'll be begging to come home. Two nights tops, I reckon. Any longer than that . . . ?" I gave my best shit-eating grin. "Call the President."

I went outside to the Minnie Winnie. Salisbury gunned the engine as I climbed inside. "I thought that damned skunk ape would die of old age before you'd be ready," he said.

"Just drive," I said, and as we pulled away, I glanced in the wing mirror and saw Walt raising his hand in farewell.

At least, that's what I'd thought at the time. Later I'd realise he'd been clutching my cellphone—and our only connection to the outside world.

*   *   *

Bigelow will never be mistaken for a metropolis, but as the Minnie Winnie left town, and we ventured out into the Sticks, I was struck by the palpable sense we were leaving civilization far behind us. Perhaps I was getting carried away. It'd been some years since I'd hunted or camped in the Sticks, and I'll admit I was excited. The woods were deserted, not a soul in sight. Despite most townsfolk having decided by now that Lester murdered Ned and then blamed it on the skunk ape to cover his tracks, it seemed no one was taking any chances.

Salisbury was driving, Eliza riding shotgun. She wore cutoff denim shorts, the scratches on her legs like scabby fishnet stockings, and a cowgirl shirt knotted above the navel. Her bare feet were propped on the dashboard as she painted her toenails Pepto-Bismol pink. Every once in a while she'd glance up from her piggies and tell Salisbury left or right or straight on. Salisbury didn't seem to appreciate taking directions from a woman, nor that she had her feet on the dash, but he needed someone to navigate, because by now Lester was half past shitfaced, and so even less reliable than a lady navigator.

I was trapped with Lester at the camper's kitchenette table. Lester was wearing a Bigelow Baboons cap and a T-shirt he'd doctored with a Sharpie pen so it read THE SKUNK APE DID IT! All he'd brought with him were his video camera, to document our skunk ape safari, and a rapidly diminishing crate of Keystone. He seemed marginally comforted by Salisbury's arsenal of skunk apeing weapons—and the beer was emboldening him—but it didn't stop Lester from whining. Between slurps of beer, Lester took pains to remind me that he was here under duress, and against his wishes, and that we all should be grateful he had deigned to join us—

"For pity's sake, Lester," I said. "Would you shut the fuck up?"

We reached the clearing around noon. I recognized the place from Lester's video. There was the log over which Eliza had been splayed while Boogaloo Baboon had his way with her. The log seemed sullied somehow. I averted my eyes and glared at Lester. "What?" he said.

Salisbury ground the Minnie Winnie to a halt and killed the engine. He marched past Lester and me to the back of the camper and began rummaging through his supplies. Then he hauled out a rifle the size of a Howitzer.

"What the hell is that?" I exclaimed. "An elephant gun?"

Smiling proudly, Salisbury said: "Mr. Levine, I'd like you to meet the Nitro Express .700 double-rifle, the most powerful hunting gun in the world." He began loading the giant gun with shells the size of Cuban cigars. "Each shell weighs 1,000 grains, hitting the target at 2,000-feet per second. That's 9,000 foot-pounds of muzzle energy. You could stop a charging bull-elephant with a single shot, make ole Dumbo fly without his magic feather."

"Hoooleee shit," Lester said. "Can I fire it?"

I answered for Salisbury: "No fucking way."

Salisbury chuckled and said, "I'm afraid not, son. Each one of these bullets costs a hundred bucks. A hundred bucks which, not to be unkind, you don't have."

Lester ceded the point with a nod.

"Besides," Salisbury said, "this bitch has gotta helluva kick. Ten times anything you've ever fired. She's liable to wrench your arms clean out of their sockets."

As he climbed from the camper, Salisbury told us: "Now stay behind me."

Lester took those words to heart and refused to move from the camper until I shoved him out the door. I considered leaving Walt's shotgun in the camper. Compared to Salisbury's cannon, I was a little ashamed of it. Plus I wasn't sure if we were hunting skunk ape or snipe here, and I figured the fewer jumpy idiots waving guns around, the better. But in the end, like a good American, I brought it with me.

We watched in silence as Salisbury stalked the clearing with the elephant gun braced before him. He scanned the ground for tracks; sniffed the air for a scent. Eliza pointed a trembling hand towards the thicket of brush where the skunk ape had run off with Ned. Hesitating outside the thicket, Salisbury cocked his head and listened intently. He made a 'follow me' gesture and inched forwards into the brush, sweeping bushes from his path with the enormous barrels of his gun. Eliza went after him. I glanced behind me. "Let's go, Lester." We followed behind Salisbury as he stalked through the brush with the elephant gun thrust before him—

Suddenly he stopped, holding up his fist.

We froze; I grabbed Lester's shirt to stop him fleeing back to the camper.

"What is it?" I whispered to Salisbury.

He crouched down on his haunches and untangled a burr of black fur that was snagged in some thorns. He wafted the burr under his nose, inhaling deeply. His nostrils flared and his head jerked back reflexively. "Christ on His throne!"

"Let me see that," I said, crouching down beside him.

Salisbury passed me the burr like he was eager to be rid of it.

I took a quick whiff, turned my head and heaved.

"That's no skunk ape," I gasped, "that's Ned's Boogaloo costume."

"You're sure?"

"Absolutely," I said. "You never forget that."

I looked back at Lester and Eliza.

"Randy-Ray should have found this. Didn't he search back here?"

Lester shook his head bitterly. "Randy-Ray and his searchers hardly moved from the clearing back there. Loafing around on the log, laughing about the Eliza and Boogaloo part of the video. One of the sonsofbitches was pumping his hips in the air like he was getting him some imaginary Eliza. I bet them bastards had already made up their minds I killed Ned out of jealousy."

"What about the coonhounds?"

"Ned's Boogaloo outfit must've thrown 'em off."

I could see, not to mention smell, how that was possible.

I brushed the fur ball from my hands and wiped my palms on my jeans. When I sniffed my fingers, I could still smell Ned's Boogaloo suit on them, and my guts lurched. How Eliza had stomached the stench, I did not know. Nobody could deny that she'd paid her dues on her quest to become a porn starlet.

"Well?" I said to Salisbury.

"Quiet!" he hissed.

He handed me the elephant gun. My knees stiffened under the weight. Damn thing weighed a ton. Never mind an elephant, you could've clubbed a T-Rex to death just with the stock. Salisbury unsheathed the machete-sized knife on his hip and began hacking at the brush. Raking the trimmings aside, he clawed away the undergrowth to reveal a monstrous bare footprint cratered in the earth.

"And *that*, Mr. Levine?" Salisbury's eyes blazed zealously. "Is *that* from a 'Boogaloo Baboon' costume?" I could only shake my head; I'd never seen the like of the huge print. When I placed my foot next to it, it dwarfed my size 12s. The size of the print, it might've been left by the Monty Python foot. "Lady and gentlemen," Salisbury declared, "we have us a skunk ape."

Lester said, "We're gonna need a bigger Winnebago—"

I said to him, "Get a shot of this with your camera, dumbass."

Lester warily approached, the video camera shaking in his hands, as if he expected the footprint would somehow come to life and kick him in the butt.

I saw Salisbury striding away. "Where are you going?"

"Back to the camper, there's much work to be done."

"Wait—uh—don't you want to take a plaster cast of this print?"

He looked at me like I was stark raving mad. "Whatever for?"

"I don't know . . ." I said, sheepishly. "Science or something?"

He gave a savage laugh.

"Once I deliver the beast dead," Salisbury said, "the scientists can study it to their hearts' content."

"You're just going to kill it?"

"And then empty my bladder on its stinking carcass."

He strode towards me. "Let's get something clear right now, Mr. Levine. I'm not here to capture or chronicle this creature. I'm here to return it to hell where it belongs."

"What about Ned?" Eliza said.

"And perhaps to get your friend back alive," Salisbury added as an afterthought.

"Now," he continued, "any man or woman who has a problem with that ought to say so now—"

Lester raised his hand. "Yeah, I wanna go home."

"Because once we're out there on its trail," Salisbury went on, "once the hunt is joined, there's no turning back—"

Lester said, "If you could just drop me off at The Henhouse—"
"Your lives will depend on you doing exactly what I say when I say it—"
"Why's no one listening to me?" Lester whined.
Salisbury fixed his gaze upon me.
"Are we clear?"
I nodded.
He grinned. "Then let's go bag this bastard."

10.

Now I'm no skunk aper, but I've hunted before, mostly squirrel, and it wasn't long before I began to question Salisbury's methods, and wonder what the hell we'd gotten into here.

Salisbury was manning the lawn chair fitted to the camper's roof. His feet were propped on the loudspeaker. The stock of the elephant gun was nestled against his crotch, the barrels jutting up from between his thighs like a magnificent steel phallus. Scanning the woods through binoculars, gnawing a stick of beef jerky to maintain his energy levels, Salisbury barked directions over the engine noise.

Eliza was driving the camper. At Salisbury's command, she'd press a button on the dashboard console to activate the loudspeaker, and a godawful honking yowl would echo over the woods. It sounded like Ric Flair being sodomized by a moose with its pecker greased in pepper spray. Salisbury claimed it was a close approximation of a skunk ape's mating call—or at least, the best impression he could do. And who were we to argue with him? He was the expert.

Lester had by now passed out drunk. I might've been grateful for the brief respite from his endless whining, except that left me alone on bait detail.

The camper's rear window was raised, and I was pouring out slop from the bait buckets, gagging at the foul stench despite the bandana covering my nose and mouth. A rancid stream of rust-colored slurry glistened in the wake of the Minnie Winnie. So far the stench had failed to attract the skunk ape, and if there was a skunk ape out here, it seemed impossible he could have missed it; what it *had* attracted was a biblical swarm of flies, trailing the camper like gulls behind a fishing trawler.

It was at times like this that I wondered what my old friend Boar Hog Brannon was up to nowadays. After he whipped me, I'd followed his progress in the boxing journals. I might have felt better about the loss if he'd gone on to have a long and illustrious career, retiring undefeated as light heavyweight champion of the world. But after steamrollering me, Boar Hog made only a brief appearance in the top twenty ranks, losing a wide points decision to Chick Estevez, before he vanished into obscurity. Still, a guy like Boar Hog always landed sunny side up. I imagined he probably owned a successful restaurant or car dealership. He lived in a nice big house, had a wife with nice big jugs, and sired a litter of husky piglets. Wherever Boar Hog was now, I felt confident he wasn't slopping out buckets of shit that smelled worse than the River Styx.

I was prising the lid off another bait bucket when the camper hit a bump on the trail. Sludge spewed from the bucket, slopped over my boots.

"Damn it, Eliza!" I kicked the shit off my boots. "Watch where you're going!"

"Sorry, Mr. Levine." She gave me a sheepish smile in the rearview.

With an angry glance at Lester, I considered waking him, letting him take his turn on bait detail. He was sprawled across the kitchenette's bench seat, snoring like a bear gone down for winter. "Mind if I ask you something?" I said to Eliza. "What exactly do you see in this clown?"

She gazed adoringly at Lester. "Oh, you don't know him, Mr. Levine. No one knows Lester like I do. He's my knight in shining armor."

As if on cue, Lester scratched his nuts, cut a long fart like a sheet being torn in half, rolled over on the bench seat, and then continued to snore.

A chivalrous knight? I couldn't see it myself.

"Lester rescued me from the mongoloid hospital," Eliza explained.

"Oh . . ." I managed to say.

I wondered if Walt knew about this. There had to be a law against hiring mongoloids as strippers, and if there wasn't, there ought to have been.

Reading my expression, she giggled. "I wasn't a patient, silly! I was a comfort nurse."

"You've got a nursing license? Then what the hell are you stripping for?"

"Comfort nurses don't need a nursing license."

"Comfort nurse . . . That's like, a hospice worker or something?"

"Oh no," she chortled, "nothing like that. Nope, I was jacking off the mongoloids."

"Come again?"

The bait fumes must have been making me heady, because it sounded like she'd said—

"Remember Melvin Stott?" Eliza went on. "When he escaped from the mongoloid hospital? They found him out at Planter's hog farm?"

I remembered, alright. The kid had butt-fucked five hogs before the squealing woke Herb, he went outside to investigate, discovered Melvin balls-deep in Bessie, his prize sow, and put him to sleep with the stock of his scattergun. Herb never recovered from what he witnessed that night, sold his hog farm and took to the bottle, drinking himself to death under the bridge on old Highway 9.

"After Melvin Stott," Eliza said, "the hospital chiefs put measures in place to ensure nothing like that ever happened again. They hired me on as a comfort nurse to take the steam off them boys." She rolled her shoulder, as if her arm had stiffened at the memory of the labor. "And I'm happy to report that we never lost another one." She raised her chin proudly. "Not on my watch."

Jesus H. Christ . . . First dopey Ned in his baboon costume, now card-carrying mongoloids. And *this* was the girl I'd figured was out of my league.

She must've seen the way I was looking at her because she said, "A mongoloid's got needs just the same as any other man, Mr. Levine. And it really wasn't as bad as you think. We just strapped 'em down to their cots. Double restraints. Cuz that retard strength, it ain't no myth. Then I pulled on the rubber glove and had at it. And not to toot my own horn, but I got real good at it too. I could finish 'em off in just a few short strokes. Shoot, sometimes they'd pop their cork as soon as they saw me pulling on the glove. The doc said it reminded him of Pavlova's dog. Said he might like to write a paper on it someday. Anyway, when I finished 'em off, they were calm as little lambs, all sweet and subdued and good as gold."

I shook my head. "I can't believe the hospital has a practice like this . . ." I also couldn't believe Eliza made being strapped down in the mongoloid ward sound like an appealing proposition.

She rolled her eyes at me. "They don't exactly advertise the fact. Well, apart from the want-ad I saw in the *Bugle*. And the want-ad was kinda vague about what the job actually entailed. Like a cryptic crossword clue . . .

"Anyway," she said, "Lester was working at the hospital as an orderly—"

"Lester Swash was gainfully employed?"

I found that harder to believe than the skunk ape.

She gave a knowing smile. "He didn't last long," she admitted. "But before they canned him, Lester would keep me company while I worked."

I'll bet he did, I thought; he probably regretted not having his video camera handy to film Eliza hard at work.

"Lester said I had talent and I should set my sights higher."

"And that'd be dancing at The Henhouse?"

Eliza nodded happily. "Lester lined up the interview with Walt, and the rest is history . . . Now here I am on the verge of making my mark in a real honest to goodness dirty movie. And who knows where that'll lead?"

I thought I had an idea.

"I know you and Walt don't approve, Mr. Levine—but sometimes I gotta pinch myself just to be sure I ain't dreaming. Cuz from where I'm from . . ." A flicker of darkness clouded her pretty face: "Believe me, I've already overachieved."

If jacking off mongoloids was a step up in the world, I shuddered to think about her family history. On a brighter note, if it turned out Eliza really *was* Walt's lovechild, she was giving me plenty of ammunition to bust his chops.

"Well," I said, not knowing what else to say, "I hope it all works out for you."

She dazzled me with a smile. "Oh, it will, Mr. Levine. You just wait n' see."

Salisbury thumped the butt of his gun on the roof of the camper, startling us.

"That's enough jawing!" he roared.

Eliza rolled her eyes at me.

"Missy," Salisbury said. "Give that bullhorn another blast!"

She muttered *Aye-aye, sir* and activated the loudspeaker.

"Levine!"

No longer 'Mr. Levine,' I noted.

"Keep running that bait line!"

I didn't know which was worse, the stench of the bait, or the skunk ape's mating call. Then I prised the lid from another bucket and decided it was definitely the bait.

11.

We camped for the night in a rough dirt clearing, choked with brush and corralled by looming pines that creaked arthritically in the breeze.

There wasn't room in the camper for us all to bed inside; given the stench of the bait buckets, nor would we have wanted to. I managed to convince Salisbury to leave the Minnie Winnie outside the clearing and upwind of our camp.

After slopping out bait all day, I looked and reeked like I'd gone skinny-dipping in a cesspool. Ducking behind the camper for privacy, I hooked a hose to the water tank, stripped down to my undershorts and hosed myself down. Why I felt the need to protect Eliza's modesty, I do not know. Given everything she'd told me, the sight of me in my drawers was unlikely to trouble her, though maybe I was flattering myself.

As clean as I was ever going to get, I fetched a change of clothes from my bag and rejoined the others. Lester had gathered some wood, built a campfire, and commandeered the coziest spot in front of it. Eliza was cooking a pot of beans over the flames. "Where's Salisbury?" I asked them.

"Went off to lay down some traps," Eliza said.

I considered seeing if Salisbury needed help—thought, *Fuck it*—plopped myself in front of the fire with a tired groan, and watched Eliza as she stirred the beans. The stench of the bait was still fresh in my mind, not to mention my nose, and I wasn't sure I'd ever eat again, but one whiff of the beans and I was surprised to hear my stomach growl. While I waited, I picked a twig off the ground and used it to scrape away the bait caked beneath my fingernails, and then incinerated the twig in the fire.

Having laid his traps around camp, Salisbury returned from the woods in time for supper. He seated himself Indian-style in front of the fire. Eliza doled out the beans and we ate in silence, watching the flames of the campfire dance. We did our *Blazing Saddles* impressions, and then Lester shared out cans from his crate of Keystone. Only Salisbury refused one, with a fussy shake of his hand. I recalled what he'd said to Walt about not drinking alcohol. Imbibing, as he'd called it. A skunk aper needed his wits about him. I had no such scruples.

Lester raised his beer can in a toast.

"To Ned," he said in a choked voice, tears welling in his eyes.

I regurgitated the last mouthful of lukewarm beer back into the can, raised it in a toast, spluttered "To Ned," and then gutted down the same mouthful.

"You think he's still alive?" Lester asked Salisbury.

"I hope so, son," the skunk aper said. "I hope so . . ."

But his eyes told a different story.

Before the atmosphere turned grim, Lester drained his beer can, fished a harmonica from his pocket, and began blowing a brave attempt at a tune. I expected Salisbury to object—Lester's harp sounded little better than Salisbury's recorded skunk ape calls—but he didn't. Maybe he thought it might attract the skunk ape?

As Lester blew his harp, Eliza snuggled up next to him and rested her head on his shoulder. For a moment, they looked almost sweet sitting there, and I wondered why the hell I was still living alone. When I finally recognized the tune Lester was murdering, I broke into a grin. Clearing my throat, I started to sing along—badly—but my singing was no worse than Lester's playing.

A-hunting we will go, a-hunting we will go
Heigh-ho, the derry-o, a-hunting we will go

Lester winked at me over his harp and kept playing. Eliza joined me for the chorus. I suspected Salisbury wanted to join in too—a tight smile peeked through the bristles of his beard—but he had his reputation to uphold.

Lester finished playing and took a little bow as Eliza applauded.

Maybe Lester wasn't such an asshole after all? I thought. Then I remembered why I was there and decided the beer must have gone to my head.

Looking pleased with himself, Lester put away his harmonica, cracked open another beer, took a slurp, wiped his lips with the back of his hand, and then blurted out to Salisbury with a drunk's childlike tactlessness: "So how'd you get your scar, Jimmy?"

Eliza slapped his arm. "Lester!"

"What?" he said.

Salisbury looked like he couldn't decide if he was offended more by the question or that Lester had called him 'Jimmy.'

But now that Lester had pointed it out, none of us could help sneaking peeks at the vicious scar bisecting Salisbury's beard, and he felt obliged to tell us the story.

"I was in the wilds of North Carolina," Salisbury said, "tracking a skunk ape to what I believed was its lair in the ruins of an old civil war fort. There, much to my surprise, I encountered not a skunk ape, but one very ornery cougar. The thing about skunk apes, they're crafty devils—and they *are* devils, make no mistake about that. In retrospect, I'm convinced the skunk ape knew I was hot on its heels and deliberately lured me into the lion's, or rather the cougar's den.

"Before I had time to fire off a shot, the cougar pounced on me, knocking the rifle from my hands and then raking my face with its claws. Like the Roman gladiators of old, I wrestled the big cat with my bare hands, until finally, on the verge of exhaustion, with the beast's hot breath on my throat, I freed my kukri knife from its sheath—" Quick as lightning, Salisbury snatched the knife from its sheath and slashed it through the air above the campfire: "—and beheaded the brute with a single blow."

"Whoa!" Lester said.

Salisbury returned his knife to its sheath.

Lester admired the fangs decorating his hatband. "Those're cougar teeth?"

Salisbury nodded. "Took 'em as a trophy," he said, "and to remind me of the sheer cunning of my *true* enemy . . . the North American skunk ape."

"I oughta get me one of them cookery knives," Lester said. "Gotta problem with cougars myself." He waggled his eyebrows. Eliza glared at him and he quickly wiped the leer off his mug.

Salisbury glanced at me. "You're no stranger to scars yourself, Levine."

"Comes with the job," I said.

"But you didn't always . . . ?" He searched for the word.

"Bounce? Sure feels like it sometimes."

"I noticed your news cutting behind the bar."

"Hell, I didn't put that there. Not exactly something I'm proud of."

"You were a prizefighter?"

Lester announced me like a ring emcee, "'The Bigelow Bleeder' Reggie Levine!"

"I thought I was . . ." I said, "Once."

"What happened?"

"You saw the cutting," I said, maybe more huffily than was necessary. "I got my fucking ass kicked."

* * *

Salisbury took the watch, while the rest of us bedded down for the night.

Lester and Eliza were cocooned inside a ratty single sleeping bag. I'd pitched my bedroll on the other side of the campfire. I lay back and stargazed, trying with little success to ignore the racket Lester was making. After complaining at length that he wouldn't sleep a wink, Lester had promptly passed out, and was now snoring loud enough to, if not wake the dead, at least ensure I couldn't sleep. Eliza was apparently accustomed to the noise; nestled in the crook of his arm with a peaceful look on her face, perhaps dreaming of the opportunity that awaited her in Austin, Texas, if we could only catch the skunk ape. Soon she was softly snoring, too. I wondered if instead of sheep, she counted ejaculating mongoloids to help her doze off.

I preferred thinking about the skunk ape. *Was it really out there?* I thought back to when I was a kid and my Momma first warned me about the shaggy-furred beast with the devil-red eyes that stalked the Bigelow Sticks. I remembered how easy it was to dismiss such things in the cold light of day. But the night has a funny way of clouding rational thought, and I moved Walt's shotgun a little closer to my bedroll.

I glanced around the clearing for Salisbury, but couldn't see him anywhere. He might have been stalking the woods, patrolling the camp perimeter, watching over us from the boughs of a tree. For all we knew, he'd retired to the Minnie Winnie and was sleeping in relative luxury. But somehow I didn't think so.

As the campfire crackled, and Lester snored, and night noises echoed from the woods, it suddenly occurred to me that Salisbury had left the three of us staked out in the open clearing like sacrificial goats, and I recalled what Walt had said about not trusting the skunk aper, and a chill shivered down my spine. Forcing the thought from my mind, I shut my eyes and tried willing myself to sleep.

But Lester's snoring made that impossible; it sounded like Leatherface was rampaging through the camp with his chainsaw. "Lester, keep it down!" In frustration, I hurled one of my boots at him. It thwacked Eliza on the head and she woke with a startled curse, lurching up in the sleeping bag and checking the sky for more falling footwear. Fortunately she was too groggy to link the boot to me, and I was able to feign sleep until she settled back down. Actual sleep was out of the question; after all that excitement, I needed a piss.

Earlier that night, I'd watched in disgust as Lester had whizzed into an empty beer can. I might not have said anything, had he been subtle about it. But he was whizzing all over the place, even getting some in the can. I said, "You can't find a tree? We're in the damn woods!" He'd siphoned the last few drops into the can and said, "With that thing out there? You must be crazy." Faced with the prospect of venturing alone into the pitch-black woods to pee, I could now see his point.

I looked around camp, but couldn't find any more empties. Maybe Lester was hoarding them for his own future use? I dreaded to think what might happen when he needed a dump. I tried holding out till dawn, but it was no use.

With a sigh, I climbed from my bedroll, fetched up Walt's shotgun, pulled on one boot, retrieved the other boot with which I'd clobbered Eliza, and then I went out into the woods to pee. I chose a tree, propped Walt's shotgun against the trunk beside me, and was emptying the Keystone from my bladder, sighing with relief . . . when I heard stealthy footsteps stalking through the brush towards me. My senses screamed a warning siren and I whirled towards the noise, the last few drops of piss spattering the leaves at my feet. "Salisbury?" I hissed into the darkness. The footsteps stopped abruptly at the sound of my voice.

Then a breath of wind whispered through the trees and I smelled a musky animal odor that prickled the hairs on the nape of my neck.

I glanced down at the tree where I'd left—

Walt's shotgun wasn't there!

Had someone—or something—stolen it while I was peeing? No, I must have knocked it to the ground as I whirled towards the footsteps; it had to be lying somewhere on the shadowy forest floor.

But before I could search for it, the footsteps started towards me once more.

And they were no longer stealthy, they were gathering speed, as whatever the thing was, and it sounded big, sounded huge, charged me from the darkness.

With a panicked cry, I turned and ran—

Into an overhanging tree branch that clotheslined me like a wrestler.

Splayed on my back, dazed, I could only watch in helpless terror as the monstrous silhouette loomed through the woods—before the beast burst from the brush with a bellowing roar. Rearing onto its hind legs, the monster towered above me, slashing powerful arms, claws glinting in the moonlight, saliva spraying from the fangs within its cavernous maw. I cowered against the ground, ducking my head as the wicked claws raked the air above me. Tensing itself to pounce down upon me, the creature took a step forwards—

And sprang the trap that lay buried in the leaves between us.

Monstrous steel jaws snapped shut around its waist, nearly cleaving the creature in two, and its roar became a keening cry of agony. It began thrashing wildly to free itself from the trap, but the vicious steel teeth only dug deeper into flesh and bone, blood steaming in the cold night air. Its struggles slowly weakened, the creature gave a pitiful sigh, and then it thudded to the ground and lay motionless.

Before I could catch my breath, I heard footsteps crashing through the brush behind me. Human, this time. I looked around and saw a flashlight beam ghosting through the woods towards me. "Levine!" Salisbury cried. "Here!" I called back, staggering to my feet as Salisbury and the others broke through the brush and found me. Salisbury shone his flashlight at me and gave a cry of horror and I feared the beast must have gored me.

Then he said, "Damn it, Levine— Put yourself away, man!"

I glanced down and saw my johnson flopping from my open zipper. I hadn't had time to tuck it away before the beast bushwhacked me. I quickly zipped myself up.

Lester grinned and said, "Cold tonight, huh?"

He'd found Walt's shotgun and I snatched it away from him.

"Shut up, Lester."

Eliza gave a sudden gasp.

I double-checked my zipper.

"Mr. Levine! You're hurt!"

Blood was dripping into my eyes; I must've cut my forehead when I ran into the tree branch.

"It's nothing," I said, because that's what you say, but the wound was already starting to throb. I turned towards Salisbury. "Where the hell were you? The damn thing almost killed me!"

Salisbury shouldered past me, shining his flashlight down at the trap.

Lingering back with the others, I said, "Is it . . . ?"

"It's dead," he said.

He raised his flashlight, shining the beam into the woods.

"I just hope the mother isn't out there."

"Mother?" I said.

"Christ, how many of these things *are* there?" Lester said.

I warily approached where Salisbury was crouching in front of the trap.

Clamped between the steel teeth was a little black bear. The critter looked as cute and harmless as the star of an old Disney nature flick. Not a cub, but definitely a juvenile, and probably the runt of the litter at that.

"Oh, Mr. Levine . . ." Eliza said. "You killed Yogi Bear."

"Yogi, my ass," Lester cackled. "That thing's smaller than Boo."

"It . . . it all happened so fast," I said. "I was on the ground . . . It looked much bigger in the dark." Nobody said anything. "*Huge*," I insisted.

Salisbury released the trap and wrenched the carcass from its jaws.

"Jesus—" I said, looking at the trap in horror. I realized how close I'd come to taking the last piss of my life. "One misstep and that could've been me."

"In future," Salisbury said, "perhaps you should check with me first before blundering through my perimeter in full dark to relieve yourself."

"Or start whizzing in cans," Lester suggested.

I could barely bring myself to look at the little dead bear.

"We should bury it," I said.

"What's this 'we' shit?" Lester said. "*You* killed it."

Salisbury looked at me curiously. "Should we say a few words, too?"

I said, "I meant we should bury it before any game wardens find it. Even if it was bear hunting season, which it isn't, I'm pretty sure there's laws against killing . . . you know . . ." I trailed off.

"Cubs?"

I hung my head in shame and gave a heavy sigh. "Ah, hell."

Salisbury considered for a moment.

"Very well," he decided, "bury it."

But first he unsheathed his knife, sliced the bear's belly open, and began removing its entrails and tossing them splat at my feet.

"For the bait buckets," he said.

Made sense, the bear guts smelled ripe enough for the job; I kicked them to Lester. "For the bait buckets," I told him.

"The what?" he said, because he'd been passed out and had missed all the fun.

"Oh, you'll see, Lester . . ." I said. "You'll see."

One day on bait detail was plenty enough for me.

Lester said to Salisbury: "Could you cut me off a piece for a trophy?"

I didn't hang around to see what piece he chose.

I staggered back to camp and fetched a shovel to bury the bear.

And yeah, I did say a few words, mostly how goddamn sorry I was.

12

The next day I was still feeling foolish and guilty about the bear, and my head was pounding where I'd thumped it against the tree branch. I was cranky-tired from lack of sleep, and starting to think our great skunk ape safari was in fact nothing more than a wild-goose chase. But hey, at least I was driving.

Lester and Eliza were on bait detail.

Eliza was doing the lion's share of the work, her sleeves rolled up and her hair tied back like Rosie the Riveter, as she slopped out the buckets from the back of the camper. Even splattered in Salisbury's godawful bait concoction she still managed to look defiantly pretty. And surely the porn biz couldn't fling anything worse at her than *this* goop. She seemed to be enjoying the adventure; compared to relieving randy mongoloids, or gyrating topless at The Henhouse, it must've been a refreshing change of scene.

Lester was taking to the task with far less enthusiasm. He could barely manage to prise the lids from the buckets and pass them to Eliza before the stench of the bait overwhelmed him and he started heaving. In half-assed emulation of Salisbury, he'd adorned the crown of his Bigelow Baboons cap with the bear's teeth—its milk teeth, I noted, with another pang of shame.

I called out cheerily, "How're you getting on back there, Lester?" Then I gave the loudspeaker a good long blast of the skunk ape's mating call to drown out the sound of him cursing me.

But the novelty of driving, less so Lester's discomfort, soon wore off.

By midday, the scorching sun had turned the camper into a sweatbox on wheels. There was no escaping the stifling stench of the bait. The fetid fumes fogged the windshield; dirty brown pearls of condensation jeweled the roof of the camper, dripping down over my head like a Chinese water torture.

Worse than that, I had no idea where the hell we were.

Before setting off that morning, I'd removed Salisbury's map of the Bigelow Sticks from the wall above his camping bed, and placed it on the passenger seat to guide me. But as Salisbury barked directions to me from his rooftop hunting deck, seemingly at random, it soon became apparent we were completely and hopelessly lost.

I patted down my pockets, searching for my cellphone. When I couldn't find it, I recalled Walt waving to me as the camper left The Henhouse.

I'd thought he was saying: *Fare-thee-well*. Turns out it was: *Don't forget your cellphone*. I called back to Eliza. "You bring your cellphone?" I knew better than to ask Lester.

Still slopping out the bait buckets, Eliza glanced back at me and blew a stray strand of hair from her eyes. "Who you calling, Mr. Levine?"

Not wanting to panic them, I said: "Just figured to let Walt know where we are."

Or vice versa.

And if we really were lost, Walt would need time to muster a search party.

Eliza fished her cellphone from the pocket of her cut-offs and thumbed it on.

"Let me guess," I said. "No signal?"

"Nope," she said. "All five bars—"

Then the camper hit a bump on the trail, the phone slipped through her greasy fingers and landed with a plop in an open bait bucket, submerging beneath the sludge. Eliza shouted, "Shitfire!"

I muttered, "That's just great . . ." Then I hit the brakes.

"Levine!" Salisbury barked, as the Minnie Winnie lurched to a stop. "Why are we stopping, man?"

Lester and Eliza took the opportunity for some fresh air. Lester staggered from the camper and away down the trail, dropped to his knees in the trailside brush and began puking violently. Eliza rubbed his back like she was burping a baby.

"That's it, get it all up," she encouraged him, *pat-pat-pat*.

I climbed from the camper and looked up at Salisbury on the roof.

"Enough's enough," I told him, "we're just going 'round in circles here."

Salisbury gave a snort of contempt. "*Kills one bear cub, the man thinks he's a skunk aper* . . . No one said this would be easy, Levine. I warned you as much before we set off."

"Exactly how long do you plan on staying out here for?"

"As long as it takes," Salisbury said.

"That's what I was afraid of," I said. "Eliza and me have jobs to get back to."

"Hey—" Lester said, defensively: "I got shit to do too, you know."

Salisbury said, "The three of you are welcome to walk back to town."

"Well, we might at that," I said, "except none of us knows where the hell we are."

Salisbury grinned. "Maybe you could ask the skunk ape for directions? You start walking now, I reckon you might just run into him around nightfall."

I looked at Eliza and Lester. "I've had enough. You guys coming?"

"What about Ned, Mr. Levine?" Eliza said.

But I reckon she was thinking about her acting career, too.

"Once we get back to town," I said, "I'll go see Randy-Ray myself. We'll figure something out—"

Lester wiped the bile off his chin and said, "I ain't walking nowhere with that thing out there."

"I thought you wanted to go home?"

"I did—I do—hell, I didn't even wanna come to start with! But Jimmy's got the big gun, Reggie. No hard feelings."

Salisbury gave a throaty chuckle. "Well," he said, "looks like you'll be walking home alone, Levine."

"One more night," I said, glaring at him, "one more night and then we're heading back to town."

He didn't say anything.

Not until I started turning away.

"Might've known you'd be the type to tuck tail and run . . ."

I turned back around. "What's that supposed to mean?"

Salisbury climbed down from the roof of the camper. We butted chests like boxers at the weigh-in. "It means you're a quitter, Levine. The first sign of adversity and you fold like a lawn chair. Inside *and* outside the boxing ring."

It seemed like everything in my life always came back to Boar Hog Brannon.

"I lost that fight fair and square," I said.

"The measure of a man's not in how he loses, it's in how he handles defeat."

"How 'bout I kick your ass and we'll see how *you* handle it?"

Eliza wedged herself between us and said, "Stop it! Both of you!"

Then Lester said, "Hey . . ."

He was holding up what looked like a baseball.

Then I realized what it was, and shuddered.

Reading my expression, Salisbury said, "Mean something to you?"

It was a plastic doll's head, the eyes black and cigarette-scorched.

The last time I'd seen it, it was hanging on a necklace worn by Baby Doll as she and the rest of her Motorcycle Club kicked the crap out of me.

"Where'd you find that?"

"Right here where I was puking," Lester said, with unmistakable pride. He wiped some upchuck off the doll's head onto his shirt, like he was polishing an apple to give to teacher.

A search of the area revealed a mess of tire tracks.

I'm no Injun tracker, but I didn't need to be to recognize the tracks as belonging to motorbikes. Five different treads, five different bikes, one of them fitted with a sidecar.

"What would those Damn Dirty Apes be doing way out here?" Eliza asked me.

"Whatever it was," I said, "it looks like they ran into some trouble."

"Couldn't have happened to a bigger bunch of assholes," Lester said.

I wasn't exactly cut up about it, either.

"Where're the bodies? The bikes?" Eliza said.

"Over here . . ." Salisbury said.

He was crouching on his haunches by the trailside, staring gravely at a great mound of foul-smelling scat. On either side of the dung heap was a monstrous bare footprint, where the creature must have squatted to empty its bowels. They were a perfect-match for the footprint we'd found at the spot where Ned was abducted. Salisbury glanced at me challengingly. "You're the expert all of a sudden. Care to explain this?"

I shrugged sheepishly. "When you gotta go, you gotta go."

Lester was staring in horror at the big pile of shit. "My God . . . Is that—is that those Damn Dirty Apes? Is *that* all that's left of 'em?"

Salisbury prodded his pinkie into the shit like he was testing the temperature of a pie, flicked his tongue across his scat-smeared finger, his face crinkled in revulsion and then he spat in the dirt and said, "Fresh." He glanced at me and then gestured to the shit, letting me know I was welcome to taste it for myself.

"I believe you," I assured him.

Salisbury stood up and scanned the woods choking the trail.

"You think it's out there?" Eliza said.

Salisbury said, "Oh, it's out there alright."

"Maybe Reggie's right," Lester said. "Maybe we ought to head back to—"

But Salisbury cut him off: "We camp here tonight."

13.

That night, the tension between Salisbury and me crackled like the logs on the campfire. Glaring at each other over the flames, Salisbury whittled a branch with his kukri knife, and I ate my beans supper with little enthusiasm and farted with even less. Lester took out his harmonica and tried raising our spirits, but he only seemed to know the one song, and the harp's mournful wail only added to the grim atmosphere, and so he put it away and just opened another can of Keystone.

I brooded over what Salisbury had said; that I was a quitter. Last night, when the bear charged me, before I realized what it was, my life had flashed before my eyes—and it was like watching a loop of interminably dull CCTV footage of any old night at The Henhouse. There I was: Slumped at my regular spot at the slab with a bottle of Coors and *The Ring* magazine, occasionally rising from my stool to check an ID, turf out a drunk, fetch another beer, or take a piss, mostly the last two. Maybe Salisbury was right; maybe I had set my sights a little low since losing the Brannon fight? Not that I planned on admitting as much to him.

I watched as he whittled the branch with his knife, carving the wood into a vaguely simian shape that looked like the sinister fetish doll of a skunk ape-worshipping savage. "You really hate them . . ." I said. "Don't you?"

He looked at me sharply. Then tossed his simian carving into the fire, watching as it crackled and burned in the flames, belching fiery ash up into the night sky.

"*Hate*, Levine? That's all a skunk ape knows. All they deserve . . . *Hate*."

"What happened?"

Salisbury didn't answer at first; I didn't think he'd answer at all.

Then he told us.

* * *

My father, Robert Salisbury, 'Bob' to his friends, plain old 'Pop' to me, was a good man—some might say a great man—but a man of mercurial temperament.

When he lost his job at the camping goods store, where he had worked all his life, he was devastated. At home, sequestering himself in his basement den, Pop shunned all human contact, taking his meals on trays that my mother left outside the locked door, and refusing my pleas for us to play catch in the yard. Mother assured me that Pop would soon reemerge from his funk. He always did, she said. Sure enough, she was right.

Three months later, one dead of night, Pop awoke us in a state of great excitement. Rousted from our beds, we assembled in the living room for an urgent family meeting where Pop told us his plans. Much to Mother's astonishment, he had sold our home and all our worldly possessions, any creature comforts he deemed superfluous to our new lives. The family station wagon had been traded for the used pickup truck sitting gassed and ready to go in the drive. Still wearing our bedclothes, Pop herded us out to the truck, and off we drove into the night. Not wishing to spoil the surprise, Pop refused to speak a word to us, ignoring our many questions and turning up the radio when Mother began to badger him.

After driving through the night, we finally reached an acreage of stinking swampland in the Florida Everglades where stood—or rather sagged—a ramshackle cabin. Ushering us inside the creaking, cobwebbed hovel, Pop welcomed us to our new home. Mother wept what Pop assured me were tears of joy. We were standing—Pop said—in what would soon become the world-famous "Salisbury Skunk Ape Sanctuary," where visitors from across the globe would flock to observe these remarkable hominids in their natural habitat. And leave their tourist dollars at the café and gift store, he added, smiling slyly at Mother to assuage her concerns. He'd clearly given this a great deal of thought. We were going to be rich.

Pop's enthusiasm was infectious. I could hardly wait to get started and see my first skunk ape. Pop was appalled to discover we had not been taught about them in school biology class, and vowed to write an outraged letter to the education authorities. I had many questions for him; so too did Mother, though her questions were less about skunk apes, than the lives we'd left behind and our future prospects. She lured him away to a closed room, where I heard her sobbing and pleading with him—then a fierce slap—followed by Pop's stern reassurances that he knew what was in the best interests of the family.

Despite her initial misgivings, to Mother's credit she pitched in and tried to make the most of it. We spruced the place up for the tourists, making repairs where required, which was most everywhere. Pop painted a SALISBURY SKUNK APE SANCTUARY sign to display outside. Mother stocked the gift store with pretty handicrafts. Pop and I built an enclosure—akin to a batting cage—in which to house our first skunk ape. And then we set about capturing one.

Every night, Pop and I would roam the swamp with tranquilizer rifles—and real guns, just in case Pop had underestimated the dosage required to incapacitate a skunk ape, and the animal charged us.

And every morning at dawn we would return empty-handed.

When the sanctuary finally opened to the public, we had still yet to capture our star attraction, and it quickly became clear that visitors would not be satisfied with an empty cage and Pop's assurances that skunk apes dwelled in the wetlands. We needed a skunk ape; our very livelihoods depended on it.

Pop and I began stalking the swamp day and night, and yet the damnable creatures continued to elude us. We caught shadowy glimpses of them, found their tracks, smelled them all around us, of course, and endured their mocking catcalls . . . But always at a distance, always out of rifle range. It was as if they were tormenting us—for as well as devious animal cunning, every skunk ape has a cruel callous mean streak at its heart.

Our failure to capture a skunk ape slowly wore down my father. Within a year his enthusiasm for the sanctuary deserted him as suddenly as it had arrived. He stopped bathing, allowed his hair and beard to grow long and wild, and would spend long lonely hours brooding inside the cage we had built for the skunk apes. Mother tried desperately to raise his spirits. She begged him to see a doctor. When that failed to elicit a response, she threatened to take me to stay with my grandparents. But to no avail. Pop was beyond help, communicating only in guttural grunts and growls. The skunk apes had broken the poor soul.

It was left to me to restore order and salvage our beleaguered family. Using every bit of skunk apeing guile my father had taught me, I began hunting the swamp alone. They were out there, of that I was certain. As I stalked the wetlands—their foul stench choking the air—I often sensed their creeping presence slyly shadowing my movements, dogging my footsteps . . .

But when I turned I saw nothing but shadows.

Then one evening, returning home for supper after yet another day's fruitless hunting, I had my first close encounter with a skunk ape. The creature was crouching behind the cabin with a bloody branch clutched like a club in its hand. Mother's lifeless body lay sprawled at its feet. Her skull had been shattered like a melon. My cry of horror alerted the beast. Its head snapped up. Baleful red eyes glared at me through the filthy matted hair masking its face. It bellowed and flailed the bloody club above its head. I raised my rifle and fired. I had long ago given up using the tranquilizer rifle. The shot tore through the creature's chest. The club slid from its grip. The beast crumpled to the ground. Rifle raised, I warily approached, and with the toe of my boot I rolled the creature onto its back. When I saw what I had done, I screamed.

As I fell to my knees beside my poor mother and father, weeping over their lifeless bodies, an infernal chorus of bestial howls arose from the wetlands.

They were laughing; the devil's skunk apes were laughing at me in their malicious triumph. Screaming back at them, screaming myself hoarse, I fired my rifle blindly into the woods, and when the chamber clicked empty, I cursed them. Two days later, a travelling salesman discovered me, still cursing and dry-firing my rifle, as the bodies of my parents lay stiff and gathered flies at my feet.

In the years that followed, I sensed it was in my best interests to cooperate with the doctors at the psychiatric hospital. I agreed with them that yes, *of course* there weren't any such thing as skunk apes; that my father—*a very sick man*, they told me—had *transferred his delusions* onto me, an *impressionable young boy*. In time, satisfied with my progress, the hospital released me.

But I knew the truth. I'd never forgotten the demonic cacophony of the skunk apes laughing at me and mine, and I vowed, upon the graves of my parents, that one day I would have my revenge, and wipe the hateful smiles from their faces.

* * *

"Ever since then," Salisbury said, "I've been hunting skunk apes, investigating every sighting—from the Florida Everglades, the wilds of North Carolina, the Louisiana swamps . . . and now here in the Bigelow Sticks.

"And as God is my witness, we shall *see* who has the last laugh."

A pinecone popped in the campfire, startling me back to my senses.

Salisbury had finished his tale, or said as much as he was going to.

I was troubled by what he'd told us.

As delicately as possible, I said: "Salisbury—in all the years you've been out there hunting them—have you ever actually *seen* a skunk ape?"

Firelight blazed in his eyes, twin visions of hell.

"No," he said. "And I'll never rest till I do."

And with that, Jameson T. Salisbury: Skunk Ape Hunter hauled himself to his feet, propped his elephant gun on his shoulder, said: "Now get some sleep, we've got a big day ahead of us," and then he strode away into the night, the darkness embracing him like an old friend.

14.

I'm sure you can imagine how well I slept.

We were on a snipe hunt being led by a certified lunatic.

A dangerous one? I didn't know. Nor did I care to wait around and find out.

Feigning sleep, I opened my eyes to slits and glanced around camp.

Salisbury was nowhere to be seen. But no doubt he'd be close—stalking the woods, patrolling the perimeter, checking his traps—there wasn't much time.

Climbing soundlessly from my bedroll, I fetched Walt's shotgun and bellied across camp to Lester and Eliza's sleeping bag. I shook Lester's shoulder until his eyes snapped open and he bolted upright in alarm. I clamped my hand over his mouth before he could scream. Raised a finger to my lips. He nodded warily.

I removed my hand and whispered, "We're leaving."

"Is it morning already?"

I shook my head. "We're leaving now."

He reached for an empty beer can. "Lemme take a leak . . ."

Eliza woke with a yawn and a cat-like stretch.

"But what about Mr. Salisbury?" she said, when I told her what was happening.

"Maybe you two haven't noticed," I said, "but the guy's batshit crazy." They just looked at me like *I* was the nut. I shook my head in exasperation. "There's no time to explain right now. Just get your boots on, get dressed, and let's get the hell out of—" That's when the cold steel .700 barrels of the elephant gun prodded sharply against the back of my skull. I'd been feeling pretty take-charge up until then. I glared at Lester and Eliza. "Thanks for the heads-up."

In their defense, Salisbury was wearing camouflage. His face was blackened with boot polish, and he was clad head to toe in a ghillie suit, festooned in leafy branches that made him look like a walking human shrub.

"Drop that peashooter in the dirt." I dropped Walt's shotgun to the ground and he kicked it across the clearing. "Now on your feet— Slowly! Keep your hands where I can see 'em . . ." I did what he said, wondering how much he'd overheard and hoping he hadn't taken my 'batshit crazy' comment to heart.

He thrust the elephant gun into my face, my nose swallowed up in the cavernous muzzle. My voice echoed as I said, "Take it easy, Salisbury. We were just heading back to town to fetch more men." I glanced at Lester and Eliza. "Right, guys?"

Eliza said, "That's the God's honest truth, Mr. Salisbury."

Lester said, "Huh?"

Salisbury said, "You must think I'm a damn fool, Levine."

"Nope. Just a little nuts—"

"You're not going anywhere . . ." Salisbury snarled. He whipped the gun barrels towards Lester and Eliza. "None of you are!" Before I could make a move for the gun, the barrels swung back towards me. "Not now that I'm *so close* . . ."

"Whoa!" Lester cried. He thrust his arms above his head. Piss sloshed from the beer can he was holding. "The fuck's going on here, Jimmy?"

I said to Salisbury, "Tell them."

"Tell us what?" Lester said.

"Bait . . ." I said. "He's using us as bait."

"Is it true, Mr. Salisbury?" Eliza said.

"Nothing personal, missy . . ." Salisbury said. "And you were safe within a ring of steel. But I warn you—you're just as much use to me dead as you are alive."

"Well, you rotten bastard," Eliza said—and she snatched the beer can from Lester's hand and flung the contents into Salisbury's face.

The skunk aper staggered back with a cry of disgust, blinded, mopping Lester's piss from his eyes. I'd caught some splash-back too—*gross*—but it was all the distraction I needed. I kicked the elephant gun from Salisbury's hands, and it crashed to the ground at Lester's feet, and then I socked the crazy bastard across the jaw. As he reeled from the blow, I hurled myself at him and tackled him hard to the ground. We fought in the dirt like wild dogs—baring our teeth and snarling and spraying piss and spittle. Salisbury snatched his kukri knife from its sheath. I grabbed his wrist and we fought for the knife, rolling towards the campfire, until there was nowhere left to roll. I was on my back and Salisbury was on top of me, bearing down on the knife with all his weight, the tip of the blade inching down towards my face.

On the edge of my vision I saw Lester struggle to aim the elephant gun. He buckled under the weight. Could barely raise the barrels. "I can't get a clear shot!"

I shouted, "It's an elephant gun, you moron—there IS no clear shot—you'll kill us all!"

But I saw his finger teasing the trigger . . .

That's when a rocket flare swooshed up into the night sky, exploding like a firework and bathing the clearing in sputtering red light as it parachuted back down to earth.

"The tripwire—" Salisbury gasped. "It . . . it sprung the tripwire!"

'It' could have been anything—a squirrel, a raccoon, maybe even the bear cub's momma—but whatever it was I owed that critter a big sloppy kiss—or an apology—because Salisbury's weight eased off the knife as he looked up at the flare. I jacked my knee into his groin. He woofed in pain. The knife slipped from his hands and dropped to the ground. I heaved him off me—

And then a bestial howl echoed over the clearing, the same blood-freezing howl I'd heard on the video of Ned's abduction. Eliza pointed and screamed. Lester cried out: "Oh shit, oh fuck— *There it is*!"

Whatever the thing was, it was no bear cub.

The beast was huge—far bigger than a man—it was snared in a web of cargo netting, suspended high above the ground from the jutting branch of a pine tree. It must have been stalking towards camp when it tripped the trap. Screeching like a banshee, the creature thrashed wildly to free itself from the webbing. The net yo-yoed from the tree branch, the limb bending under its weight. It wouldn't hold for much longer.

Then I saw Lester raising the barrels of the elephant gun.

"Lester, no!" I cried.

"Swash, no!" Salisbury cried.

But it was too late; he didn't hear us, or was too panicked to listen.

The cannon roared and belched fiery smoke.

The recoil ragdolled Lester back off his feet. He thudded to the ground and tobogganed through the dirt, skidding to a stop where he lay dazed and winded.

The devastating impact of the .700 bullets cored the base of the tree in a blast of shrapnel and splinters. The tree lurched violently. The branch supporting the beast in the snare net sheared away from the trunk with a thunderous *crack!* The net plummeted to the ground. The beast thrashed free from the webbing and scrambled away into the darkness. The tree creaked and shuddered above the clearing like a bowling pin—then began toppling down on the camp.

Salisbury scrambled away on his hands and knees. Staggering to my feet, I hurled myself at Eliza, leaping clear across the campfire and tackling her to safety. But Lester—the poor bastard, pinned down beneath the weight of the elephant gun—could only scream as the tree came crashing down and crushed him like a bug beneath a giant flyswatter.

A shockwave of leaves and dirt erupted through the clearing. The campfire was snuffed out like a candle. Shielding Eliza's body with my own, I raised my forearm to protect my face from the shrapnel of pine needles. When the dust cloud cleared, I raised my head gingerly.

Salisbury was hacking at the felled tree with his kukri knife, breaking branches and raking foliage aside. There wasn't a hope in hell Lester could have survived. Then I realized Salisbury wasn't looking for Lester. Digging through the foliate rubble, Salisbury hacked away another branch and threw it aside to reveal Lester's shattered body. I told Eliza not to look. Lester's face was buried beneath branches, but I could see he still clutched the elephant gun to his chest. The impact of the tree had crushed the heavy weapon into his ribcage. Salisbury wrenched the gun from Lester's dead fingers, and then he charged off into the woods in pursuit of the beast, bellowing a war cry, a man possessed.

Eliza wriggled free and clambered to her feet. She stared down numbly at the felled tree. "Lester?" she said, in a tiny cracked voice. "Quit playing now, baby." She choked back a sob as she realized this wasn't some kind of elaborate prank.

"Eliza," I said to her, softly. "We have to go. Right now." I put my arm around her and began ushering her away from the tree like a sylvan funeral director.

"We can't just leave him here, Mr. Levine!" She fought free of my arms and threw herself on top of the tree, grasping one of Lester's hands and kissing it as if she could bring him magically back to life. "I'm not leaving him," she sobbed.

We didn't have time for this. I glanced into the woods where Salisbury had gone after the skunk ape. The crazy bastard could come back at any minute with that damn cannon of his. "Go start the camper, Eliza. I'll figure something out."

"You promise we won't leave him?" I promised. "Thank you, Mr. Levine." She kissed Lester's hand once more and then scurried off towards the Minnie Winnie.

Once Eliza had gone, I clawed away the rest of the foliage to reveal what was left of Lester. Just as well she wasn't there to see it. The poor bastard had hemorrhaged when the tree pulped him. His mouth was frozen in a silent scream. His eyes bugged from his skull on bloody stalks. Propping my foot against a thick branch for leverage, I sucked a deep breath, gripping Lester's arms at the wrist, then I pulled with all my strength, and his shoulders dislocated with a horrific pop of gristle and bone, and I cried out in disgust but kept on pulling, until I finally managed to drag his body out from under the leafy rubble.

Without pausing for breath, I zippered the corpse inside Lester and Eliza's sleeping bag, slung the burden over my shoulder, and then staggered to the Minnie Winnie. I clambered aboard, thumping Lester's head on the doorway as I entered. "Sorry, Lester . . ." I lowered him carefully onto the kitchenette's bench seat, a little more gently than I might have, had Eliza not been watching me in the rearview. Then, gasping for breath, I collapsed down onto the passenger seat beside her. "You okay to drive?" Eliza nodded, adjusted the rearview so she could see Lester's sleeping bag-shrouded shape in the mirror, and then she keyed the ignition, the engine growled to life, the headlights blinked on—

Salisbury stood blocking our path with the elephant gun leveled at Eliza. The muzzle seemed as big as the Holland Tunnel. At this range, we'd be vaporized.

"Missy," Salisbury said, "ease your foot off the gas, nice n' slow."

But Eliza started pumping the gas and revving the engine like a bull raking its hoof in the dirt. Glaring at Salisbury, she was about to throw the camper into gear and mow the bastard down, when I grasped her arm and said, "Don't."

Eliza flinched and looked at me in surprise. She'd apparently forgotten I was even riding bitch. She glanced in the rearview at Lester's sleeping bag-shrouded corpse, tears welling up in her eyes. Then she nodded, her hand dropped grudgingly from the gearstick, the engine whined down as her foot slid from the gas pedal, and she slumped over the steering wheel and started sobbing.

Salisbury grinned at me fiercely. Removing one of his hands from the elephant gun—I had to admire the crazy bastard's strength, that he could wield the cannon one-handed—he held up his palm in the glow of the headlights.

It was coated thickly in blood.

"It's hurt."

15.

We followed the trail of the beast's blood through the Sticks.

Eliza drove in numb silence, white-knuckling the wheel, her eyes wide and glassy with grief. Salisbury rode elephant gun, the barrels of the cannon propped on the headrest of the passenger seat, aimed directly at me. Staring into the muzzle was like looking down a long dark tunnel with no light at the end of it, just the pearly white gates if I made a wrong move. I was sitting next to Lester on the kitchenette's bench seat. His head was lolling fondly on my shoulder, like an easy girl at the drive-in. Every bump on the trail, the shrouded corpse would slump across me, and when Eliza wasn't watching in the rearview, I'd elbow him back into a sitting position. "Lester might've pulled the trigger," I said to Salisbury, "but you good as killed this boy yourself."

"The drunken fool cost me my skunk ape," he said. Eliza glared daggers at him. "I regret the boy's death," Salisbury allowed, with little feeling, "but in any war there are casualties. And rest assured," he warned us, "if you or Miss Tuttle stand in my way I will not hesitate to remove you with lethal force."

"I was wrong about you..."

He cocked his eyebrow.

"You're even crazier than I thought," I said. "When we tell the law what happened out here, you're going back to the nuthouse."

Salisbury hacked out a hollow laugh. "I don't give a damn what happens to me. Look around you, Levine." He gestured about the filthily cluttered camper. "What kind of life do you think I have? Do you think I care about fame or material rewards? No. Slaying this beast is all that matters."

With that, Salisbury looked away from me and gazed through the windshield at the blood trail, disappearing into the darkness beyond the headlights.

* * *

Grey dawn light filtered through the forest canopy as the Minnie Winnie jounced across the uneven terrain. Eliza wrestled the wheel, slaloming between trees that loomed suddenly before us. Branches whipped the camper, raking the windshield like twiggy fingernails. The grill guard chewed through the brush like threshing teeth. And then we burst through a tangle of bracken—emerging without warning onto a narrow shelf above a plunging ravine, the chasm yawning before us like the edge of Flat Earth.

I cried out a warning. Salisbury's grip tightened on his gun. Eliza hit the brakes and we were pitched forwards in our seats. Lester's shrouded head slammed down upon the kitchenette table. The camper slewed to a shuddering halt at the foot of a ramshackle wooden truss bridge.

I let out my breath and sat Lester upright. His head was cocked at a quizzical angle—I think he'd broken his neck when he head-butted the table—he looked like he was wondering what we were going to do next. Eliza asked me if he was okay. I thought, *Apart from being dead.* I told her: "He's fine."

Salisbury considered the challenge before us and growled, "Damn it all to hell . . ."

"Nothing else for it," I said. "We'll have to find another way across."

But if I'd thought something so simple as a suicidal bridge crossing might give Salisbury pause, I had underestimated his obsession.

"No time," he said. "I won't lose him, not now I'm so *close*."

He herded us from the camper with the gun at our backs.

The ravine cleaved the woods in two like an axe wound. Craggy rock walls plunged thirty-feet down onto whitewater rapids. Jagged rocks studded the river like the spine of a wallowing stegosaur. The bridge looked like something an insane hobbyist had built using matchsticks; a fallen Jenga tower of rotten timber trussed together with rusted steel cables and fraying snakes of rope. Bloodstains spattered the bridge path. The creature's fart-in-an-elevator stink still lingered in the air.

But for the first time, I felt a glimmer of hope; I knew where we were. The Bigelow Skunk Ape had long been rumored to haunt Strickland Bridge—and other local death traps parents sought to frighten their children away from. If Eliza and me could somehow give Salisbury the slip, I was confident we could follow the river and blunder our way back to town. Of course, that was easier said than done with a maniac holding an elephant gun to our backs.

Salisbury nudged Eliza towards the bridge.

"Guide us across, missy," he said. "You're driving, Levine."

"Are you nuts?" I said, rhetorically. "No way that bridge is gonna hold us."

Salisbury shoved the gun in my face and said, "If you prefer, I could jettison some weight—a bouncer and a stripper's worth, say—and make the crossing myself."

"I'll be fine, Mr. Levine," Eliza assured me. She was eyeing the bridge speculatively. "Just don't forget to buckle up."

I started saying, "Road safety's the least of my concerns right now—"

Then she winked at me; a sly wink that scared me as much as Salisbury's gun. God help me, Eliza had a plan. At least, she *thought* she did. Because unless I'd misinterpreted that wink, and her advice that I buckle up, it was a plan straight out of the Lester Swash playbook. She had to be dumber than Lester and crazier than Salisbury if she thought it would achieve anything other than killing us all.

But before I could try and reason with her, she'd already turned and stepped cautiously onto the bridge. Inching across the path, her arms outstretched like a tightrope walker, she tested each rotten beam with her foot before entrusting her weight to it.

Salisbury frog-marched me back to the camper. I slumped down behind the wheel, not quite believing what I was about to do. Salisbury sat beside me and jammed the gun barrels under my armpit. I fastened my seat belt and keyed the ignition and the engine growled to life. I glanced at Salisbury. He wasn't wearing his seat belt. He seemed to hold them in the same disdain as Quint the shark fisherman held for life jackets.

Salisbury offered me this sage advice, "Nice and easy now, Levine."

"You think?"

I swiped the sweat off my palms on my jeans, shifted the Minnie Winnie into gear, and then I teased my foot down on the gas pedal, clutching the wheel in a white-knuckle grip as the camper crawled onto the bridge.

The entire structure shuddered violently. Rotten wood groaned and sagged under the Minnie Winnie's weight, or just crumbled to sawdust beneath the slow-rolling tires. The cables and ropes squealed like an orchestra of tautly stringed instruments. Eliza guided us forwards like a traffic cop, steering me left and right and halting my snail's pace-crawl with urgent hand signals and animated facial expressions. And somehow, by some miracle, the bridge was holding.

"You see, Levine?" Salisbury cackled. "God loves a skunk aper!"

Then we reached the middle of the bridge—Eliza winked at me—there was a thunderclap of rotten wood, and the camper gave a violent downwards lurch like a submarine performing an emergency dive. The camper's nose chewed through the bridge path like a giant ravenous termite. The rear-end seesawed off the ground, tires spinning in space, as the Minnie Winnie tore through the underside of the bridge in a blizzard of sawdust. For a moment, we hung suspended in a tangled net of ropes and cables, like an insect trapped in a spider's web. Then one by one they snapped with a musical twang—and then suddenly we were freefalling . . . A kamikaze camper plummeting thirty-feet down towards the river and the rocks.

16.

The camper cratered onto the rocks, the hood crumpling like a tin can, the windshield shattering on impact. A hailstorm of broken glass tore through the cab, studding my arms as I raised them to shield my eyes. The impact pitched me forwards in my seat. My seat belt bit sharply into my chest, snatching the air from my lungs. My neck whiplashed, my forehead thumping the steering wheel.

Not wearing his seat belt, Salisbury thudded against the dash like a crash test dummy. The gun was wrenched away from my armpit.

Then the camper rocked forwards and crashed onto its roof and the world turned topsy-turvy. Lester's shrouded corpse was hurled about the camper like a scarecrow in a hurricane. The bait buckets spilled like cans of paint, decorating the camper like a demented Jackson Pollack.

Pinned to my seat by my belt, I dangled upside-down, watching helplessly as Salisbury peeled himself from the upturned roof. How the hell he'd survived the crash, I didn't know; maybe he was right, God really *did* love a skunk aper.

Then I saw with horror he was still clutching the elephant gun.

"Goddamn you, Levine . . ."

Racked with pain, furious he was losing his quarry, Salisbury raised the barrels towards me—and then a high-pressure spray of water tore through the camper and punched out the rear window and he was blasted outside like a Wet N' Wild ride. So too was Lester; I saw him in his sleeping bag, being swept away downriver like a sea burial.

The camper was flooding fast, bait buckets bobbing in the water like putrid fishing lures. I sucked a deep breath before the fast-rising water enveloped my head. Then I fumbled to unfasten my— *My seatbelt was jammed!* I couldn't release the lock. Panicking, I thrashed and flailed against my restraints like a condemned con riding Old Sparky, screaming bubbles in the icy water. A startled fish swam past me. For a moment we locked eyes, before it darted away. Then I saw Salisbury's slouch hat floating by. I snatched the hat, tore one of the cougar's fangs from the hatband, and used its sharp edge to saw frantically through the belt strapped across my chest. My lungs burned for air, gray clouded the edge of my vision . . . and then the fraying strap broke away from my chest and I floated free from my seat. With a last effort, I propelled myself through the broken windshield, kicking upwards, clawing towards the sunlight, exploding to the surface and sucking in great gulps of air.

The upturned camper sank amid a seething froth of bubbles, until only the tires were visible. Flotsam popped to the surface around me. Clinging to a rock to avoid being swept away downriver, I searched for Salisbury but couldn't see him anywhere. Drowned, I hoped. Peering up at the bridge, I was amazed to see it was still standing. A gaping hole in the midsection had collapsed where the Minnie Winnie had torn right through it. The foot-ends jutted like gangplanks on either embankment. I couldn't see Eliza above me.

Paddling to shore, I dragged myself hand-over-hand onto the bank, slithering through the mud like some strange creature in the process of evolution. I slumped in exhaustion against the sheer rock wall, trying to catch my breath. It was hard to believe I'd survived. Staring at the wreckage of the sunken camper was like an out-of-body experience. I felt dog-tired all of a sudden. All I wanted was to curl up on the bank and take a long nap. My head lolled, my eyelids drooped. Then I heard a scratching sound above me.

Raising my head, I saw a length of rope snaking down the rock face, until it coiled in the mud beside me. "Eliza . . ." I said. "What the hell were you thinking?"

"Didn't you see me wink 'Jump'?" Eliza called from above.

Then she said, "Tie the rope around your waist, Mr. Levine!"

She was flattering me if she thought she could pull my ass up. Even at my fighting weight, I'd fought at light heavy—and that was many beers ago. But I tied the rope around my waist and told Eliza to anchor the other end around a tree that would take my weight in the likely event that I slipped and fell. I was searching the rock face for handholds to begin scaling the cliff—when the rope snapped taut and I was hoisted off my feet and began being winched up the wall.

The girl had freakish strength.

It was only when I reached the top of the cliff that I realized she'd had help. Rough hands dragged me onto the precipice and rolled me onto my back. Then a familiar smiling face loomed over me—and I wondered if maybe I'd died in the camper wreck after all, died and gone straight to hell.

17.

The last time I'd seen him, he'd been on his hands and knees, scrabbling for his rotten teeth on the floor of The Henhouse. Now he was sporting a pair of Gary Busey-big dentures that didn't quite fit his mouth. "Oh, I prayed to God I'd run into you again," Smiley said. Before I could react, he booted me in the guts. As I hacked for breath, he grabbed hold of my shirt, dragged me to my feet, and jammed the barrel of an AK-47 under my jaw. "Remember me, motherfucker?"

"I never forget a pretty smile."

Clearly sensitive about his new teeth, he tried to close his lips around his whopping dentures, and couldn't quite manage it. "Laugh it up while you still can, asshole. Cuz I aim to return the favor with a fucking claw hammer."

I glanced at Eliza. Another Damn Dirty Ape—Blubberguts—had his beefy arms wrapped around her. He was kneading her breasts like he was trying to coax music from them, but the only sounds it produced were Eliza's moans of disgust.

"I'm sorry, Mr. Levine. They just came out of nowhere. I couldn't stop 'em."

"You okay?"

She nodded sadly.

Smiley patted me on the shoulder. "She's fine, Palooka."

Blubberguts haw-haw-hawed as he honked her breasts. "She's *real* fine."

As Eliza squirmed in Blubberguts's grip, my eyes darted to the sawed-off shotgun with the pistol grip the big man wore in a leather bucket holster on his thigh.

I bunched my fists by my sides. "If you hurt her," I said, "so help me, I'll—"

Smiley ground the barrel of the AK-47 into the underside of my jaw. "You'll do *what* exactly?" Sneering, he said, "Trust me, Palooka—pretty soon you're gonna be too busy wishing you was dead to even *think* about playing hero." He glanced at the broken bridge; peered down over the cliff edge at the camper submerged in the river below. "Now what the fuck are y'all doing out here?"

I was wondering the same thing about them. I'd thought the skunk ape had devoured and excreted the bikers. But I figured what the hell and just went ahead and told him. "Hunting skunk ape."

Blubberguts haw-haw-hawed. "Hunting skunk ape, he says."

Smiley gave a snort of amusement. "Find any?"

"Just the Damn Dirty kind."

Smiley snatched a knife from a hip sheath and cut the rope from around my waist. Gripping my shoulder, he spun me around, and jammed the barrel of the AK against my spine. "Get walking." He encouraged me with a kick in the ass.

As I staggered forwards, I said to Eliza, "It's gonna be okay."

Smiley said, "He's lying to you, princess."

They marched us into the woods, Smiley with the barrel of the Widowmaker glued to my spine, Eliza saddled over Blubberguts's shoulders. Conversation was limited to "Keep walking, asshole," punctuated with a shove or a kick in the ass and a haw-haw-haw from Blubberguts. I glanced once again at Blubberguts's sawed-off, but wasn't convinced I could snatch it from his thigh holster before Smiley gunned me down, so I just kept walking, trying to stay out of range of those kicks in the ass.

* * *

After hiking for some time, we broke through the brush and emerged into an overgrown farmyard. A derelict farmhouse and a scattering of tumbledown outbuildings loomed before us. The rusted hulks of junk farming equipment lurked in the tall grass and weeds. I remembered the place from a recent conversation with Eliza. This was Herb Planter's old farm—where the fugitive Melvin Stott had come to sate his mongoloid lust on Herb's hogs. The place had fallen to rot and ruin since then. The only people who came here now were local kids: Drinking beer, smoking weed, honing their graffiti skills, and boosting the teenage pregnancy stats. A fleet of five motorcycles leaned on kickstands outside the porch. A sidecar was fitted to the bike on the end. I couldn't see the rest of the bikers anywhere; the other Damn Dirty Apes must have been inside the house.

A sharp chemical smell choked the air. "Mmm-hmm . . ." I said. "Just like momma used to make." Things were starting to make sense. The Damn Dirty Apes were cooking crystal meth out here. They must have heard the Minnie Winnie wreck. Smiley and Blubberguts had been sent to scout the commotion.

Smiley gave me a shove towards the house. He stuck two fingers in his mouth and attempted to whistle, but with his dentures, could only achieve a sloppy sputtering sound. He glared at me, daring me to crack wise.

"We got company!" he hollered at the house.

The Damn Dirty Apes emerged from the house. Shitface and Baby Doll were wearing gas masks, and the same MC vests they'd worn that night at The Henhouse. Chains—rusted neck chains, Old Dixie do-rag, and a six-shooter holstered gunfighter-style on his hip—was last to appear. He peeled the gasmask from his face and let it hang around his neck like a fetish collar.

"Ain't that the knucklehead from the titty bar?" he said when he saw me.

I played it cool and said, "Sup."

Smiley forced me to my knees.

Blubberguts dropped Eliza down in the dirt beside me.

Chains finished ogling Eliza and then returned his attention to me.

"The fuck're you doing out here, boy?"

Smiley couldn't wait to share the joke. "Hunting skunk ape."

The Apes laughed their asses off.

Chains grinned at me. "That true, boy? You hunting skunk ape?"

Stalling for time, praying God would see me in my time of need, and divinely intervene, I told Chains and the rest of the Apes the whole sorry story.

It was a big hit with the Apes. They were all howling with laughter; even Smiley was almost in tears, covering his mouth to stifle his laughter and stop his dentures popping out. By the time I was done, I was cackling along with them. Saying it out loud, I had to admit the whole thing sounded fucking crazy. Like I'd smoked the whole batch of what they were cooking up inside.

Still chuckling, I said, "So you see, whatever you guys are doing out here, it's none of our business. And what happened at The Henhouse—well, you already got your licks in. As far as I'm concerned, that's all water under the bridge—"

"Like hell it is," said Smiley, his dentures clacking like maracas.

"You can just let us go, and we'll be on our way," I said. "We won't say a word to anyone."

Chains scratched his stubble like he was seriously considering it.

Then he said, "Or we could just fucking kill you?"

My shoulders slumped. "There's that, I suppose." I cut an anxious glance at Eliza. "At least let the girl go." Reggie Levine: Chivalrous to the bitter end.

"Let her go?" Chains cackled. "Shit, son—we been cooking all week. Reckon we deserve us a ree-ward for all our hard work." He played to the Apes. "What d'you say, fellas?" I guessed that included Baby Doll. "Soon as we cook up this last batch we take Blondie here for a train ride." The Apes howled like lusty wolves.

Eliza looked at me pleadingly.

I couldn't meet her eyes. "I'm sorry, Eliza . . ."

She slumped forwards in the dirt, raking her hands in the earth.

"What about *this* asshole?" Smiley said.

He prodded me in the back of the skull with his AK.

Before Chains could answer, I jerked my head to the side, and the barrel of Smiley's AK slid past my shoulder. I grabbed the barrel and yanked it, pulling Smiley down towards me as I sprang to my feet and slammed the back of my skull into his chin. His dentures shattered with a sound like Fast Eddie Felson breaking pool balls and he crumpled to the ground. Clutching the AK by the barrel, I swung it like a club against Blubberguts's skull. The stock impacted with a meaty thud, jarring the gun from my hands. The big man avalanched down on top of Smiley. There was no time for me to retrieve the AK. Eliza flung double fistfuls of dirt into the faces of Chains, Shitface, and Baby Doll, and as they staggered back, blinded, choking on dust, I grabbed Eliza's wrist and we ran.

As we jinked through the maze of junk farming equipment, someone fired a gun, and the shot pinged off a tractor with a flash of sparks.

"Don't shoot!" Chains cried. "You'll blow us all sky-high!"

I dragged Eliza towards the barn. We scrambled inside and slammed the door and bolted it shut with a horizontal bar. Seconds later, the Apes started hammering and hurling themselves against it, the door shuddering violently under the assault. Then Smiley must have found an axe from somewhere. He started hacking at the door like Jack Nicholson doing his "Here's Johnny!" number. Smiley glared at me through the splintered slats, his lips bloodied and torn by his shattered dentures. "Muggerfugger! Goo broge by teeb! Again!" He continued hacking his way through the door. It wasn't going to hold for much longer.

I looked around wildly for a weapon. Just cobwebs and straw—unless the Apes were arachnophobic, or suffered from hay fever, we were shit out of luck. The barn was too dingy for me to see much of anything else. On either side of us were livestock stalls. At the end of the barn, a rickety ladder led up to the hayloft. I started dragging Eliza towards the ladder—when in doubt, *climb*—but she dug in her heels and refused to move. "Mr. Levine!" She gripped my hand till the knuckles popped. "That smell . . ." I was about to tell her that the funky odor was the least of our problems, when I recognized the stench, and I glanced into the livestock stall from which it was wafting.

Huddled in the gloomy stall, curled in a fetal ball, was Ned, still wearing his Boogaloo Baboon costume. If simians have a hell, Boogaloo called it home. His blood-matted fur was ripped out in mangy patches. His tail had been yanked off at the root. The once proud red-cushion ass of the baboon costume was torn out to reveal Ned's skinny butt, which looked in even worse condition than the costume, his buttocks scratched and caked with blood.

"Ned?" I gasped.

What the hell had the Apes been doing to the poor bastard?

Boogaloo flinched at the sound of my voice; Ned whimpered inside the baboon mask. "Please . . ." he rasped. "Please, no more . . ."

"Ned, it's me." I crouched down beside him. "It's Reggie."

Grunting with effort, Ned raised the heavy baboon mask off the ground. A hole had been gouged through it. A glazed eye peered out at me. It reminded me of the photos I'd seen of Vietnam vets returning from a tour of duty. The thousand-yard stare.

"Reggie?" Like he wasn't sure if he was imagining things. "Is . . . is it really you?"

And then he started to sob, a pitiful broken sound.

"It's okay, Ned," I said. "You're gonna be okay." Not strictly true—not with the Apes breaking down the barn door—but at least now Ned wouldn't die alone.

"Oh, thank God—" Ned bawled, clutching at me. "I thought . . . I thought that thing was gonna hump me to death."

I frowned.

"What thing?"

That's when the skunk ape dropped down from the hayloft.

18.

It landed with a heavy thud behind Eliza and me. With a terrified shriek, Ned scuttled to the far end of the stall and curled himself into a protective ball. I whirled towards the beast, shielding Eliza behind me. I had time to think: For a skunk ape, the damn thing looked a lot like an orangutan—And then it snatched my head in a huge leathery paw, Eliza's in the other, and smashed our skulls together like cymbals, and down I went like a TV with the plug pulled.

When I came to, I was flat on my back in the yard outside the farmhouse. Eliza was sprawled in the dirt beside me, out-cold. A nasty-looking lump, where the skunk ape had cracked our skulls together, protruded through her hair like a pink anthill.

I forced myself to sit—regretted it instantly—clutching my head as if afraid it would crumble to dust in my hands. Shielding my eyes from the sun, I saw the barn door clapping open and shut in the breeze, and a rutted trail in the dirt where the skunk ape must have dragged us from the barn to the farmhouse.

Except it wasn't a skunk ape.

It was an orangutan—just as I'd thought before it put me to sleep—wearing calf-length cargo shorts, and a biker vest with the Motorcycle Club's patch on the back. His shoulder was bandaged, the gauze sodden with blood, where he must have been wounded by the shrapnel of splinters when the elephant gun cored the tree. The first thing that struck me was the stench—it staggered me back like a physical blow—the ape reeked like a Grizzly had excreted a whole colony of skunks before wiping its ass on his fur. A halo of flies buzzed drunkenly above his head. He was an ugly brute, too. Maybe even harsher on the eye than Baby Doll. His face was hashtagged with battle scars, the skin leathery and cracked like an old cowboy's saddle, or Charles Bronson in one of the later *Death Wish* pictures. His filthy fur was tangled into ruddy brown dreadlocks. The whiskers around his muzzle were salted gray like a silvery Fu Manchu mustache. His dull amber eyes seemed only slightly less human than the rest of the Damn Dirty Apes. And they were sizing me up in a way that made my balls shrink to the size of chickpeas, as if he couldn't decide if he wanted to fight me or fuck me. I could scarcely imagine the living hell poor Ned must have endured as this monster had its way with him.

Chains said, "There's your skunk ape, asshole."

So far I'd mistaken a black bear and an orangutan for a skunk ape; and yet never once had I looked in my shaving mirror and mistaken myself for George Clooney. The only thing I can say in my defense was that the beast *smelled* like you'd expect a skunk ape to smell; like a wet pack mule saddled with shitty diapers.

Chains said to the orangutan, "Say hello to our guests, Mofo."

Things were plenty weird enough already; if the orangutan actually started talking, I thought I would scream. Mercifully, the ape just blew a raspberry and flipped me the bird. Exactly like he did to Walt from the sidecar, that night at The Henhouse—and just like that, the final piece of the jigsaw fell into place.

The only thing I still couldn't figure was that big pile of shit and the bike tracks we'd found in the Sticks. I guessed the Apes had been on their way out to Herb's farm when they'd stopped for Mofo to pinch a loaf. Who knows how Baby Doll lost the doll's head from her necklace? And hell, I really wasn't giving it much thought, focused as I was on the big-ass ugly orangutan glaring at me.

"We won him in a game of cards from a fella runs a roadside zoo," Chains said. "Mofo's been riding with us for years now." He jerked a thumb over his shoulder at the sidecar attached to his hog, just in case I thought the orangutan had his own bike, although right then, nothing would have surprised me. "Full-blood member. Somewhere under all that fur, he's even got the ink."

It was all I could do just to shake my head in disbelief.

"We was holed up in a motel outside Jasper," Chains explained, "try'na figure out where we was gonna cook. Shawna's got the TV playing—" He glanced at Baby Doll. "What was it you was watching, girl?"

Baby Doll thought long and hard. "*Mike & Molly*?"

Chains rolled his eyes and sighed. "After *Mike & Molly*, you dumb cunt."

"Oh," Baby Doll said.

Chains stressed to me, "We wasn't watching *Mike & Molly*."

"Sure you weren't," I said.

Chains looked like he wanted to press the point.

Then Baby Doll said, "*The Unexplained Files*."

Chains snapped his fingers. "*The Unexplained Files*," he nodded. "It just come on the TV like a sign from God. A special 'bout the Bigelow Skunk

Ape. 'Cording to the show, moonshiners made him up to scare folks away from their whiskey stills. An' that's when it hits me. Alls we need is for the Bigelow Skunk Ape to make a reappearance, and then the Sticks is ours to do with what we please. We can cook up our shit without nobody coming out here n' bothering us. Just like the moonshinin' days. So we send Mofo off to scare the shit outta some dumbass yokels. Figured it'd be a fisherman or a hiker or something." Chains looked at Eliza reproachfully. "Not a buncha freaks making a fuck-flick . . . Anyway, sure enough, word spreads about the 'Skunk Ape' and folks stayed away—until now."

"You would've got away with it too," I said, "if it wasn't for us pesky kids."

Chains grinned at me. "Something I didn't count on," he said, "there'd be anybody damn fool enough to come looking for the fucking thing."

"He kidnapped a friend of ours," I said.

"That wasn't part of the plan," Chains admitted. "But in Mofo's defense, your friend was dressed provocatively in that baboon costume. Mofo took one look at that big red butt and fell in love. When he brung the fella back here, I didn't see no harm in letting Mofo have some sport. And it's a braver man than me who'll stand in the way of a randy orangutan and his mate."

I glanced at the orangutan, shivering in the heat of its gaze.

Mofo peeled off his biker vest and tossed it to Shitface. He started pacing the dooryard, stomping his huge feet, pinwheeling his arms and chinking his neck.

"Whoa—" I said. "The hell's it doing?"

"Limbering up," Chains said.

Sick fear shuddered through me. "Limbering up for what?"

Chains gave a throaty chuckle. "Take it easy, sport. Unless you're planning on slipping into your buddy's baboon costume, I reckon you're safe."

Then he grinned at me and said, almost purring, "*Reggie Levine . . .*"

I tried not to show my surprise that he knew my name.

"You know," he said, "I saw you fight Boar Hog Brannon."

"If you could call it that," I said.

"Always wondered how Boar Hog's fists took all that punishment."

"My head wondered the same thing."

"Heard you hung up your gloves after that?"

"Figured I'd quit while I was behind."

"Never tempted to lace 'em back up?"

I cut an anxious glance at the orangutan.

"Nope," I said, not liking where this conversation was going.

"Shame," Chains said. "It took true grit sticking it out with Boar Hog for as long as you done . . ." He turned to the other Apes. "In fact, I reckon 'The Bigelow Bleeder' Reggie Levine could last . . . oh, let's call it four minutes versus Mofo."

"Four minutes?" Shitface scoffed. "Bullshit! I'll take me summa that action."

The Apes started placing bets. I noticed that none of them were betting on me to win. They were wagering how quickly Mofo would beat me to death.

"Wait a minute—" I staggered to my feet. "You don't honestly expect me to fight an orangutan, do you?"

"What's the problem?" Chains said. "Mofo'll give you a fair fight." He seesawed his hand. "Ish." He shadowboxed a few lefts and rights. "Taught him myself."

"This . . . this is crazy," I stammered. "I'm not fighting a fucking monkey!"

Chains nodded like he understood perfectly. "Then I guess you're getting beat to death by one."

Eliza came awake with a groan. Reaching for her head, she hissed in pain as her fingers prodded the lump on her skull. She glanced around at the Apes. Then she saw the orangutan and her eyes bugged with shock. She clutched at my leg.

"Mr. Levine?" she whispered. "Do you see that orangutan doing stretching exercises over there?"

I assured her I did.

She sighed with relief, like she wasn't going crazy after all.

"Mr. Levine?"

"Yeah."

"The hell's going on?"

I just shook my head.

"Mr. Levine?"

"Yes, Eliza."

"Am I dreaming?"

"I think we both are."

Chains was enjoying himself so much, he decided to be generous. "Tell you what, sport. You beat Mofo—" The other Apes hooted with laughter at this preposterous notion: "—I'll let you and your lady friend and even Mofo's little fuck-buddy leave here alive." He held up his hand: "Scout's honor."

What the hell other choice did I have? Way I saw it, I could just curl in a ball and allow myself to be torn limb from limb by an orangutan, or I could throw a few punches for pride's sake, and then be torn limb from limb by an orangutan.

I sucked in my gut, stripped off my shirt and handed it to Eliza.

"Good luck, Mr. Levine."

"You get a chance," I whispered to her, "run."

I forced myself to look at my opponent. My mouth went dry and I swallowed hard and my Adam's apple tried to choke me. The orangutan was pacing at the other end of the yard, bunching his wrecking ball fists, his knuckles popping like firecrackers. He glared at me contemptuously and I knew he could smell my fear. Scared as I was, all I could think about was Boar Hog Brannon and the beating he'd given me the last time I fought. Sure, there'd been bar brawls and parking lot punch-ups since then, but nothing like that painful night in the prize ring.

And of course, nothing like this.

Smiley was smiling a bloody smile and waving his axe like it was a Mofo pennant. Watching me get beaten to death by an orangutan was clearly a more fitting demise than anything he could have devised himself. "Fuggim ugg, Moofoo!" he cried around his shattered dentures. The other Apes crowded around the dooryard, baying for blood and barking their support for Mofo.

Chains dragged Eliza to the porch steps and sat down, pulling her onto his lap.

I glanced at him, started saying, "What are the rules here—?"

Then the orangutan's arm cleared the length of the dooryard like a long hairy bargepole, and he speared me with a jab that snapped my head back and to the left like the JFK kill shot. The blow shuddered down through me, buckled my knees and made me pigeon-toed. Before I even knew what hit me, the orangutan was charging, kicking up dust as he thundered across the yard towards me. I tried to cover up, but my arms refused to cooperate. I could only watch helplessly as the orangutan threw a long looping uppercut that exploded on my chin and hurled me back off my feet like a ragdoll. I hit the deck with a grunt, skidded back across the dirt like a skipping stone, thumping my head against a rusted engine block and jerking to a stop. The orangutan loomed above me, waving his arms above his head like Clay taunting Liston.

The Apes cheered.

"Rules?" Chains cackled from his perch on the porch steps. "Protect yourself at all times, slugger!"

Splayed on my back in the dirt, my entire body was numb, prickling with pins and needles. I would have been content just to lie there and let the orangutan beat me to death. As long as it didn't do to me what it had done to Ned, I could live with that. Except I hadn't managed to throw a single punch yet, and God help me, I still had a shred of pride. I glanced at Eliza and saw the fear shining in her eyes. That was enough to stoke the furnace. I climbed to my feet—staggered but stayed up—brushed myself down. I pawed my face to check that my nose was still there. My fingers prodded a vaguely nose-shaped lump of putty that flared angrily. I snorted blood and spat it out on the dirt. Then I raised my mitts and nodded to the orangutan, acknowledging the shot that'd floored me.

"Not bad," I said, "but let's see you try that again—" The words had barely left my lips before he swarmed back in. I tried to block the barrage of blows, but he smashed through my guard like a battering ram at the castle gates, and I started eating lefts and rights like I was starving for them. But I held my ground, tucked my chin to my chest and soaked up the punishment—my one saving grace was I had a chin like George Chuvalo, and a noggin like a fucking rock—praying to the boxing gods that the orangutan would soon run out of gas.

The stubborn bastard refused to tire. I was fading fast myself. I wrestled him into a clinch, hanging on for dear life. The stench of his fur made me retch. I was grateful for my broken nose, that I couldn't get a proper whiff of him. Tying up his arms, I pounded his ribs with crunching hooks. He just shrugged and threw me off him. As I staggered back, flailing my arms to keep my balance, my fist connected with his wounded shoulder and he let out a roar of pain.

The sound was music to my ears.

I'd hurt the sonofabitch; if he could be hurt, he could be beat.

Leastways, that's what I was hoping.

Keeping out of range of his long arms, I started circling him like a shark scenting blood, preying on that wounded shoulder with popping jabs. The old training started coming back; I bobbed and weaved, darted in and out, sticking his shoulder with stinging shots and dancing away before he tagged me back.

I didn't know how long we'd been fighting, but I heard Smiley curse as his bet went to shit, and I got cocky, couldn't resist winking at him—

That was a mistake.

The orangutan rocked me with a right I never saw coming.

I did see the left; that's the one that dropped me.

I lay there pole-axed, eyes pinballing around in my skull, my vision blurred; I saw a whole colony of orangutans waddling forwards leisurely to finish me off.

I glanced at Eliza. Mouthed, *I'm sorry.* Her eyes brimmed with tears and she bowed her head like Talia Shire in the *Rocky* movies. Usually that's enough to inspire the Italian Stallion to one last onslaught, and victory. Not me. I was done.

But somehow I managed to drag myself up off the ground; when the orangutan killed me, I wanted to die on my feet, not lying in the dirt like a dog.

Mofo gave me a little nod—a mark of grudging respect, as if I'd given him more than he'd bargained for. Then he cocked his fist like he was drawing back on a hunting-bow, and as he let it fly—I dipped my head and caught the punch on the rock-hard dome of my skull. The orangutan shrieked as his knuckles fractured. He staggered back in pain, nursing his injured right paw, unable to even clench his fist. I swarmed him, and he covered up, jabbing weakly with his left to fend me off. But the damage I'd done to his wounded shoulder was money in the bank, and there was no strength in the shots. Bobbing and weaving past his pansy jab, I bulled my way forwards and worked his body, chopping him with hooks that cracked his ribs and made him gasp. He covered up his midsection—leaving his head unguarded—and then I pounced at him with a leaping left hook filled with fifteen years of bitterness and self-loathing, regrets and what ifs.

I never threw a sweeter shot. It landed right on the button, clean on the point of the chin. His head damn near rotated like the girl's in *The Exorcist.* He went down hard, like the tree that pulped Lester, out-cold before he hit the ground. A great cloud of dust billowed up and I sank to my knees at his feet. I'd put everything I had into that punch and didn't have the strength left to even raise my arm in victory. But maybe that was just as well. Judging by their shocked expressions, the Damn Dirty Apes would not have appreciated me showboating.

Eliza wrestled free from Chains's arms and scrambled across the yard to embrace me. "You did it, Mr. Levine!" "You bet," I gasped—and then celebrated by puking in the dirt.

I caught my breath and then looked up at Chains, who was glaring daggers at me from his stoop on the porch. "We had a deal, right?" He didn't answer. Just climbed to his feet and went over to Mofo. He shook his head in disgust at the unconscious ape. "Fucking fleabag don't deserve to wear the ink," Chains muttered. He snapped his fingers at Shitface. "Drag his sorry ass inside."

Shitface crouched over the orangutan and started slapping his face. Mofo snorted awake, blinking in confusion and shaking his head as if to clear the stars from his eyes. Shitface hauled the orangutan to his feet, slung an arm around his waist, and helped him stagger inside the farmhouse. Chains returned his attention to me.

"About our deal?" I said, a little less optimistically.

"Deal's off," Chains said.

Then he nodded to Smiley. "Kill this motherfucker."

19.

Eliza clung to me. "No! You can't!"

"Sweetheart," Chains said with a sigh, "you oughta be worrying 'bout what we're gonna do to you."

Baby Doll stepped forwards and slapped the curse that was forming on Eliza's lips. Then the biker bitch grabbed her by the hair and dragged her over to where Chains was standing at the foot of the porch.

Smiley and Blubberguts loomed in front of me. Blubberguts snatched the sawed-off from his thigh holster and started raising it to my head. Smiley deflected the gun with his axe, the rusted blade clanging off the barrels. The big man frowned at Smiley in confusion. A rope of congealed blood was dangling from his ear where I'd clobbered him with the AK. But compared to what I'd done to Smiley's mouth—shredded lips, chunks of false teeth embedded in his gums—Blubberguts looked in great shape. The big man seemed to acknowledge this and holstered his sawed-off. I was all Smiley's. *Shit.*

Smiley planted his feet like a golfer and then measured me with the axe for the blow that would cleave my skull in two. Hefting the axe high above his head, he was about to bring it slicing down—when a deafening cannon roared and Blubberguts's upper torso suddenly burst like a blood-filled piñata, his head smashed away as if by an invisible wrecking ball. Smiley and me were splattered in gore like we'd just done the Ice Bucket Challenge in a washtub of hog guts. Blubberguts's lower body remained intact. His intestines unspooled in thick red ropes. He rocked back on the heels of his biker boots. Then his legs did a little Elvis shimmy and his bottom half thudded to the ground beside me, his feet twitching and raking the dirt.

For a moment, as the echoing roar of the cannon faded over the farm, time seemed to stand still; no one moved, frozen in shock.

Then I mopped the viscera from my eyes and looked across the overgrown yard.

My first thought was not how Salisbury had survived—I remembered him saying that God loved a skunk aper—but to wonder if he'd waited to see how my fight with the orangutan panned out before springing into action.

Still, I was glad to see the crazy sonofabitch, especially that elephant gun of his.

Smoke billowed from the barrels as he strode towards the farmhouse.

"Unhand the woman, you fornicating barbarians!"

Salisbury fired off another shot. The porch upright next to Chains exploded into sawdust and splinters. A huge hole was blasted through the wall of the farmhouse. The porch roof buckled and collapsed. Chains leapt out of the way before he was buried beneath an avalanche of timber. Half his face was studded with wooden shrapnel, the wounds oozing blood. He hit the ground in a combat roll. Came back up with his six-shooter blazing. Skinning the hammer like a Wild West gunfighter. The sound of the six-shooter was nothing compared to the elephant gun—a chain of firecrackers to an H-bomb—but Chains's aim was truer. Salisbury was reloading as the shots struck his chest and he staggered back with a cry and collapsed beneath the line of the tall grass.

I glanced back at Eliza. That girl was no pushover. She'd taken advantage of the chaos and was now rolling around in the dirt with Baby Doll. They were going at it like wildcats in a sack, pulling hair and clawing eyes and yowling. Eliza rolled on top of Baby Doll and started throttling the bitch with her own necklace. When Baby Doll lay still on the ground—choked out—Eliza tore the necklace from her neck and gave a primal scream, waving it over her head like a trophy.

I shouted, "Run, Eliza!"

"What about Ned?"

"Just get the hell out of here!"

Still clutching her trophy necklace, Eliza scuttled away from the house and dove into a thicket of tall grass, ducking for cover behind a rusted feed trough.

Satisfied she was safe, I scrabbled through the dirt towards Blubberguts's remains . . . and the sawed-off in his thigh holster. Smiley—streaked in gore and frozen in shock—saw what I was doing, snapped out of his inertia, and began raising the axe to hurl it at me. There was no time for me to wrench the sawed-off from the holster, so I just aimed Blubberguts's leg at Smiley and pulled the trigger. The shot tore through the bottom of the holster and obliterated Blubberguts's foot before it punched a ragged red hole through Smiley's stomach. The axe dropped from his hand and he splashed to the ground in a pool of his own blood and guts, his toothless mouth popping like a fish.

Now I wrestled the sawed-off from Blubberguts's holster—

A long length of chain snaked around the barrels and the shotgun was snatched from my hands. I looked up in surprise. Chains had removed the biggest of the chains from around his neck and was wielding it like a bullwhip. With an expert flick of his wrist, he sent the sawed-off clattering away in the dirt far from my reach; another flick of his wrist and then the chain whistled through the air towards me. The heavy steel links smashed into my chest, punching the wind from my lungs. As I hacked for breath, Chains darted forwards and started whipping me with the chain like a junkyard Indiana Jones. It was all I could do just to curl into a ball, shielding my skull as he flogged me with the chain.

Sheltering behind the feed trough, Eliza saw me in trouble and hatched a plan to rival the bridge fiasco, a plan that would have been the envy of the late Lester Swash. Digging a Zippo lighter from her pocket, she set fire to the plastic doll heads on Baby Doll's necklace. As their nylon hair caught light, they burned like marshmallows, and she fetched up a rock and pitched it through the farmhouse window. Then she hurled the flaming necklace like a bola. It sailed above Chains and me . . . through the broken window . . . straight into the Apes' shake-and-bake meth lab.

In the Mark Wahlberg movies, you see old Marky Mark swaggering away from Hiroshima-sized explosions without a care in the world, the blast tousling his hair like a shampoo commercial, the flames giving his complexion a healthy glow.

But this was nothing like that; this was like Armageddon had arrived.

The farmhouse exploded like a cherry bomb inside a mailbox. A monstrous fireball punched out the walls and roof, spewing wood and glass and shingles. The Apes' bikes, parked in front of the porch, were scattered like toys hurled by a brat. The blast tossed Chains and me across the yard like dice flung from a gambler's hand. Still curled in a ball, I bounced across the yard until I woofed to a crunching stop against a junk refrigerator lying on its side in the weeds. I didn't see what happened to Chains. He'd been standing when the house exploded and took the brunt of the blast; the last I saw of Chains he was on fire, soaring through the air like a human cannonball stunt gone wrong. The force of the explosion was too much for most of the outbuildings to withstand. The barn collapsed like a house of cards. I hoped Ned had got out in time.

Reasonably sure I remained intact, I hauled myself upright and sat slumped against the refrigerator. My ears were ringing from the explosion. I surveyed the devastation. Fiery debris rained down from the sky. I saw Eliza poke her head above the feed trough to witness the hell she had wrought.

Her eyes were wide with shock. Looking like a prankster whose prank had spiraled out of control, she ducked back down sheepishly behind the trough.

I was about to call to her when my eyes found Salisbury. The skunk aper was splayed on his back in the tall grass. His teeth were bloody and bared in pain. He'd clamped a hand to his ruptured chest in a futile attempt to staunch the blood flow. As his lifeblood gushed through his fingers, he looked at me, and his eyes filled with shame. He rasped: "Forgive me, Levine . . . I—I was wrong about you . . . You—you're no quitter . . ." And then he smiled at me strangely before lapsing into a lung-shredding coughing fit that spattered his beard with blood.

I told him, "Just hang in there, Salisbury." I looked around the smoldering farmyard. I still couldn't see Chains anywhere. It didn't know what had happened to Shitface and Mofo. They'd been inside the house when it exploded and I figured they must have been incinerated in the blast. Then I heard a whistling sound above me, and I rolled my eyes slowly upwards.

"You gotta be shitting me . . ."

20.

For those of you unfamiliar with the sound a burning orangutan makes as it falls from a great height, take my word for it; there's nothing quite like it.

Salisbury's eyes widened in horror as he saw the plummeting ape. Its shadow cloaked him, growing larger and larger, like a falling safe about to flatten Wile E. Coyote in a Road Runner cartoon. When Salisbury realized there was nothing he could do to prevent what was about to happen, he sighed, shook his head ruefully and said, simply, "Shit—"

I turned my head and looked away before it struck him, but I heard the sickening crunch as it landed, and felt the shuddering impact through the soles of my boots. I wished I hadn't looked back. What I saw of Salisbury and the orangutan's remains looked like a failed experiment of Dr. Moreau.

Before the echo of the orangutan's crash landing faded away, a second shadow fell, over me this time. I searched the heavens for Shitface, expecting to see his flaming corpse rocketing down towards me like a man-shaped missile.

But it was Chains. He'd been flame-grilled like a Whopper. His eyes glared hatefully from his barbecued face. The jagged splinters puncturing his cheeks and scalp were also charred black. Smoke coiled like ghostly puppet strings from the scorched rags of his biker vest. He was clutching Smiley's axe.

Chains snarled at me in rage and lashed out with a boot, kicking me onto my back like a turtle. Then he raised the axe above his head to strike. Flat on my back—winded, exhausted, helpless—I waited for Chains to bury the axe blade in me. I had no more fight left. All I could do was pray death came quickly.

Then some kind of animal roared, and behind Chains, I saw a monstrous black shape loping through the smoke like a demon summoned from the fiery pits of hell. *Was it—? Could it be—?* Of course not, dumbass. But it was only when the creature pounced on Chains, clinging to his back like a giant hairy leech, that I realized it was Boogaloo Baboon.

Ned wrestled Chains to the ground. The axe fell from Chains's hands. Ned got his paws on the axe, raised it above him in a wide arc, and then brought the blade thudding down into Chains's chest. The biker gave a gurgling scream as Ned wrenched the axe free, and then brought it down again, and again, hacking with a feral fury. Through the ragged holes in his baboon mask, the look in Ned's eyes was more animal than human. He continued hacking long after Chains had stopped screaming, or even breathing. Exhaustion finally overwhelmed him and Ned sank to his knees beside the shattered carcass.

I warily approached him, and managed to prise the bloody axe from his paws. He bowed his head and I heard him weeping inside his baboon mask. I went to remove the mask but he growled at me. I let him alone and just patted his shoulder. "It's gonna be okay, Ned." What else could I say?

Eliza came and returned my shirt to me. Through all this madness, I'd been running around shirtless; if I'd been in better shape, it might've even looked heroic. I put my shirt back on. "You alright?"

She nodded. "Is Ned okay?"

"He'll bounce back," I said, though after everything he'd been through, I wasn't sure about that.

I picked through the wreckage of the farm, satisfying myself that all the Damn Dirty Apes were dead, and that nobody else, neither man nor beast, was likely to crash-land on us from the heavens. There was still no sign of Shitface. He must have been cremated in the explosion; either that or his corpse was currently residing on the moon. It looked like Chains's motorcycle, the one with Mofo's sidecar attached, was the least damaged of the bikes. Eliza helped me haul it upright. I tried the engine. After everything I'd been through, I wasn't expecting any favors, but wouldn't you know it, the bike roared to life the first time I cranked the throttle. Little late in the day, but maybe God was finally starting to cut me some slack. Eliza led Ned by the paw to the bike. We helped him into the sidecar. He sank gingerly into the cushioned leather seat, hissing in pain. "We'll get that butt looked at just as soon we get back to town," I told him. Then I straddled the hog, Eliza climbed on behind me and cinched her arms around my waist, and I hit the throttle. The bike revved away from the smoldering ruins of the farmhouse and the mushroom cloud of smoke rising over the horizon.

21.

That's about the size of it; that's my story, the one I sold to the Hollywood movie people. These days they'll make a movie about any old nonsense.

Eliza talked me into selling my story rights. I agreed under one condition: That the role the movie producer had promised Eliza contained no nudity. The producer wasn't happy about that. Eliza would be playing herself in the movie and the guy made a convincing argument that nudity was integral to the character of a topless dancer. But I put my foot down and he finally relented.

The last I heard, the movie is scheduled for release next fall. Oscar-winner Nic Cage is playing yours truly. Could've been worse, I guess; I understand Shane Moxie was briefly in the running. I'm curious to see what hairpiece Cage brings to the role.

Eliza wrote me from Hollywood, where she's living the dream. She's shacked up with the movie producer—rather him than the nice man from Austin, Texas at the sleazier end of the market. She invited me out to the premiere. Ever since he saw the invite had a plus one, Walt keeps badgering me to take him. I just tell him, "We'll see." I'm still a little ticked off with Walt, or letting him think I am.

When Eliza, Ned and me got back to town from the Sticks, and I skidded Chains's bike to a stop outside The Henhouse, and then climbed off the hog and collapsed in the parking lot, Walt had scuttled outside with a big beaming smile and the first thing he'd said was: "Good news, Reggie! Henrietta-Sue and me! I got my dates wrong! Eliza ain't my you-know-what!" Eliza asked me what he'd meant. I told her she'd just dodged a bullet. Then Walt said, "Where's Salisbury? Where's Lester? Ah shit, Reggie— Where's my shotgun?" The old skinflint docked it from my next paycheck. Eventually he did get around to asking how I was. He claimed he'd never had a doubt I'd be okay. "You're like the cat who came back, Reggie."

If that's true, I've got to be all out of lives by now.

While I was laid up hospital, Constable Gooch came to take my statement. Given how crazy it all sounded, I half-expected the feisty little lawman to start swatting me with his hat. But Eliza backed up my story—Ned still wasn't talking much—and despite himself, Gooch seemed impressed by my derring-do.

Legally speaking, for my part in the deaths of the Damn Dirty Apes, not to mention Lester and Salisbury, I escaped with little more than a slap on the wrist. Mofo the orangutan was another matter. The A.S.P.C.A. brought me up on charges of animal cruelty, and I was lucky just to be fined. Had they learned about the black bear—I left that part out of my statement—I might've been looking at some serious jail time.

After extensive surgery on his ass, and a long spell at the Shady Oak nervous hospital, Ned Pratt did indeed bounce back from his ordeal. Well, maybe not 'bounce' exactly. He still walks with a pronounced limp, and carries a donut cushion for when he sits, but without Lester around to lead him astray, Ned's a changed man. On the advice of his therapist, Ned ritually burned his Boogaloo Baboon costume, and is learning to let go of the past. He's become a committed churchgoer, and unlike the rest of those sinners, we rarely ever see him at The Henhouse anymore. I understand there's a horror movie producer interested in telling Ned's version of events. Who the hell would want to watch two hours of an orangutan sodomizing a man, I do not know. But then again, until recently I'd been unaware of the demand for skunk ape porn, so maybe I'm just out of touch?

Lester Swash was exonerated of having murdered Ned, and his name (if not his good name) restored around town. Lester's body—you may recall I last saw it in a sleeping bag, floating downriver like a Viking funeral—was never recovered. Maybe bears fished it from the river; or it sank and was eaten by flatheads? But I like to think the body made it all the way out to sea. I picture Lester floating out over the horizon as the reflection of the setting sun shimmers on the ocean waves.

The *Bugle*'s front-page story on Eliza and me, calling us heroes, was a business boon for Walt. He framed the news cutting and put it on the wall next to my other one. I would've preferred if he'd *replaced* the other one, but he claimed they complimented each other. For a spell, folks flocked to The Henhouse to hear me tell the story in person, which I could usually be coaxed into doing for the price of a beer or the slim chance of getting laid. Less welcome were the people who started coming to me with their problems, like I was some kind of one-man A-Team who could help them, and not just a shit-magnet who'd survived Mofo and the Damn Dirty Apes only by the skin of his teeth.

Little could I know that the news coverage would catch the eye of a skeleton from my closet; one morning, Boar Hog Brannon rolled up to visit me.

Now with a name like Boar Hog, you don't expect a fella with matinee idol looks, and Boar Hog didn't have those, then or now—but he was radiating such rude health that it shamed me to glance at my sorry-ass reflection in the back-bar mirror. Wearing a crisp polo shirt tucked into jeans, Boar Hog paused at the entrance and glanced around the bar like he was viewing a grisly crime scene. Then he saw me perched at my spot at the end of the slab and grinned. "Reggie?"

"Boar Hog," I said, unable to mask my surprise.

He chuckled bashfully. "Oh . . ." he said, "no one calls me Boar Hog no more. It's plain old Clarence nowadays." He hovered at the entrance like a vampire waiting for an invite; maybe he just didn't like the look of the joint, and wanted me to come join him outside. But I just plastered a welcoming smile on my mug and said: "Well, hell . . . Get on in here, Boar— *Clarence*." He came inside warily—eyes darting—like a Christian entering the lion's den. I offered him the stool next to mine at the slab.

"How long's it been?" I said, knowing full well how long it had been, to the day.

"Fifteen years and change, I reckon."

"And change," I said. "What're you drinking?"

He tore his eyes away from the liquor display. "Club soda," he said.

Walt glanced at me—cocked his eyebrow—and then poured the club soda in silent judgment, placing the glass on the slab in front of Boar Hog.

I toasted Boar Hog with my breakfast bottle of Coors. "Here's to you."

Boar Hog hesitated, wetting his lips with a flick of his tongue as he ogled the pearls of condensation jewelling my beer bottle. Then he chinked his glass against it.

"You're looking good," I told him.

He nodded magnanimously. Then thought to say, "You too, Reggie."

We both let the lie slide; I heard Walt give a little snort.

"So what brings you here?"

"I saw your picture in the paper," Boar Hog said. "That, uh . . ." He rolled his wrist like he was searching for the right words. "Skunk ape thing."

I told him I recalled the skunk ape thing he was referring to.

"Heckuva story," he said. "Did it really happen like the papers said?"

I smiled enigmatically. "Well, you know how they like to exaggerate things."

He nodded. "It sounded kinda far-fetched . . .

"Anyway—I saw you in the paper and realized I'd plain left you off my list."

I shot a nervous glance at Walt.

"What list would that be?" I hoped it wasn't a shit list.

Boar Hog bowed his head in shame.

"The list of all the people I've hurt," he said softly.

I frowned. "Not sure I'm following you, B.H."

Boar Hog gave a heavy sigh. He glanced longingly at my beer and then took a birdlike sip of soda, grimacing in distaste. "I'm in the program," he said. "A.A. God willing, next month I'll be three years clean and sober."

"Yeah? That's great. Good for you," I said, raising my beer in congratulations.

He nodded grimly. "I've been working the steps, trying to make amends for all the hurt I caused—"

I realized where he was going with all this and cut him off. "Hell, Boar Hog—" I had a slight buzz going now, and I'd forgotten he'd asked me to call him Clarence. "You don't owe me nothing. We're fighters, man. Hurt comes with the territory."

He shook his head. "You don't understand, Reggie." He sighed like he'd been gut-punched. "When we fought, I was . . . I was wearing loaded gloves."

"Say what?"

"Plaster," he said. "On my hand wraps. Christ, I was hitting you with sledgehammers that night. For the life of me, I don't know how you took it for as long as you did. It damn near killed me just to *land* that many shots. The ref hadn't stopped it when he did, I don't think I could've climbed off my stool for another round."

"Loaded gloves . . ." was all I could say.

He nodded sheepishly. "I'm sorry, Reggie. Truly I am."

I glanced at my beer like it was giving me counsel.

Boar Hog said, "I guess you probably want to take a swing at me?"

"Ah, what the hell's that gonna solve?"

But I slugged him to the floor all the same.

He peered up at me, blinking and rubbing his jaw. "Guess I deserved that."

I offered him my hand and helped him back to his feet.

"We square, Reggie?"

I sighed. "You can cross my name off your list."

Boar Hog beamed like a pug-ugly cherub, blood glistening on his split lip. "Thanks, Reggie."

We made some more small talk, but he'd come here to say what he wanted to say, and The Henhouse was no place for a recovering alcoholic—or a borderline functional one, now that I think of it—and pretty soon he left.

I walked him to the door and we shook hands.

"No hard feelings, Reggie?"

"You bet."

I watched him drive away and then I sat back down at my regular spot at the end of the slab, thinking things through the only way I knew how, with a beer in my hand and a dumbfounded look on my mug.

Walt started wet-ragging the slab all around me, not saying anything.

"Just say it," I said.

"Loaded gloves, huh?"

I nodded. "Loaded gloves . . ."

"And you *still* took that big bastard life and death."

The thought had already occurred to me, but I didn't say anything.

"So what d'you reckon, kid?"

I glanced up at Walt.

"Any gas left in the tank?"

I sucked in my gut and squared my shoulders, looking long and hard at my reflection in the back-bar mirror. And then I let out my breath and deflated.

"I'm too old for that shit," I said.

And it's a funny thing—but for the first time I was okay with just wondering what could've been.

* * *

No next of kin came forward to claim the body of Jameson T. Salisbury. I felt a pang of compassion for the crazy bastard—that there was no one to mourn his passing. If it wasn't for Salisbury, those Damn Dirty Apes would've killed me. Of course, if it wasn't for Salisbury, I wouldn't have been caught up in the whole sorry mess to start with. I continue to have mixed feelings about the man.

All the same, I paid for his funeral service and a small headstone with some of my movie money. Salisbury was buried in a modest grave in Bigelow cemetery. The boneyard is on the far side of town, way out by the Sticks. Shortly before she decamped to Hollywood, Eliza and me drove out there to pay our respects. I didn't know Salisbury's date of birth, or much else about him except that he was certifiably insane. But I couldn't put that on the headstone, so the marker just read SKUNK APE HUNTER, which you might argue is a roundabout way of saying the same thing. Still, I reckon he would've approved of that epitaph.

Eliza and me didn't have much to say in the way of kind words, so we just stood silent vigil at his grave for as long as propriety demanded. We were turning to leave when suddenly an unearthly howl rose from the depths of the Sticks.

As the chilling cry echoed over the boneyard, Eliza gasped: "Is that . . . ?"

I could only shake my head. "Can't be . . ."

But as the cry faded away—and we hurried from the cemetery—I couldn't help thinking that what we had heard was the Bigelow Skunk Ape paying his own respects to the greatest foe his kind had ever known.

DIE DOG OR EAT THE HATCHET

PART ONE

"I'm the most cold-hearted sonofabitch you'll ever meet."
—Ted Bundy

MAY 16, 1993

The night of the massacre, Luella was foraging for comfort food in the refrigerator she shared with her sisters at the Kappa Pi sorority house.

It had been a shitty day for Luella. First the results of her term paper—all those weeks of hard work for nothing but a lousy B—then, as she commiserated over chocolate-chip cookies in the cafeteria, she'd overheard Todd Greenway make a cutting remark about her figure—"Check it out: Feeding time at the zoo"—that caused his hangers-on to howl with laughter. As she raided the refrigerator that night, the cruel laughter still ringing in her ears, Luella knew stuffing her fat disgusting face with Krispy Kremes was no way to help matters, but she was powerless, shoveling down donuts in the secret darkness of the kitchen.

The knock at the door startled her. She jerked her head guiltily from the refrigerator. Glanced at the clock on the kitchen wall. Almost one a.m. She'd thought her sisters were all present and accounted for and sleeping soundly in their beds, scolded herself for not making sure of it before she crept downstairs to raid the refrigerator. Peeking outside, she saw a young man standing on the back porch. He had his arm slung around what at first glance Luella thought was a life-size mannequin. Then she recognized the long frizz of Irish-red hair hanging over the mannequin's face and sighed.

This wasn't the first time Susan had come home shitfaced. Usually whichever guy had been loading her with booze dumped her home in the morning after getting his money's worth. Luella supposed it was a checkmark in *this* guy's favor. Susan's partying was getting way out of hand. She'd been warned if she kept it up she risked flunking out. Luella liked Susan. Hoped she'd see sense and pull back from the brink before it was too late.

She unlocked the door and opened it.

The young man smiled at her sheepishly. "I think your friend had a little too much to drink," he said, like he had no idea how it might've happened.

Luella sighed again. "She does that."

She gestured for the man to bring her inside.

"Do you mind?" she whispered. "If the house mother sees her like this again she'll freak."

The man hesitated a moment. Glanced about the yard. Luella figured that before he'd seen the light of the refrigerator, he'd been planning to leave Susan on the porch-swing and scram. But he nodded dutifully and lugged her inside and Luella closed the door softly behind him.

In the dim light of the kitchen, Luella saw he was older than she'd first thought. Late twenties at least. Boyishly handsome, with long lashes and blowtorch-blue eyes, his sharp features faintly lined, Luella found herself flicking her hair reflexively and hoping she didn't have any Krispy Kreme frosting smeared around her lips. Not that he'd be interested in *her*. And that depressing thought would require another donut (or two) after he left.

The man started saying: "Where—?"

Luella raised a finger to his lips. Mimed: people sleeping upstairs.

"Where do you, uh . . . want her?" he whispered.

"Can you bring her through to the lounge?" Luella said. "I should probably try and sober her up."

The man laughed softly. "Good luck with that."

She led the way to the lounge and motioned for him to set Susan on the couch. He lowered her gently onto the cushioned seat, and then slumped down beside her to catch his breath. *It could've been worse, buddy*, Luella thought. *You could have been carrying* me. She kneeled in front of Susan and took her hands to try and rouse her. "Christ, she's freezing."

The man nodded. "It's cold out."

Luella brushed Susan's long red hair from her face.

Couldn't help snickering. "She is *totally* wasted—"

And then Susan's head lolled back against the headrest, flopping to the side at an angle that made Luella wince, the bone of her broken vertebrae bulging grotesquely from her neck. Luella glanced in sudden terror at the smiling young man with the piercing blue eyes. Before she could scream, the knife in his hand glinted in the gloom, and her scream became a sigh that sputtered and hissed from a slashed throat. She slid soundlessly to the rug, clutching at the gushing wound, the warmth bleeding out between her fingers as the man stalked upstairs to wake her sisters.

1.

If Billy Joe Carrick was running the world, a mad dog killer like Terrence Hingle wouldn't be seeing out his days in no cushy state nuthouse. He'd be deader than Old Yeller and it would've been Billy Joe Carrick who put him down. A bullet for every girl he killed. Unfortunately, Billy Joe wasn't running the world. A bunch of liberal assholes were. And so, on the fourth anniversary of the Kappa Pi Massacre, like he did every year the old cop made the long drive out to Pine Grove State Hospital to try and get the sonofabitch to talk.

Against his better judgment, when Hingle was committed, Carrick had made a solemn vow to the families of the victims that come hell or high water he'd bring Hingle to account. For the grieving loved ones, perhaps the cruelest cut of all was that no one knew why this young man, with no criminal record or history of violence, had suddenly snapped and butchered five girls. It just seemed so fucking senseless. But four years later, and the families were no closer to knowing. Hingle still hadn't uttered a word—not to Carrick or to anyone else. And now that fool promise he'd made was eating away at Billy Joe like a cancer.

He was one year shy of being pensioned off the force, and he dreaded not keeping his word. Even worse was not knowing himself why Hingle had murdered those girls, and restoring some semblance of reason to this gone-to-shit world. Carrick could picture himself in retirement: Staying up nights and brooding on it endlessly, with only his pistol and a bottle of hooch for company. What he'd seen at that crime scene would gnaw through his brain like a worm in a rotten apple. If he couldn't get Hingle to talk, Carrick gave himself three years tops before he ate his own pistol.

Carrick tried not to let his desperation show as he stared at the mad dog sitting opposite him. The two men were locked inside a cramped concrete box that had all the charm of the Black Hole of Calcutta. Sallow light smeared the room; the light fixture was filled with the husks of dead flies, the bulb buzzing like their ghosts. The stark white walls were Rorschach-blotted with faded nicotine stains in which Carrick saw the faces of the dead girls. He could almost hear them whispering to him . . . *Why?* Begging for the answers that would lay them to rest.

The mad dog was slumped in his chair like a puppet with its strings cut. Wearing striped hospital pajamas and a ratty blue robe, his glazed eyes stared across the table, straight through Carrick, and a thousand-yards yonder. Mouth hanging open, a rope of drool dangled from his bottom lip, dripping like a leaking faucet. His hands were folded neatly in his lap; slender and ladylike, it was hard to believe those dainty little hands had butchered five sorority sisters.

"Terrence," Carrick said. "You might've fooled that old judge and these headshrinkers, but you don't fool me." He crinkled his face like a cornpone Columbo. "Now how much longer do you plan on playing possum for?"

Another drip-drop of drool.

Carrick sighed.

The headshrinkers called it—when they weren't using fancy words—a complete mental breakdown. As if the horrors Hingle inflicted on those sorority sisters had driven him plumb out of his mind. Carrick understood how that was possible. Just viewing the crime scene had damn near had the same effect on him. A thirty-year veteran of some of the worst godforsaken shitholes in the state, he'd thought he'd seen every depravity that one human being could inflict on another. He was wrong. Dead wrong.

He remembered that night at Kappa Pi. Arriving to find the sorority house awash in the flashing lights of the cop cars and the EMS vehicles swarming outside. Remembered entering the hall and his feeling of icy dread as the rich red carpet squelched beneath his shoes and he realized what he was standing in. Hanging by her hair from the landing rail above him was Luella Potton. Carrick thought she was smiling, at first; a big crimson ear-to-ear smile carved across her throat. He'd followed the trail of blood upstairs to the room where the remains of the other girls were heaped like something a gator had upchucked. The same room where Hingle had been caught in the act by the college cops, literally red-handed, as he garroted the last of the girls with her roommate's intestines—

Carrick pushed the memory away. He couldn't get Hingle to talk and he'd have the rest of his life to dwell on what he saw that awful night. He loosened his tie and rubbed at his throat. Rolled up his shirtsleeves and stole a glance at his wristwatch. Quarter to five in the p.m. The seconds were ticking down on his career as a po-lice. Just fifteen more minutes before his last hour with Hingle was up. Fifteen minutes to keep his word to the families and get answers.

Carrick glanced over his shoulder at the closed door. Checked that the orderly posted outside wasn't watching through the Judas hatch. Fetched his hipflask from the pocket of the coat draped over his chair back. Poured a generous shot into the Styrofoam cup of cold coffee on the table next to the file folder. Took a nip from the cup, baring his teeth as he choked it down.

Then he flipped the file folder open.

No reaction from Hingle.

The crime scene photos were paperclipped together. Carrick thumbed loose the paperclip. Placed it on the table next to his coffee. He started tossing the photos across the table like he was dealing cards. Didn't look at the photos himself. No need. All he had to do was shut his eyes.

"Look at them, boy," Carrick growled. He'd coddled this degenerate punk long enough. "By Christ, you're gonna look at these photos if I have to claw the eyeballs out of your skull—and then you're going to tell me why . . . WHY?"

He thumped his fist down hard on the table, knocking over his cup, black coffee bleeding across the crime scene photos. With a curse, Carrick righted the cup and then fished in his pocket for a snot-rag to mop up the mess.

Behind him, the Judas hatch clanged open. The orderly's eyes peered through the slit. "Everything okay?"

"Fine," Carrick grunted, and waited for the hatch to clang shut.

When he looked back at Hingle, the mad dog had one of the photos in his hands. He was gaping at the image, eyes blinking rapidly, his pupils shrinking to pinpricks and swelling to black balloons as he struggled to focus on it.

Carrick nearly lurched in surprise from his chair. For all the animation Hingle had shown on his previous visits, the madman might well have been tap-dancing on the table. Was this it, at long last, was the sonofabitch finally going to crack?

Carrick quickly composed himself. "You see, Terrence?" he said. "You see what you done?"

Hingle raised a hand from his lap. Swiped the drool from his lips. His eyes darted between the other photos on the table. Like he was spoiled for choice and didn't know which one to pick up next. He fanned them out before him. Hunched over the table to peer at them closely. His mouth began working soundlessly. His cheeks flushed with color. He bull-snorted breath. Shoulders hitching spasmodically as if a great cry was building up inside him.

"That's it," Carrick encouraged him. "You remember now, don't you, boy? Now tell me why?" He reached across the table and gave Hingle a reassuring pat on the hand, suppressing a shudder as he remembered those hands had been elbow-deep in girl-guts. "Why? Why'd you do it?"

Hingle's head jerked up. He looked the lawman cold in the eye.

"More . . ." he croaked, his neglected voice barely audible.

Carrick frowned. Four years, and that's the first thing he says? He didn't understand. Christ, were there other victims? *Before* Kappi Pi? Keep him talking . . . "More?"

And then he let out a cry of disgust as he realized what Hingle was doing.

Carrick lurched to his feet, chair clattering to the floor behind him. On the other side of the table, the sick sonofabitch had his dick in his hand and he was beating it like it owed him money. Hingle bared his teeth at Carrick in a bestial grin, and then he hunched back over the photos, his hand drumming the underside of the table as he jerked himself, moaning as he neared climax.

Carrick shook his head in numb horror. He'd hoped the photos might wrench some kind of reaction from Hingle. But *this* . . . Rage boiled up inside him.

"Fuh—fuck . . . fucking . . . ANIMAL!"

Carrick heaved the table aside and hurled himself at Hingle.

Hingle's chair overturned. They crashed down onto the grimy tiled floor.

Carrick landed on top of him. Gripped his head in his hands. Started beating the back of his skull on the floor. Five blows for five dead girls.

Susan Donnelly (BAM!)—

Luella Potton (BAM!)—

Katherine Marsh (BAM!)—

Donna Hastings (BAM!)—

Francine Chung (BAM!)—

The door exploded open behind them. A pack of white-uniformed orderlies dog-piled inside and dragged Carrick off him, kicking and screaming from the room. Carrick's cries echoed down the corridor like he was just another nut checking into the nuthouse.

Hingle lay splayed in a daze on the floor, the crime scene photos strewn about him like storm debris—Hurricane Billy Joe—and as he waited for the orderlies to haul him off to the infirmary, Hingle closed his fist around the paperclip.

2

When Hingle regained consciousness later that night, he found himself cuffed to a steel-framed cot in the infirmary, shackled at each of his wrists to either side of the bed frame. The steel bracelets bit painfully into his flesh. Canvas restraints strapped down his legs. His skull was cocooned in bandages. His head throbbed like a hammered thumb. And yet he smiled.

The old cop was nothing if not predictable. Visiting him at the nuthouse every year on the anniversary of the murders. Having Hingle hauled from his cell and then dragged to the same stifling interview room. Shoving the crime scene photos in Hingle's face like he was rubbing a dog's nose in its own mess.

Expecting Hingle to be *ashamed* for what he'd done.

The old fool didn't realize: His precious memories of those Kappa Pi girls were the only thing that'd kept him going all this time.

For four long years, he'd existed as a slack-jawed zombie, not speaking a word to anyone, just staring into space, drooling and soiling himself like a wet-brained wino—all the while secretly dreaming of the day he could be free again.

His only regret was being arrested; he'd been having so much fun playing doctor with those sorority girls, he didn't hear the college cops until it was too late.

Hingle could've kissed the silly sonofabitch who clubbed him half to death with his nightstick. That use of excessive force had been the difference between the needle and his committal at Pine Grove. And oh, how Hingle had inwardly laughed at the public outcry when he escaped good Christian justice.

All things considered, the nuthouse wasn't so bad. It sure beat being put to sleep like a dog. But Hingle had no intention of staying here.

And so he'd waited, watched, and every year the tired old cop, reeking of desperation, would come to interview him . . . until Hingle finally saw his way out.

Maybe once he was footloose and fancy free, he'd send the dumb bastard a thank you note, carved into the belly of the next gal he met.

Hingle gazed across the infirmary at the orderly posted on the door. The man's chin rested on his chest. He was snoring softly. Just the two of them in the room.

A splinter of steel from the paperclip was buried beneath the skin of Hingle's palm. He'd secreted it there while the orderlies were dragging the old cop off him. Curling his left hand inwards, careful not to clang his cuffs against the bed frame and wake Sleeping Dumbass, Hingle tweezed the splinter free with his thumbnail. He wiped the blood off the splinter onto his sheets, and then inserted it into the keyhole of the cuffs, and as he worked the lock with his improvised pick, searching for the sweet spot, his mind wandered back to when he'd first learned the trick.

*   *   *

Terry Lee Hingle was ten years old, living with his momma and the monkey on her back, and all the uncles a young boy could ever want, in a white trash ghetto apartment that made darktown look like Disneyland.

Momma's pimp was a vice bull, Little Cyril Dupree, the kind of guy who pulls the wings off flies till he's old enough to break arms and he takes up the badge.

He came for the rent every week, and for a piece of momma whenever else he felt like it. He'd toss his hat down on the table. Unbuckle his gunbelt and hang it like a saddle on the back of his chair. Sit in the kitchen, drinking and counting his cut and searching momma's face for signs she was holding out on him. Dipping a hand in his pocket, he'd dig out a few wraps of whatever he'd scrounged from the evidence locker, or shaken down from street dealers, scatter the junk on the floor and watch with amusement as momma snatched up the wraps like a pigeon gobbling breadcrumbs. And then he'd cuff Terry Lee to the drainpipe under the sink and take momma back to the bedroom for the rest of the rent.

Chained like a dog to the drainpipe, huddled on the stained linoleum floor among the rotting food cartons and the cigarette butts, the empty beer cans and bottles, the dead roaches and the rat shit, Terry Lee would listen to Little Cyril rut his momma, or bounce her head off the bedroom walls if he was too drunk to fuck, sometimes both—dreaming up ways to way to fix that fucking pig's wagon.

The next time Little Cyril came and cuffed him to the pipe, Terry Lee was prepared. He'd glued one of momma's hairpins behind the drainpipe with a wad of gum. Little Cyril went out back with momma. Terry Lee started picking the lock with the hairpin. It wasn't as easy as the cop shows on TV had led him to believe. There was a knack to it. He didn't get it right away. It took several more visits from Little Cyril before one night, the hairpin clicked in the lock, and the steel bracelets slid almost by magic from his wrist.

When Little Cyril emerged later from the bedroom, it took him a drunken moment to register that the kid wasn't cuffed to the drainpipe, that his gunbelt drooped impotently over the chair back, and that his pistol was no longer in the holster. He turned in time to see the boy aiming the barrel at his open fly.

Terry Lee squeezed the trigger. Little Cyril crashed to the floor, squealing like a stuck pig, clutching his crotch as what was left of his junk gushed through his hands. The boy shot him once more in the chest. Little Cyril thudded back against the pantry door and his high hog-like squeals stopped. Terry Lee wiped his prints from the gun with his tee shirt, just like he'd seen on the TV cop shows.

Momma clattered through the curtain beads behind him, stopping in her tracks when she saw him crouching over Little Cyril to remove the .22 from his ankle holster. "What—oh, baby—what have you done?"

"Take this, momma," Terry Lee said, calmly handing her Little Cyril's pistol.

She was still staring at the gun in her hands when Terry Lee fired the .22 and knocked her back into the bedroom. He heard the heavy thud as she crashed to the floor. He wiped his prints off the .22 and then forced the gun into the stiffening claw of Little Cyril's hand.

Then he went and cuffed himself back to the drainpipe and waited for someone to come and find him there.

It took longer than he expected.

The flies came first.

Then the rats.

They stripped Little Cyril's skull to the bone, until all that was left was a grinning death's head mask, topped with ragged clumps of hair, and black-hollowed eyes that seemed to bore into Terry Lee. The rats burrowed under Little Cyril's clothes, his shirt and pants billowing and bulging, blooming with blood as they gnawed their way inside him. Next they went after momma. Terry Lee listened to the sound of claws tearing flesh, incisors scraping bone, the frenzied squealing as they feasted and fought over scraps; watched as the vermin scuttled back from the bedroom, fur slick with blood, carrying away pieces of momma—a finger here, an ear there—like she was takeout food.

After two days, still shackled to the drainpipe, Terry Lee began to have serious doubts that anyone was ever going to come for him. The kitchen was a storm of flies, the air choked with the stench of blood and death. Little

Cyril was barely recognizable as human, and momma had run away with the rats, piece by piece. The vermin turned their attention to the helpless boy. Terry Lee deeply regretted having tossed away that fucking hairpin. As the rats crept towards him, he saw his reflection in their beady black eyes, like a nightmare house of mirrors. He screamed, thrashing against the drainpipe and kicking desperately to fend them off. He was still screaming and thrashing and kicking when the cops came and found him and freed him from the cuffs, and as they carted him away in an ambulance, and for months at the orphanage he still woke screaming and thrashing and kicking from nightmares in which the cops arrived too late.

* * *

The splinter clicked in the keyhole. The cuffs snapped open. The orderly didn't stir. Hingle freed his hand from the bracelet, and then used the splinter to work the lock on the second set of cuffs. With both hands free, he unbuckled the strap restraining his legs, slowly peeled back his sheets and then lowered his bare feet to the floor. His eyes never strayed from the sleeping orderly. He unraveled the thick surgical bandages from around his skull. His fingers brushed the stitches lacing the back of his scalp together. The wound flared angrily, but the pain only sharpened his senses. Like a cat stalking a bird, he padded across the room towards the sleeping orderly. Looming behind the man, Hingle looped the bandages around his neck like a gauze garrote, and put him to sleep forever.

There was no time to get creative on the corpse. He switched his hospital pajamas for the dead orderly's uniform. Swiped the man's keys and the billy club hooked to his belt. Hingle used the keys to proceed through the maze of locked gates, and the billy club to brain the fatass guard on the front desk. The guy never looked up from the titty magazine he was ogling, blood and brains splattering the centerfold bunny like clotted crimson jizz.

* * *

The escape siren didn't start sounding until Hingle was already pounding away through the vast acreage of forest from which Pine Grove State Hospital got its name. A storm was raging, the rain lashing down, soaking him through to the bone. Lightning flashed across the night sky like yellow sutures on black velvet. His orderly whites were mud-soiled and torn where he'd clawed his way through the wilds. It had been years since he'd expended more energy than it took to zombie-walk about the hospital. His lungs burned. His legs cramped. A stitch gouged his side. And yet he barely paused for breath, energized by the storm as he plunged on through the woods.

The trees began to thin as he reached the far fringes of the forest.

The lights of a diner glittered into view. BIG BOB'S EATS, the sign said. Replete with a neon-lit likeness of Big Bob who licked his lips when the lights flashed. In the parking lot were a trucker's Peterbilt rig, a Kawasaki motorcycle, and an old beater Volkswagen Beetle. Hingle matched the people he saw through the diner window to the vehicles. There was the trucker at a window booth, sipping a cup of coffee. A tired-looking waitress in a red check apron sat leafing through a magazine at the end of the counter. She didn't look much like a biker. The hog had to belong to the short order cook Hingle could see through the kitchen service hatch behind her. That meant the Beetle was hers.

Ted Bundy had driven a Bug; Hingle took that as a good omen.

He worked his way around the building to the rear. An open restroom window clattered in the wind. A dumpster was pushed up against the wall. All it'd take was to give the dumpster a little nudge—after checking it first for rats: Nasty little bastards—and he could boost himself up inside the window. Hingle grinned to himself.

Returning to the front of the building, he hunkered down in the shadows of the forest line, and then he bided his time and waited, watching the waitress with a hungry gleam in his eyes.

It had been four long years since he'd had a woman, and though she wasn't really his type—a little older than he liked 'em—Terrence Hingle aimed to catch up for lost time.

3.

The diner was quiet as an Edward Hopper painting.

Tilly was perched at her regular spot at the end of the lunch counter, flipping through a celebrity scandal-rag some customer had left behind. In the kitchen behind her she could hear Earl scraping grit off the grill with a spatula. Glancing up from the magazine, Tilly checked to see how her only customer was getting along with that cup of joe he'd been nursing for damn near an hour. Alone at his window booth, the trucker was stirring his coffee in time to the slit-your-wrists country ballad warbling from the juke between the doors to the restrooms. Tilly hoped the guy didn't ask for a refill so she could close the diner early. Business wouldn't pick up on a night like tonight and she was beat from having already worked the day shift.

It should've been Mathilda Mulvehill's night off; Tilly would think about that many times in the hours to come. Not that she'd had any grand plans. Just another night curled on the couch watching TV with Marmalade the cat and a *ménage a trois* with Misters Ben & Jerry. She hadn't even changed out of her day shift uniform when Big Bob called her at home and asked her to cover his shift tonight, with his usual empty promises of a raise. Of course, she'd agreed.

Scolding herself for being such a pushover—though it was her mother's voice she heard in her mind—Tilly had ignored Marmalade's despairing glance as she crammed her aching feet back inside her crepe-soled work shoes. She trudged outside the trailer through the rain to her Bug. The car seemed to have more backbone than its owner, refusing to work at first—but a few more turns of the key and old Betsy Bug finally putt-putted to life.

As she passed through town on her way to the diner, not for the first time Tilly sighed and asked herself what she was still doing in this place. There was nothing keeping her here since mom died. Hadn't the plan been to save up enough money to go back to school; what had happened to that plan?

A pushover and a coward . . . her mother's voice said.

Tilly turned on the radio to shut up the voice.

What happened to that plan was Lizette Mulvehill.

Sometimes Tilly wondered if her mother started drinking because her father walked out on her, or if dad bugged out because mom started drinking. The story tended to change every time Lizette told it, which was often. What never changed was that Brandon Mulvehill was a no-account piece of trash and that Tilly was her daddy's daughter and destined to turn out just the same way.

When she went to college she thought she'd finally escaped. But it was less than a week before the phone calls started. Begging her to come home. Saying she was sick. *Real* sick this time. Asking how—after everything she'd sacrificed to raise her daughter right—*how could Tilly leave her own mother to die alone?*

Another month of calls and Tilly buckled and went home to do her daughterly duty. It turned out her mother wasn't *quite* as close to death's door as she'd led Tilly to believe. It would be another five long years before Lizette drew her final hateful breath. By then Tilly's dreams of college and bettering herself hung in tatters. Mom had seen to that.

The trucker finally gave up on his coffee. He tossed a few bills on the table to cover the check, and then shuffled to the door. Turned up the lapels of his jacket before braving the rain, the bell above the door tinkling as he left. Tilly glanced at the clock above the lunch counter—quarter to ten. Putting down her magazine, she hopped off her stool and went and locked the door. She flipped the sign in the window to CLOSED. Rain needled her tired reflection in the glass as she watched the trucker's Peterbilt rumble off into the night. She was a petite young woman—more mousy than cute—with a heart-shaped face, freckles dusting her nose and cheeks, her eyes hiding beneath sandy lashes, and shoulder-length strawberry blonde hair scrunchied back in a ponytail.

Tilly cleared the trucker's booth. Stuffed the tip the cheap bastard had left in the apron bib of her uniform. Earl shoved his head through the kitchen service hatch, wearing his cook's hat like a rumpled paper crown. "I thought he'd never leave," Earl said. "You mind if I scoot, Tilly? Leave you to lock up?" The question was of course rhetorical; Earl was all but already out the door and buzzing away home astride his Kawasaki.

"Go ahead," she sighed.

"You're—

(*such a pushover*)

"—a doll," Earl said.

The kitchen door banged shut behind him; she heard the waspy whine of his bike tearing away from the lot.

Tilly turned off the juke. If she heard one more country song tonight she thought she'd scream; the dreary lyrics were like her life set to music. She fetched the menus off the tables. Piled them at the waitress station at the end of the lunch counter. Stacked the chairs on the tables. Considered sweeping and mopping the floor before she remembered she was working again first thing tomorrow and deciding it could wait until then. She checked the windows in the restrooms were locked. The ladies room window had blown open, clapping in the wind. Tilly had to stand on tiptoes and lean outside—and was rewarded with a ripe whiff from the dumpster—before she could drag the window shut.

Returning to the diner floor, she took the cash float from the register and went to Big Bob's office to stash it in the safe. In the corner of the office was the staff closet. Big Bob also kept a surplus of waitress uniforms and kitchen whites and a change of his own clothes, because even on cold days, Big Bob would sweat like a racehorse. Tilly took her parka off the rail, car keys jangling in the pocket as she shrugged it on. She fetched her bag from the closet. Slung the carry strap over her forearm. At the bottom of the closet was a crumpled cardboard box with LOST & FOUND Sharpied on the side. Customers were always forgetting their hats or scarves or—

"Alone at last," said a man's voice behind her.

4.

Tilly whirled towards the voice, thudding back against the wall and knocking the EMPLOYEE OF THE MONTH photo to the floor. The glass frame shattered and a crack zigzagged through the Tilly-in-the-photo's timid smile.

Silhouetted in the doorway stood a slender young man with brilliant blue eyes. His dark hair was slicked back with rain. Tilly thought he was wearing kitchen whites at first. Then she realised it was some kind of uniform, like a hospital orderly or a male nurse might wear. His white shirt and pants were soaked through, soiled with mud and torn in places, as if he'd crawled through hell just to get here—and Big Bob's coffee wasn't *that* good.

The man grinned at her with huge white teeth, the Big Bad Wolf wearing human skin. As he crept towards her, trailing mud and rainwater across the carpet, Tilly saw one of Earl's fillet knives clutched in his fist. She gave a low moan. In the event of a robbery—please God, that's all this was—there was a procedure she was supposed to follow. But the only thing she could think was

KNIFE!

"Muh-money's in the safe," she said, in panicked staccato.

The man nodded calmly. "That your car in the lot? The Bug?"

He had a soft Southern accent. All that was missing was the stalk of prairie grass in his mouth, maybe LOVE and HATE tattooed on his knuckles.

It took a moment for his words to register. Then she clawed through the pockets of her parka, found her car keys and held them out. The keys jangled in her shaking hand. "Tuh-take it."

He took the keys and she snatched her hand back to her chest.

"Ted Bundy drove a Bug." The man grinned. "Did you know that?"

No. No, she hadn't known that. What person in their right mind *would*? Fear shuddered through her. "Oh god, please, don't hurt me—"

He whipped up the knife and pressed the cold blade to her lips.

"Hush now," he said. "You do what I say when I say it, me and you are gonna get along famously. Now why don't you open that safe you mentioned?"

Removing the knife from her lips, he backed up a step. With a flourish of his arm, he gestured for her to move past him to the safe—a gesture that might have been gentlemanly had he not been clutching a big-ass fucking knife.

He parked his butt casually on the edge of Big Bob's desk.

Tilly glanced at the telephone beside him—

He stabbed the knife down into the desk, blocking her view of the phone.

"You get any bright ideas like that," the man warned her, "you'd best remember you're just a waitress at a greasy spoon diner and not Brain of the fucking Year."

He nodded at the safe. "Go on now."

She kneeled in front of the safe. What was the combination? She couldn't remember. Her mind had gone blank. For the life of her she would not have been able to unlock the safe with a gun to her head . . . or a knife to her throat. And then it suddenly came back to her. Nearly sobbing with relief she entered the combination and unlocked the safe and dragged the heavy door open.

She took out the money float and placed it on Big Bob's desk. Backing away to the wall, her legs turned to jelly and she slumped to the floor beside the safe. She dragged her legs to her chest, laced her arms around her shins to stop her body from shaking, watching as the young man clawed the bills from the cash drawers.

"That's it?" he said.

"We banked our week's takings yesterday."

"How about you?" he said. "What's in that bag of yours?"

She kicked her bag across the floor to him.

He upended the bag over Big Bob's desk and started rooting through all the junk she'd collected—her makeup bag and compact, wadded tissues, losing Lotto tickets, a few too many candy bar wrappers—the clutter of a miserable wage-slave existence. He found her purse and read the name on her photo ID aloud.

"Mathilda Mulvehill."

"Tilly," she said. Maybe if he started thinking of her as a person, and not a victim, he wouldn't hurt her? "My name's Tilly." It was printed in capital letters on the nametag pinned to the breast of her uniform.

"Tilly . . ." he said, taking the name for a spin. "Well, then you can call me Terry." He grinned his toothy grin. "Terry n' Tilly: It's almost cute."

He returned his attention to her purse. Added what little money he found to his swag from the cash float. "That'll have to do it, I guess."

Then he glanced down at her and kept on looking.

Tilly choked back a scream as he unbuttoned his shirt, unzipped his pants.

A little snort of amusement. "Sorry to disappoint you, sis. There's no time for hanky-panky. And I'm not getting caught with my pants down again."

He peeled off his soaking shirt and pants—he was whipcord lean, muscled like a terrier—found an apron in the closet, towel dried his hair. Next to the closet on the wall was a mirror. He paused to admire his reflection. Combed his hair with his fingers. Shook his head and sighed. "Lookit what those fucking headshrinkers done to me . . ." Tilly thought he still seemed pretty pleased with himself. He caught her watching him and shot her a wink. She looked away quickly.

He snatched a pair of Big Bob's slacks from the rail in the closet; had to cuff the ankles, and bore a new notch in his belt with the knife before they fit him. Then he rummaged through the LOST & FOUND box. Salvaged a dorky ensemble of a smiley face tee shirt, a jean jacket, and a black knit beanie hat.

He gave Tilly a little twirl. "How'd I look?"

She didn't answer.

He stuffed the money from the safe and Tilly's purse in the breast pocket of the jean jacket.

Then he squatted in front of where she huddled on the floor.

Over his shoulder she could see the knife embedded in the desk behind him.

The way he was squatting in front of her she could kick him in the balls and snatch up the knife and—

"—at home?"

He was asking her something; oh Christ, what had he asked her?

He snapped his fingers in front of her face.

"You with me, sis?"

She stifled a sob and nodded.

"You got anyone waiting for you at home?" he said again.

"Yes," she said.

But she'd hesitated just long enough for him to smell the lie. "Bullshit."

Tilly couldn't help bristling in offence. Was it really so farfetched? Marmalade certainly wouldn't think so. She tried to remember if she'd fed the cat before she left for—

"Alright," he said. "Here's how it is, sister. You and me are gonna go for a little drive."

"Please, I gave you all the money—"

He reached behind him. Wrenched the knife from the desk. Pressed the blade to her lips once again. "Don't interrupt," he told her. "I don't like that." She nodded weakly. "Good girl," he said. He hooked a stray strand of hair back behind her ear with the knife. The tip of the blade caressed her earlobe.

"Now there's people looking for me, see. I'm not so keen that they find me. So now you and me are gonna go for a little drive—like I was saying before you rudely interrupted me—and you're gonna see that it doesn't happen . . .

"You help me get out of Dodge," he promised, "and all this will be over."

5.

They left the diner linking arms like lovers. Terry embraced her protectively. The knife was pressed up under her arm, the blade pricking her armpit. The rain beat down hard on the parking lot asphalt, erupting into a deluge as Terry led her to the Bug. Through the sheeting rain, Tilly could hardly see the used car dealership across the street. The married owner sometimes worked late with his pretty young secretary. But not tonight. She glanced along the street but there was no one to be seen. There usually wasn't by the time Big Bob closed his kitchen. And especially not on a night like this. *My night off* . . .

Terry unlocked the Bug's driver's-side door and hauled it open. Waited patiently for Tilly to climb behind the wheel. Then he slammed the door shut and walked around to the passenger-side. Climbed inside and shook himself dry like a wet dog. Rain pelted the car roof in a white noise roar. He placed the knife in his lap, the blade jutting from his crotch like a razor-sharp dildo. He held out his hand and offered Tilly the car keys. When she reached to take them, he teased his hand back. "Now we got us a deal, right?"

"You'll let me go?"

Earnest as a politician, he said: "You hold up your end, I will."

Tilly nodded.

He gave her the keys.

A deep breath, and then she slid the key into the ignition and turned it.

Betsy Bug grumbled awake and the radio crackled to life: "—authorities warn that Terrence LeRoy Hingle, who escaped earlier tonight from the Pine Grove State Hospital after killing several orderlies, is highly dangerous and should not be approached by the public—"

Hingle snapped off the radio.

"Well," he said, "that's the cat out of the bag."

Until then, Tilly felt she was holding up remarkably well. She'd almost managed to convince herself that if she just did what he told her this would all soon be over. But she recognized the name Terrence Hingle at once. What had the papers called him? "The Sorority Slayer." Mom had followed the Kappa Pi Massacre with ghoulish relish. She'd watched every TV crime show; read every lurid tabloid paperback. It was almost as if the brutal murder of those sorority girls was the only thing keeping her alive. "See?" she'd once said to Tilly. "I hadn't brung you home from college when I did, that might've been you."

Tilly shrank down into her seat, shaking uncontrollably.

Hingle sighed. "Now don't go getting hysterical." He popped the glove compartment. A flashlight rolled out and thudded into the footwell. He fetched it up and placed it on the dashboard. Then he rooted through the clutter of the glove box and found some Kleenex. "Here," he said, tearing off a wad of tissues. "Clean yourself up. You're no good to me like this."

She couldn't move. Hands clutching the steering wheel in a white-knuckled grip. Hingle wadded the tissues into a ball and mopped the tears from her face like the parent of a dirty child. Tilly flinched at his touch.

"You know," he told her, "there ain't a bad-looking gal under all this frump. You ought to take better care of yourself, sis."

Flattery was getting him nowhere; he frowned, offering her another tissue.

"Honk your nose," he said. "I'm not listening to you snuffle all night."

She took the tissue and trumpeted her nose.

"There," Hingle said. "All better?"

Her head was welded to her shoulders but she managed to nod, if only to prevent him pawing at her with another Kleenex.

"I can tell by the way you're carrying-on that you've heard of me?" Hingle said.

Tilly thought he sounded proud. She nodded again.

"Well, that's good, I guess. Then you'll know your best bet's not to piss me off and to do exactly what I tell you . . . Right, Tilly?"

Another furtive nod.

"Let me hear you say it, sis."

"I understand."

With a pat of her knee, "Thatta girl." He nestled back in his seat and snaked his arm around her headrest like a guy with his date at the drive-in.

"Alright then, sis. Let's roll. Not too fast, not too slow."

As the Bug pulled from the lot, and turned onto the empty street, Tilly glanced in the rearview mirror and saw the neon sign of Big Bob leering and licking his lips.

Mathilda Mulvehill was finally leaving town.

6.

The Smokies had erected a roadblock on the county line. A fleet of cop cars was parked on the shoulder. Emergency road flares blazed on the blacktop, fizzling red in the rain. The troopers were stopping traffic and checking vehicles with flashlights. Soaked sniffer dogs glanced up at their handlers as if to say *I hope you're not expecting me to smell anything in this shit?*

Seeing the blockade up ahead, Hingle fidgeted excitedly in his seat. Tilly didn't think he seemed overly concerned. "Time to earn your keep, sis," he told her. "Now you just play it like Buck and the Buckaroos: All you gotta do is act naturally." She watched from the corner of her eye as he palmed the fillet knife like a magician inside his jean jacket. He saw her watching and gave a goading grin. "Go ahead and try something," he said. "I'll open you up before they ever put the cuffs on me." She looked away quickly.

The Bug joined the end of the short line of vehicles. The interior glowed red in the brake lights of the pickup in front of them. A state trooper wearing a waterproof poncho and a rain protector over his hat came towards them. Twirled his finger for Tilly to unwind her window. She rolled it down and he leaned towards the gap. Rain dripped off the brim of his hat as he peered inside the car. The trooper looked all of twelve, like he was playing dress-up in his daddy's uniform. "Evening, folks," he said, with all the authority he could muster. He swept the flashlight beam across the backseat. Back at the couple up-front.

Hingle leaned across Tilly and offered the trooper a sloppy smile.

"What seems to be the officer, problem?" He gave a little snort of drunken laughter that sounded pretty convincing to Tilly's trained ear.

The trooper speared the drunk's face with his flashlight beam.

Hingle shrank back like a vampire from sunlight. "Ow! Bright!"

The trooper smirked. "Been doing a little drinking tonight, sir?" He looked like he wished he was boozing in a cozy bar himself, than freezing his ass off in the rain.

Hingle held up his hand like a boy scout. "Officer," he slurred, "I swear I only had a couple of beers." He winked at the trooper, jerking his head towards Tilly with a roll of his eyes, like he was begging the guy to play along and not land him in more hot water with his old lady. "I knocked off work, then stopped for one or two with the fellas. Law-abiding citizen that I am, I figured I oughtn't drive and so I called the ole ball and chain to come fetch me."

Tilly stiffened behind the wheel. He'd made a mistake. Had the trooper picked up on it? Maybe she could help him along . . . She drummed the steering wheel lightly with her hands, like she was impatient to get her worthless drunk husband home so she could chew him out. Trying to draw the trooper's attention to her left hand. The one not wearing a wedding ring. She prayed the trooper would notice; that he'd put two and two together and quick-draw his sidearm before Hingle had time to—

(*open you up*)

—react.

But instead he just said to the drunk, "Smart thinking. Last thing we needed tonight was to be scraping you up off the road."

The trooper didn't see what Tilly was doing; but Hingle did. He reached across the car and clapped his hands over hers and then planted a sloppy wet kiss on her cheek. "Don't know what I'd do without you, honey."

The trooper grimaced at Tilly sympathetically.

"You folks headed home now?" he asked her.

Tilly nodded, resisting the urge to wipe her face where Hingle had kissed her.

"Well, when you get there," the trooper said, "make sure you lock up safe. You probably heard already—one of them Pine Grove nuts has escaped."

"Another one?" the drunk exclaimed. "What in the hell are we paying our taxes for?"

The trooper ignored him. He saw Tilly shudder and was quick to reassure her. "I'm sure you'll be fine with your fella here to protect you." He looked at the drunk sternly. "Right, chief?"

The drunk snapped off a smart salute. "Yessir. Roger that."

"Alright." The trooper waved them along the line. "Go on home now. Just mind what I said to secure all your windows and doors. And try not to worry, ma'am. We'll catch him again soon enough, and when we do he'll *know* he's been caught."

Tilly thanked the trooper and started easing the Bug forwards. The jovial drunk called back to him, "Happy hunting!"

The young trooper just shook his head and spit in the rain and then glanced about sheepishly, hoping none of his buddies had seen the wind spit it right back in his face.

7.

An hour had passed. It was closing in on midnight. They'd barely seen another car on the road, let alone more cops. The rain was letting up, dotting the windshield, the wipers grating across the glass. Tilly watched the headlights spear the wet two-lane blacktop, driving in numb silence. Hingle still hadn't said anything about her attempt to alert the trooper. He'd found a crinkled road map in the glove compartment and was studying it by flashlight. Tilly knew some kind of reprimand must be coming. Awaited her punishment like a battered housewife dreading the sound of her husband's key in the door.

The Bug grumbled along miles of country road; puttered through the occasional sleeping small town. The last place they'd passed through was a mostly boarded-up backwater called Camborne. The ancient wooden town sign was rotting away, listing like a neglected tombstone.

They drove on past the town.

The silence was torture; Tilly couldn't stand it.

Finally she said, in a cracked voice: "Okay?"

Hingle glanced up from the map. "Okay, what?"

She blinked back tears, trying to keep her composure.

"I did what you said, didn't I? I got us through the roadblock—"

Hingle arched his eyebrow. "Well now, Mathilda . . ." he said, folding the map and placing it on the dash, "so far as I recall I didn't tell you nothing about trying to warn that Smokey Bear back there?"

And there it was.

Tilly choked back a cry. "I was scared— I *am* scared— *Please*!" She thumped the steering wheel with her hand; Betsy Bug tooted in sympathy. "Just take the car and let me go!"

Hingle glanced outside at the near-black wooded road. "*Here*? You want to get out *here*?" He chuckled. "Hell, any old psycho killer might come along." He pointed the flashlight beam under his chin, shadows crawling across his face.

She bowed her head, sobbing like a child.

"But you . . . you pruh-pruh . . . promised—"

The Bug swerved across the lanes. Hingle had to grab the wheel to stop them plowing into the woods. "Alright," he sighed. "Alright, pull her over."

She looked at him, not trusting he meant it.

"Go ahead, sis," he said. "A deal's a deal and you kept up your end of it. You want to get out here, who the hell am I to stop you? Now pull her over before you wreck us."

Betsy Bug shuddered to a stop on the shoulder.

"Th-thank you," Tilly sobbed, fumbling to release her seatbelt.

Hingle nodded magnanimously. "A man's only as good as his word, I reckon."

She unfastened the seatbelt and reached for the door handle.

Then he said, "The problem you got is I'm *not* a good man."

He flipped the flashlight in his hand like he was twirling a baton and then clubbed the heavy handle across her temple. The flashlight broke open and spewed its batteries, the light blinking out. Her head snapped back and struck the driver's-side window, fracturing the glass in a splintered star. She sagged against the door, blood gushing from the gash in her forehead and into her eyes. And then he clubbed again and white fireworks exploded across her vision and Tilly followed the light down into darkness.

8.

Hingle stared at the out-cold waitress slumped beside him. It always amazed him how a bitch could be so blinded by dumb fear; it was like a Judas cow leading 'em straight into the slaughterhouse. She must have known this wouldn't end well. Knowing who he was—*what* he was—had she truly believed he'd just let her go? Yet beyond her pitiful attempt to warn the Smokey Bear she hadn't even tried to escape. She was pathetic, really.

Hingle traced his forefinger slowly along her legs. The hem of her uniform had ridden up her thighs. His jagged fingernail slit her nylon hose. She moaned in her sleep as his fingers spidered across her flesh. He cupped his hand gently over her left breast, catching the dull thud of her heart in his palm.

She'd keep.

He climbed from the Bug and stretched the stiffness from his legs. Glanced about the barren road. Welcome to Bumfuck, USA. He popped the trunk at the front of the car—damn quirky Beetles—then went and hauled the waitress from the driver's seat. Carrying her like a sleeping child, he folded her neatly inside the trunk. There was no spare tire in the trunk, and she was a such a tiny little thing that she fit easy. He pulled off her shoes and tossed them inside with her. Peeled her pantyhose from her legs and used them to bind her hands tightly at the wrists. Reaching up under her skirt, he clawed off her panties, inhaled her scent like he was bagging glue, and then stuffed them down her throat to gag her.

She looked almost peaceful lying there. Well, that'd change soon enough.

He slammed down the trunk lid and climbed back in the Bug. Gunned the engine and continued driving south, placing the map on the passenger seat to guide him. He glanced at the fuel gauge and saw that the car was near running on fumes. No problem. He had more than enough money to cover the cost of gas and a pack of smokes too. He'd stop at the first place he saw.

9.

The filling station was a decrepit wooden shack that looked about a termite or two from collapsing into kindling on the side of the road. Hingle pulled the Bug alongside the rusted pumps. Weeds sprouted through the cracks in the concrete forecourt. Above the ragged screen door the weathered red paint of the RITTER GAS & TOW sign had faded scar-pink.

Through the grimy storefront window, Hingle saw a man snoozing behind the counter. The glow of a portable TV flickered across his gaunt unshaven features. The man's mouth was open, catching flies. The brim of a baseball cap was slanted down over his eyes like a sleeping mask. When Hingle honked the car horn, the man's head jerked up like a dog surprised by its own fart. Prodding up the brim of his cap, he peered out the window and saw the Bug on the forecourt.

As the man sat and stared at him, it flashed through Hingle's mind he'd been recognized, and he fingered the knife inside his jean jacket. Was the TV news showing his mugshot? More than likely, Hingle supposed. Then the man raised his hand in a lazy wave and Hingle decided he just hadn't seen any business for some time—any people at all, for that matter.

Hingle watched as the man hauled himself up from his stool and started ambling around the counter. For a few moments he lost sight of the guy within the gloom of the store. Then the screen door butted open and he stepped outside, snapping a chamois leather from the bib of his coveralls.

"Evening, sir!" DWAYNE was stitched on the breast of the coveralls. He was a scrawny runt with a beach ball-size beer gut. BAYWATCH was printed over the brim of his cap, along with the silhouette of a ludicrously proportioned beach babe. He did something with his mouth that might've been a smile if he'd had enough teeth.

"Fill her up?" Hingle said, with a dubious glance at the rusted pumps.

"Yessir!" Dwayne doffed the brim of his *Baywatch* cap. "You want I should clean the bugs off your windshield too?" Hingle was about to tell him that the rain had beaten him to it, when the man snickered, said, "Clean the bugs off your Bug?" And then he threw his head back and started braying like a jackass.

Hingle wondered how many years he'd been waiting to tell that joke.

"Just the gas is fine," he said, not smiling.

Dwayne managed to compose himself. He looked a little disappointed as he stuffed the chamois leather back in his coveralls. Like cleaning the bugs off windshields was the highlight of his day. And shit, Hingle thought, living out here in the willywags, maybe it was. Hingle unlocked the fuel tank and then moved aside to let the pump monkey start filling her up.

Dwayne worked the pump one-handed, grinning at Hingle like a garrulous drunk stood pissing at the urinal. "Where you headed?"

"South," Hingle said.

Dwayne saw the splintered driver's-side window. "Whoops, what happened here?"

Hingle didn't miss a beat. "Bird flew into it. This gonna take long, buddy?"

Dwayne bristled at his tone. "Shoot, mister. Just flapping my jaw is all. Making conversation. We don't see many out-of-towners no more. Not since they closed the string museum."

String museum? Hingle thought. *Shit, and I bet folks were lining up.*

He sighed. No reason to raise the guy's suspicions. Last thing he needed was this shit-kicker dropping a dime to the sheriff once he left.

He gave his most charming grin.

"Hell, I'm sorry, buddy. Been on the road too long, I guess. Must've left my manners a-ways behind me."

Dwayne nodded like he understood, but once bitten, twice shy; he still looked a little wary.

Hingle glanced at his baseball cap. "*Baywatch*, huh?"

Dwayne hesitated a moment. Then he said, "*Boob*watch, I call it. Cuz of all the titties, see. Bouncing up and down in glory-us slow motion." He puckered his lips with a wet smacking sound, sucking on the nipple of an invisible beach babe.

Hingle chuckled. "I'm guessing you're not a leg or an ass man?"

"Mister," Dwayne imparted, with a broad gummy smile, "you'd be guessing correctly."

He finished pumping the gas and slotted the nozzle back in its stand.

"How much do I owe you, buddy?" Hingle said, fishing in his pocket for his roll.

Dwayne honked his nose in his chamois leather and examined the contents with interest. "Call it twenty."

"We'll call it twenty-five," Hingle said, "you've got a pack of smokes for me inside?"

"What brand?"

Hingle was about to name his poison—

And that's when the bitch in the trunk came to, and started screaming to wake the dead.

PART TWO

"For them, an idyllic summer afternoon drive became a nightmare."
—*The Texas Chainsaw Massacre*

Magdalene Ritter was a thirteen-year old girl of plain face and plainer mind. She lived without siblings on her father, Dwyer Ritter's farm. She had murdered her mother during childbirth, a fact which Dwyer took pains to impress upon his daughter from an early age, tilling her guilt more attentively than his land. As Magdalene blossomed towards womanhood, Dwyer grew haunted by the girl's resemblance to his beloved late wife. He took to drinking whiskey, and to prowling the landing outside her bedroom door at night.

While feeding the livestock one summer's evening, Magdalene was kicked in the head by an ornery mule, and knocked unconscious. When she awoke, weeks later, with no memory of what had happened to her, the girl was with child.

Some people in town, knowing no better, blamed the mule, which Dwyer put to death with a shotgun; others suspected the negro field workers, and a few likely-looking bucks were strung from trees without trial; the local preacher, seizing enthusiastically upon the expectant mother's name, claimed it was Immaculate Conception.

But when the twin boys were born—Dwight bulldozing his way from his mother's womb, little Dwayne slopping out behind him like hog-guts—it was clear who had fathered them. Dwyer took one look at the babes, their troll-like features the perfect likeness of his own, and knew he was finished in town. He strolled outside to the yard, kneeled beneath the old oak tree where he had laid his wife to rest, doused himself with tractor diesel, tucked a Chesterfield in his mouth, and then struck a match, scattering his own ashes to the wind.

The young mother was made a pariah by the scandalized townsfolk, and left alone on the farm to raise her sons as best she could; time would prove this was not very well at all.

In Magdalene's defense, she had never been the same since that mule-kick to the cranium. She suffered ferocious migraine headaches, and was prone to fits of wild-eyed, mouth-frothing, flagellant religious mania, sermonizing in tongues as she instilled in her sons the teachings of the Old Testament; at other times she would plunge into pits of Stygian-black, godless despair from which it seemed she might never emerge, and punish the boys for their transgressions.

Long before reaching puberty, the Ritter brothers demonstrated a precocious fascination with sex, and voracious carnal appetites. Magdalene had no doubt that they had inherited this hunger from their—and indeed, her—father.

The boys collected pornography like other boys collect baseball cards. They'd been excluded from school, and local children, especially but not exclusively the girls, were warned by their parents to steer well clear of the Ritter house.

The brothers filled their days rutting their hands or each other or the barnyard animals; anything holey and moist would suffice, and even the tightest of holes could be moistened with Vaseline or spit and then probed.

As the boys matured, Dwight proved to be a dab hand at mechanics. He would occupy his time stripping down engine parts, and disassembling household appliances, curious to discover their inner workings. Dwayne was the intellectual brother, and developed an interest in history. His specialist subjects were the cruel and unusual punishments of the Roman emperors and the Nazi experiments conducted by Dr. Josef Mengele. The brothers soon coupled their interests, and began conducting pseudo-scientific experiments on the family's dwindling stock of barnyard animals, and neighborhood pets.

Magdalene despaired at what would become of her sons when she was no longer able to instruct them. She never lived to see Dwight and Dwayne achieve their full potential. While preaching to them one night in the cellar, God reached down from heaven, clutched her heart in His fist, and then crushed it like a grape. She died with the warnings of the Scarlet Woman still on her lips.

When the smell of decay at last became intolerable—though that was something they'd soon become used to—the boys dragged the fly-swept carcass from the cellar and buried it beneath the old oak tree where their father had immolated himself. Dwayne, always the gabbier of the twins, said a few solemn words. Dwight raised his can of Keystone in a toast.

Then the brothers returned upstairs to their mother's room, which they were in the process of redecorating, plastering the walls with glossy centerfold pages from their favorite issues of *Playboy* and *Penthouse*, *Hustler* and *Juggs*, getting the place all spick and span before they started looking for their first lodger.

10.

Muffled voices in the darkness above her, like the teachers in the old *Peanuts* cartoons . . . Tilly dragged herself back to consciousness. Her eyes were gummed shut with tears and blood. She forced them open, crust crumbling from her eyelashes. Wherever she was it was pitch black, choked with the stench of sweat and oil and blood and hot animal fear. Her tongue was bone-dry and swollen painfully against her inner cheeks. Except it wasn't her tongue. Something was stuffed down into her mouth. She groped upwards through the darkness to remove it. Her arms clanged against some kind of low metal ceiling. She realized her hands were bound tightly at the wrist with her pantyhose. She tried to wriggle her hands free. The hose coiled tighter, scraping the skin off her wrists. Panicking, she started to choke on the thing in her mouth. Prodding it forward with her tongue, she forced it from the back of her throat, fed it through her lips and hacked it out . . . Some kind of rag . . . Her—*oh, God*—her panties. Trying to sit, she thumped her skull against the low metal ceiling. Her head flared like a struck match and she whimpered in pain. *Where was she, had she been buried alive?* Then her eyes adjusted slowly to the gloom and she realized where she was: Betsy Bug's trunk. Her head throbbed sickly as she struggled to remember how she'd got here. She listened to the muffled voices above her— And then she recognized HIS voice and the memory of the last few hours bludgeoned her like another clubbing blow from the flashlight. Who was he talking to? Had the police stopped him at another roadblock? Why the hell were they talking about *Baywatch*? Never mind. Whoever it was they could help her. *Oh please, help me!* She'd been an idiot to trust him. She wouldn't make the same mistake again—

Tilly hammered her fists against the trunk lid, kicking up at it with her bare feet, screaming for help until her throat burned and she tasted blood and just choking it down and screeching and screaming louder.

11.

When the screaming started, Dwayne wondered for the first time if maybe he'd underestimated the townie.

He'd heard the car before he saw it: That unmistakable Beetle grumble.

As the engine drew nearer the filling station, with a peevish sigh Dwayne wrenched his pecker from the rigid 'O' of Mrs. Crenshaw's mouth, and returned the head to the spirits-filled mason jar. He screwed the lid firmly on the jar and then slid Mrs. Crenshaw back in her place beneath the counter. "We'll finish up later, Mrs. C," he assured her. Not that she complained so much these days. Never cussed, nor tried to spit no more. Happily swallowing whatever he gave her. Floating inside the jar, hair fanning around her bloated face like the fins of an exotic fish, Mrs. Crenshaw nodded in anticipation of finishing the job.

Dwayne stuffed his wilting pecker back inside his pants and listened to the Bug putter closer. He buttoned up his coveralls. Nestled back down on the stool behind the counter, unable to get comfortable with his balls aching for release.

Slanting the brim of his *Baywatch* cap over his eyes, Dwayne bowed his head and folded his arms across his swollen gut, and then made out like he was catching some Zs. He watched from the corner of his eye as the Bug tootled onto the forecourt and pulled up alongside the pumps.

Hunched behind the wheel was the kind of citified faggot who wouldn't say shit if he was choking on a mouthful of it. Real pretty fella, too. Maybe Dwayne wouldn't have to wait long to bust his nut after all. Old Lady Crenshaw would just have to sit tight and wait a while longer for hers. Dwayne grinned, his toothless smile hidden in the shadow of the brim of his cap.

He waited for the townie to toot the horn, and then pretended to startle awake like some damn fool who'd never heard a car horn before. As he stared out the window, Dwayne sized the man up and made his decision—though the fella's fate was all but written the moment he pulled up at RITTER GAS & TOW.

Dwayne hauled himself up off his stool and shuffled through the shadows at the back of the store, pausing where he knew the townie couldn't see him from outside. He fetched the phone off the storeroom wall and dialed.

When he called Dwight back at the house, Dwayne could hardly hear his brother over all the screaming in the background. It pissed Dwayne off royally that he was stuck working, with only Old Lady Crenshaw for company, while Dwight got the night off to ball with the Jarvis gal. The Jarvis gal had been all purdy and fresh when he'd left the house that morning, but Dwayne knew, a few hours in his brother's company, and Dwight'd take that new gal gloss right off her. And getting sloppy seconds was never as much fun as breaking 'em in.

But Dwayne didn't bitch about it. He quickly apprised Dwight of the current situation. Dwight sighed on the other end of the phone line; Dwayne could tell he was reluctant to leave the Jarvis gal now that he'd warmed her up and she was hot to trot.

"Can't you handle it?" Dwight whined.

"Now you know that's not the way we do things," Dwayne told him.

He hung up the phone before Dwight could protest any further.

The way they did things—and after so many years, the Ritter brothers had it down to a fine fucking art—when a fresh piece of meat arrived at the filling station, Dwayne would pump their vehicle with the Special Gas. The Special Gas was Dwayne's own concoction and he guarded the recipe as jealously as the Colonel did his secret blend of eleven herbs and spices. The meat would drive off with a full tank of the Special Gas, and Dwayne waving them fare-thee-well and see-you-again-soon in their rearview mirror. The Special Gas would quickly work its magic. The vehicle would conk out within six short miles of the filling station. That's when Dwight would just happen along in his tow truck. Coming to the rescue like a knight in shining coveralls. The meat was so pleased to have avoided the long walk back to the filling station (and there wasn't no place else within spitting distance) that they rarely questioned the serendipity of this encounter. The poor bastards never knew what hit them. Usually Dwight's tire-iron. A stunning blow upside the head. And then it was back to Casa de Ritter for some sport.

If it ain't broke then don't fix it . . . Dwayne liked to say like he'd coined the phrase. And he wasn't about to go messing with a good thing now. So he stuck to the game plan: Acting the role of country bumpkin while he pumped the townie's Bug with the Special Gas. Dwayne could tell the fella was peering down his nose at him. Smirking at his Boobwatch cap like Dwayne was some kind of asshole for liking titties. Well, he wouldn't be so high and fucking mighty in a couple of hours. Dwayne was looking forward to getting the fella back to the house and showing him the score. Cutting his snooty nose clean off his face and eating it right in front of him. Not that nose was good eating, mind you. Too gristly. Maybe he'd start with his—

The sound of screaming snapped Dwayne from his reverie. He startled back from the Bug. The car was pitching and rocking as someone in the trunk kicked and hammered at the lid. A gal, judging by the screams. "You got someone in there, mister?" Dwayne said to the townie, not altogether disapprovingly.

The townie gave an impish grin, as if driving around with a gal in the trunk of his car was the most natural thing in the world—and Dwayne wasn't exactly unaccustomed to the experience.

The townie's knowing smile made the hairs on the back of Dwayne's neck prickle with recognition. A spark of energy seemed to pass between the two men like static electricity. "You can keep a secret, right?" the fella said.

"Well sure, I guess," Dwayne said.

The townie nodded. "You want to see her?"

Dwayne wet his lips with a flick of his tongue.

Now the fella was speaking his language.

"Who is she?" he said.

The townie shrugged. "Just some hitcher I picked up," he said, "and was saving for later. But hey, share and share alike, I say." He waggled his eyebrows. "She's got a pair of titties on her just like Pammy from *Baywatch*."

Dwayne couldn't help grinning. "No kidding?"

Maybe this fella wasn't such an asshole, after all.

The townie swept an arm towards the trunk like Mickey Mouse welcoming him to the Magic Kingdom.

Dwayne shuffled forwards to take a gander.

The townie unlocked the trunk, proudly hoisted up the lid, and there she was crammed inside the trunk space. Dwayne thought her crumpled red check apron was a funny thing for a hitcher to be wearing, but he let that go. Her wrists were roped with pantyhose, her hands clasped together as if in prayer. She peered up in terror at Dwayne and pleaded for help in a cracked and rasping voice that got him hard as a rail spike.

Even all beat to hell, she was a fine one to look at. Almost as purdy as the Jarvis gal. About the only disappointing thing were her titties. Just a handful, Dwayne reckoned. Nothing like as big and ripe as Pammy's on Boobwatch. Dwayne was turning his head to tell the townie that very thing—when the blade of the knife slammed into his temple, and suddenly titties were the last things on his mind.

12.

Curled helplessly inside the trunk, Tilly could only watch as Hingle wrenched the fillet knife in the gas station attendant's temple. There was a sickening crunch of bone. The man twitched and whimpered like a dreaming dog. His eyes rolled up in his skull. Blood hemorrhaged from his nose, spattering the DWAYNE stitched on the breast of his coveralls. Hingle ripped the knife free with a savage grunt. Blood jetted from the wound, catapulting the *Baywatch* cap off Dwayne's head to reveal a thinning thatch of chimney-red hair. Before the man could crumple to the ground, Hingle deftly grabbed him by the neck, holding him upright and wiping the blood off the blade onto the shoulder of his coveralls.

Hingle grinned at Tilly.

"Room for one more in there?"

And then he shoved the dead man down into the trunk.

Tilly woofed for breath as Dwayne's deadweight pinned her to the floor of the trunk like a wrestler going for the three-count.

Hingle curled the man's arms and legs inside the trunk and then he swung the trunk lid down. It bounced off Dwayne's bony ass and rattled back up. Hingle lost all patience with Dwayne. Gripping the upraised lid for balance, he started stomping the carcass down inside the trunk like he was compacting garbage. The air was crushed from Tilly's lungs beneath the bloody corpse.

"Get in there, you scrawny sonofabitch!"

When Hingle tried the trunk lid again, it clicked shut and locked firmly into place.

13.

The dead man embraced her in the dark of the trunk.

Warm blood drizzled down from his face onto hers—blinding her—spattering the back of her throat when she tried to scream. But with the deadweight pressing down on her, Tilly could barely breathe, let alone scream, and she knew that only the madman driving her car would hear her cries. Struggling to move beneath Dwayne's deceptive bulk, grunting and gasping with effort, Tilly wormed her arms out from under him. But her hands were still bound with her pantyhose. She could only clasp them around the back of Dwayne's neck like they were slow dancing in the world's tiniest ballroom. She tried to roll him off her but he was just . . . Too. Damn. Heavy. And there was no room in the trunk. Nowhere to roll him. They were crushed together like twins in a tin womb. She was surprised the two of them had even fit in the trunk. And if she'd replaced the spare tire like she'd been meaning to, they wouldn't have.

In a flash of anger and frustration, she jacked her knees up into the fleshy balloon of his gut—"Get off me!"—and in protest the dead man belched fetid gas in her face, and then his bowels blew a raspberry as they voided, and the trunk became choked with the stink of shit.

Tilly made a strangled sound halfway between a sob and a retch.

What was she *doing* here, how had she let this happen?

Her mind was more than happy to show her where she'd gone wrong; like a sadistic movie projectionist, it replayed all the times she might have fought back or tried to escape. Driving Hingle through the woods, she could have leapt from the car and tried to hide in the forest. She should have done more to alert the troopers at the roadblock. Back in Big Bob's office—another lifetime ago—she could have kicked Hingle in the balls and grabbed the knife. She shouldn't have been working tonight, it was her night off! She should have left town when she had the chance, stayed in college and not run home to mom when the old bitch had lied about being on her deathbed. And truth be told, Tilly hadn't taken much convincing, had she? That one lonely semester of college had been more than she could bear—she hadn't belonged there, had made a dreadful mistake in ever believing she did. She'd been looking for an excuse to leave even before her mother's claws had hooked her back home and never let her go again. And why? Because she was a coward at heart, a pushover and a doormat, and now look where it had got her— *Look at you now!* Mom crowed. And suddenly it wasn't Dwayne weighing down on her, it was her mother; and this wasn't a car trunk, it was Lizette Mulvehill's casket; and Tilly screamed as she twisted and turned beneath her mother's crushing weight, cursing and clawing and fighting back as she'd never dared while her mother was alive.

14.

Hingle lit another Marlboro off the butt of the one he was smoking, flicked the dog-end out the window, took a deep drag, sighed back in his seat, and then joined Merle Haggard on the radio for a rousing chorus of *I'm a White Boy*.

Before leaving RITTER GAS & TOW he'd swiped a few cartons of Marlboro Reds and a sixer of Old Milwaukee for the road, plus what little cash money there was in the register. Nothing else worth stealing in that rat-haven, and the place stank worse than a latrine. So he'd flipped the sign in the window to CLOSED and taken off again. Now the filling station was a good half dozen miles behind him.

According to his map, he was headed south on Broke Leg Road. All he had to do was keep following this potholed dirt track and it would lead him back to the highway. Lady Luck willing, he'd be home free the rest of the way to the state line. Then he'd find somewhere to hole up. Throw himself a Welcome Home party with little Tilly in the trunk. Somewhere nice and quiet where they could get to know each other better. Hingle smiled at the thought, drumming his hands on the wheel in time with Merle. After four years locked in a concrete box, things were looking up.

He was still smiling when the Bug backfired a black cloud of smoke and started shuddering violently. The steering wheel convulsed in his hands. The engine sputtered and coughed an automotive death rattle. And then the car gave up the ghost and died, jerking to a stop in the middle of the road.

Hingle pounded the wheel in anger. He hauled himself out of the Bug. Fanned the air as he waded through the smoke billowing from the back of the car. He raised the hood and scowled at the engine, cursing himself for not having the shit-kicker check it at the filling station before he shanked the sonofabitch. He glanced about the lonely forest road and sighed, not relishing the prospect of another long hike through the woods. At least it had stopped raining.

Still cursing, he fetched the map from inside the car. Spread it out across the trunk lid and charted a course through the woods that would lead him to the highway. He folded the map and stuffed it in the back pocket of his pants.

Then he took the knife from inside his jacket, and hauled up the lid of the trunk.

The redneck was draped across the waitress like a spent lover. Her blood-spattered face peered over his shoulder. "Not disturbing nothing, am I?" Hingle chuckled. Then he caught a whiff of Dwayne's shitty drawers and staggered back, gagging. "Phew! That you or him couldn't hold it in?"

Tilly had screamed herself hoarse. "*Please . . .*" she croaked.

Hingle shushed her. "It breaks my heart, darling, it truly does. We're gonna have to cut this short. What I had in mind for you—roses, champagne, Perry Como records; the whole nine yards—I was gonna treat you like a queen . . ."

He shook his head with what Tilly thought was genuine regret. "But I'm sorry to say, me and you are gonna have to say our goodbyes right here and now."

Reaching down into the trunk, Hingle grabbed Dwayne by the back of his hair and dragged the man's head from Tilly's shoulder. She gasped for breath as the deadweight eased off her. Hingle lowered the knife to her throat. Tilly shut her eyes tight and shivered as the icy blade teased her larynx.

Then something like thunder rumbled in the distance.

Hingle raised his head sharply.

A vehicle was approaching.

When he saw what it was, Hingle almost laughed.

Lady Luck always *had* been sweet on him.

Before Tilly could cry for help, Hingle butted Dwayne's skull down hard into her face, and as she slumped unconscious, he slammed the trunk lid shut.

15.

When Dwayne called the house to tell his brother they had company, Dwight was fooling around with the Jarvis gal, and he almost didn't hear the phone ringing downstairs over all the racket she was making.

They were in Momma's old room. Momma's portrait watched solemnly from the wall above the bed. The portrait formed the centerpiece of a shrine; pages torn from porno mags plastered every other spare inch of the wall. After Momma popped her clogs, it had taken the Ritter brothers many hours to redecorate, but they were pleased with the end result. Momma looked less pleased to be glaring out amid an orgy of naked breasts and swollen labia.

The Jarvis gal was splayed across the four-poster. Buck-naked. Her wrists and ankles shackled with chains in a X-shape, like she was making snow angels on the soiled bed sheets.

Dwight loomed at the foot of the bed, stripped to his grubby undershorts, the crotch tented with excitement. His coarse pelt of body hair was dewy with sweat.

He was clutching the salesman's disembodied arm like a withered brown baton. Foul with decay, the limb was attracting the interest of the flies that whorled above the bed. A jagged stump of bone jutted from the shoulder where the limb had been wrenched from the salesman's body. Gripping the bone like an ivory handle, Dwight waved the arm above the bed as if conducting an orchestra, the flies buzzing in symphony. He scratched his nuts with the clawed hand, raked the fingers up and down his spine. Then he proceeded to jab the rotting fist between the Jarvis gal's thighs like he was plunging a blocked drain.

Her screams were music to his ears. Whenever the excitement was too much for her to bear and she passed out, Dwight gave her a good jolt from the car battery. Jumper cables trailed from the battery to the set of alligator clips that were clamped to her teats. Oh yeah, that'd wake her back up right quick; with a pop of sparks, and the sickly sweet stench of scorched flesh filling his nostrils.

Hell, sometimes he gave her a jolt just to watch her thrash about and holler.

When he finally heard the phone ringing, Dwight was tempted to ignore it, he was having such a hoot. *La-la-la, I can't hear you, Dwayne . . .* But

Dwight knew if he did, Dwayne would only be sore at him. At best he'd catch a whipping; at worst Dwayne would clamp the car battery to Dwight's nut sack. And Dwight knew from bitter experience he preferred dishing out pain to receiving it.

Reluctantly, he left the Jarvis gal and trudged downstairs to the kitchen to answer the phone. No "Hello, brother" or nothing, Dwayne just ordered him out to Broke Leg Road to fetch the meat.

Dwight returned to Momma's old room and started changing back into his coveralls, bitching to the Jarvis gal how Dwayne was always bossing him around.

"It ain't right," he complained. "I'm older than that runt by five minutes."

Well, she wasn't much of a shoulder to cry on, so Dwight just left the Jarvis gal with the salesman's arm sheathed inside her, and went outside to his truck.

Roscoe poked his head out from under the porch. The dog gave a whimper when he saw it was Dwight and ducked his head back into the shadows.

Dwight climbed in his truck and gunned the engine, the winch jangling like a butcher-hook as the truck jounced away down the trail towards Broke Leg Road.

16.

Look at this *fucking hick*, Hingle thought, as the ape clambered out of the tow truck. A squat troll of a man. Balding up top, with a mane of mullet hair. Reminded Hingle of the redneck comedian, Gallagher. Maybe the mullet was some kind of tribute? He could imagine this goon laughing his ass off as Gallagher smashed watermelons with his sledgehammer. The tow truck driver was wearing the same coveralls as his brother, but even filthier, if that was possible. And they *had* to be brothers—twins, maybe—the inbred likeness was unmistakable. DWIGHT was stitched on his breast. Hingle wondered if there was a third brother, and what his folks might've called him; there couldn't be many names left beginning with 'Dw—'.

"Car trouble?" Dwight said.

Clearly the brains of the outfit, Hingle thought, with a glance at the clapped-out Bug. Dwayne got the matinee idol looks—comparatively, at least—while Dwight was gifted with the ability to state the fucking obvious.

"Sure looks like it," Hingle said.

When he killed this hick with the same knife he'd used on his brother, Hingle figured he'd be doing the world a rare favor. Cleaning some pollution from the gene pool. But first he'd let him fix the Bug. And if he couldn't, then he'd just take his truck. Sure as hell beat hiking through the woods again.

"Well," Dwight said, "then you're lucky I happened along."

All but dragging his knuckles along the ground, Dwight joined Hingle beside the upraised hood at the back of the Bug. He frowned at the engine in that way grease monkeys do before they fleece you. "Uh-huh," he said, finally.

"Sounds expensive," Hingle said.

"Mister," Dwight said, "your first mistake's not buying American."

He scowled at the Volkswagen and shook his head disapprovingly.

"Your second mistake's right here."

He pointed a filthy finger towards the back of the engine.

"Come take a look at this . . ."

Humoring the guy, Hingle stooped forward for a closer look—

17.

—and Dwight clipped him upside the head with the tire-iron, and he slumped to the road like a sack of cement.

The townie lay twitching on his back. Blood pooled on the asphalt and haloed his head where the back of his skull had split. His eyes were in orbit, his legs drumming the ground like he was dancing a jig. Dwight waited patiently for the townie to lie still, as he knew from experience would happen right about . . . *now.*

He crouched down beside the fella to check his pulse.

Still beating strong.

A good clean capture.

Satisfied the townie would keep, Dwight hoisted the fella onto his shoulder and carried him effortlessly around the Bug. He draped him across the front seats. Blood rained from his scalp wound into the footwell. Dwight closed the door on him, slammed the hood down over the engine, and hooked his winch to the back of the Bug. Then he clapped the muck off his hands, started up the truck, and towed the car back to the house, singing tunelessly to himself.

He pulled up in the yard and unhooked the Bug from the truck. Hauled the townie from the car by his ankles and started dragging him. The fella's outstretched arms dug ruts in the dirt as Dwight dragged him to the bulkhead doors alongside the house. Dwight raised the bulkhead doors and lugged the townie down to the root cellar. A naked light bulb dangled from the ceiling. Dwight yanked the cord and dirty light shone down on the rough earthen floor.

Hanging down from the wooden rafters were two rusted lengths of chain with handcuffs at the ends of them. Dwight clapped the cuffs around the townie's wrists, and then hauled on a pulley and hoisted the chains till the fella hung suspended from the ceiling like a decrepit Christ, with only the tips of his big toes brushing the ground. The townie's shoulder blades groaned like old wood as his arms were forced to take his weight, and he gave a pained moan in his sleep.

Dwight fetched a sling blade down from the pegboard wall—some folks called it a Kaiser blade, Dwight always called it a sling blade. With a few practiced slashes, he stripped the townie of his duds and left him wearing just his shorts. He tossed the townie's clothes into the corner of the cellar.

The fillet knife fell from inside the jean jacket. Dwight didn't think much of it. A man had every right to protect himself. There were a lot of sick people out there in the world. He fetched up the fillet knife and added his new toy to the tools on the pegboard.

When the townie came to, the first thing he'd see was the pegboard. And as a new guest, he'd get to choose the first tool that went to work on him. Dwight always got a kick out of that; watching the meat agonize over which of the tools was likely to cause them the least amount of pain. They'd always be surprised. In the right hands, even the most innocent-looking tool could find your sweet spot and make you sing. Take a spoon, for instance. A spoon could crush a testicle, or scoop an eyeball right out of its socket.

Dwight made a mental note: *Spoon.*

Leaving the townie hanging from the rafters, Dwight shuffled back and canted his head like an artist admiring his work. He reckoned he'd earned a beer for his efforts. In the corner of the cellar was a refrigerator chest. Dwight hauled up the lid and reached down past the dismembered census taker. The fella's dying scream was literally frozen on his face. Dumb bastard knocked on the wrong door with his questions. *"And how many people are currently residing in this abode?" he'd asked. "Living or dead?" Dwight had replied, before he whapped him over the head with a meat mallet.* Dwight shoved the census taker's torso aside and fished a can of Keystone from the bottom of the refrigerator chest. He took a long pull and smacked his lips and nodded. "Yep." What more could you say?

Glugging his beer, Dwight trudged upstairs to the kitchen. He called Dwayne at the filling station to let him know the meat was ready and waiting to be tenderized—oh, and to fetch home more beer, they were almost out.

When Dwayne didn't answer the phone, Dwight was tempted to get started on the new fella without him. But he knew he'd catch hell if he dared. An hour later and Dwayne still wasn't answering the phone and Dwight was out of beer by now and getting antsy. "Goddamn it, Dwayne . . ." What was keeping that runt?

Stomping outside the house, Dwight leapt in his truck and gunned the engine. Hitting the gas, he was so angry with Dwayne that he reversed the truck into the Bug, cursing at the crunch of metal and glass. The Bug jolted forward, its nose crumpling against the oak tree next to the house. Deciding he'd check for damage to his truck when he returned—and vent his frustrations on the townie if he found any—Dwight threw the truck into gear and then floored it away down the trail, starting out to the filling station to see what was keeping his brother.

18.

Tilly startled awake as the Bug gave a violent jolt that pitched Dwayne's deadweight off her. She quickly braced her arms against his chest to prevent him rolling back and crushing her. Her wrists bent back painfully, her arms buckling and burning under the strain. She couldn't hold him like this much longer. She gulped greedily for air while she could, ignoring the hellish stench inside the trunk as the car continued to roll—

And then the Bug thudded to a sudden stop, striking something that crumpled the trunk and twisted one corner of the lid up into a sneer. A sliver of moonlight shone through the gap. Clean air wafted across her face. Tilly raised her head gratefully towards the gap and inhaled deeply.

Before her arms collapsed, and Dwayne fell back on top of her, she pressed her back against the floor of the trunk, kicking upwards with all her strength at the damaged trunk lid. She gritted her teeth against the pain and kicked until her bare feet were bloody . . . and slowly but surely the gap began to widen. Still kicking, she grunted determinedly as more clean air breathed inside—

The trunk lid clattered open, squealing up on its hinges. Moonlight blinded her.

Lurching up inside the trunk, Tilly released her grip on Dwayne and let him slump to the floor across her legs. She raised her bound hands to shield her eyes from the glaring light. *Where was she? Where had Hingle brought her?*

Through the cracks of her fingers she saw an overgrown yard choked with weeds, strewn with the hulks of rusted junk cars through which sprouted tall grass and sunflowers. Crickets chirred in the tall grass. A ramshackle farmhouse loomed above her. The faded white clapboard was bearded with creepers and lichen. Above the buckled porch were two windows. One window was boarded over with wooden slats; reflected in the grimy glass of the other, the lunatic eye of the moon winked at Tilly. An old oak tree sagged against the side of the house. A withered black branch overhung the porch roof. A tire-swing dangled from the branch like a fishing line with a Goodyear lure. The tire was chewed-up and mangled.

Tilly glanced at Betsy Bug's nose crumpled against the tree and knew at once that even if she had the keys, she wasn't driving anywhere. It didn't matter. All that mattered was she was free. She couldn't see Hingle anywhere . . . but that didn't mean he wasn't close. She had to get out of here. Right now. While she could—

She wormed her legs out from under Dwayne and massaged some life into them, hissing as they prickled with pins and needles. She tried to stand but her legs were still numb and refused to support her. Her bound hands made it difficult to climb down from the trunk. Clinging to the trunk like a nervous swimmer at the pool edge, she lowered herself gingerly to the ground.

Her legs folded beneath her and she landed on her butt more heavily than she'd anticipated. Her teeth clacked together, biting her tongue and bringing fresh tears to her eyes. Shattered glass from the broken car headlights crunched under her butt and gouged her thighs. Barely registering the pain, she snatched up a shard of glass, and began sawing awkwardly through her pantyhose shackles. She glanced about anxiously—the yard, the house—expecting Hingle to appear before she could finish sawing through the nylon. The way her hose always laddered, she wouldn't have thought it would be this difficult. Then the fabric tore and she clawed her hands free with a cry of relief, rubbing first her grazed wrists, and then her numb legs, the feeling slowly prickling back.

Clutching the car for balance, Tilly staggered to her feet.

Blood rushed to her head and the world teetered sickeningly around her. She shut her eyes and sucked deep breaths until the nausea passed—

Something roared in front of her. Her eyes snapped open in time to see the dog bolting out from under the porch. Its claws raked the mud as it hurtled across the yard towards her, the chain around its neck unspooling with a jangle. Its fur was matted with dried blood, standing up in spikes along the ridged muscles of its back. Its ears were pricked back on a bullet-shaped skull that was more gargoyle than pit bull. Its fangs were bared as it charged her.

There was nowhere to run, not before it pounced.

Cowering back against the Bug, Tilly slammed the trunk shut and clambered onto the lid, scrambling up the oak tree and lifting her legs out of harm's way.

The dog slammed against the trunk beneath her bare feet. It strained on its hind legs to reach her. Saliva sprayed from its chops as it snapped at her heels.

She hauled herself higher up the tree, branches raking her face and drawing blood as she butted upwards through the foliage. She found an uneasy perch upon an outstretched limb and huddled there gasping for breath and gaping down at the dog. It prowled around the tree, barking furiously at her.

Tilly shook her head in disbelief.

Treed by a fucking dog . . . What the hell next?

19.

Dwight wasn't the sharpest tool in the cellar torture chamber, but even he knew something smelled rotten at RITTER GAS & TOW. His first clue was the puddle of blood on the forecourt next to the Special Gas pump. Clue number two was lying nearby: His brother's prized *Baywatch* cap. Dwight struggled to recall the last time he'd seen Dwayne not wearing it. Dwayne was sensitive about his thinning hair. Dwight told him he just ought to take the plunge and grow it out long at the back like he did and then no one would notice. But Dwayne wouldn't listen, reckoned he knowed it all.

Inside the filling station, the store sign was flipped to CLOSED, but the door was unlocked, and the register was empty and the counter unmanned. That wasn't like Dwayne at all. Normally he'd be sitting at the counter with Old Lady Crenshaw snug on his lap, the two lovebirds watching *Baywatch* on the portable TV.

Dwight fetched the mason jar from under the counter.

"Where's Dwayne at, Mrs. C?" Shaking her up like a snow globe.

Mrs. Crenshaw silently bobbed and butted against the glass. If she knew, she wasn't telling.

The TV was on with the sound muted. Tuned to local news. Dwight was about to switch it off and lock up the store and then head back home to see if Dwayne had showed up there, when a photo of the fella he'd just hung in the cellar flashed across the screen.

Frowning, Dwight turned up the sound: "—the hunt for escaped mass-murderer Terrence LeRoy Hingle continues tonight. Hingle, also known as the Sorority Slayer, escaped earlier this evening from the Pine Grove State Hospital after killing several orderlies. He remains at large and is known to be highly dangerous. Police have warned the public not to approach him and to remain vigilant until he is apprehended—" Dwight shut off the TV.

Highly dangerous, my ass. But maybe this Hingle fella had done something to Dwayne? And Dwight didn't like the thought of leaving the Jarvis gal alone in the house with a madman. Hell, anything could happen.

He hustled from the store and back to his truck. Fetched Dwayne's bloody cap off the forecourt and frowned at it. Nope, Dwight didn't like the look of this at all. For all their bickering, Dwayne was kin, his baby brother by five minutes. It filled Dwight with dread that something might've happened to him. He leapt in the truck and hit the gas and floored it home.

20.

Hingle woke with a hiss of pain. His skull was pounding where the shit-kicker had cold-cocked him as he'd stooped to check the car engine. Oldest trick in the book—hell, he'd used it himself a time or two—and he'd fallen for it. The hick must've seen his mugshot on TV and decided to make a citizen's arrest. Except this didn't look like no jail cell. None Hingle had ever seen before, anyway.

Glancing around, his vision blurred like an old Movie of the Week flashback . . . and then the root cellar swam slowly into focus. The corners of the room were thick with shadow. A naked light bulb glowed dimly above him. In the dingy light, at first it was hard for Hingle to tell why he couldn't move and why it hurt like such a sonofabitch when he tried. Then he realized he'd been stripped to his shorts—shit, *that* wasn't good—and that he was hanging by chains from the rafters, like a goddamn puppet on strings. His arms were wrenched above and behind him, like a madman flapping his arms in an attempt to fly. His shoulders were forced to take the brunt of his weight. And they weren't happy about it, burning like they were aflame.

Hingle tried to stretch his feet to the floor to relieve the burden from his shoulders, raking the cold dirt with his toes. At full extension he managed to teeter on his big toes like some half-assed ballerina, but it barely eased the pressure from his shoulders, and the effort required was exhausting. He slumped down heavily, shoulders popping under his full weight. He stayed hanging here like this and pretty soon his arms would wrench from the sockets.

He raised his head towards the stairs leading up to the kitchen.

Was the shit-kicker up there? Had to be. What the hell was he waiting for?

"Hey . . ." Hingle croaked.

He choked down the frog in his throat and tried again. "Hey, fucker! Come on down here and cut me loose, let's you and me dance a few rounds!"

No answer; not a sound up there.

Maybe the shit-kicker had gone to fetch the cops?

Then why go to the effort of stripping him and hanging him up in chains?

Maybe . . . maybe he'd found his brother in the trunk of the Bug?

That was not the most comforting thought—especially not now that Hingle had noticed the pegboard wall cluttered with tools. Hammers and saws and chisels and drills and pliers; it was a regular hardware store down here, every tool coated in rust. Wait a minute—

Hingle squinted . . . *Was* that rust?

His balls didn't think so, shriveling in fear as he gaped at the bloody tools and saw his own fillet knife hanging among them on the pegboard.

21.

Perched on the outstretched tree branch, Tilly stared down at the dog; the dog stared up at Tilly, salivating.

"Hey! Get me out of here! Goddamn it, get me the hell out of here!"

Her head snapped towards the cries. They were coming from the house. Behind those bulkhead doors. Down in the cellar.

Then she recognized HIS voice and a chill shivered down her spine.

Why would HE be yelling like that? This was HIS place . . . wasn't it?

As if in answer came the rumbling approach of a truck engine. The hairs on the nape of Tilly's neck prickled as she saw headlights ghosting along the wooded trail towards the house. She wondered again just where she was.

Below her the dog stood against the tree on its hind legs, barking like a furry Judas, eager to reveal her presence to its master. Tilly thought about what they said about dogs and their owners, and she shivered once more. Before the truck could emerge from the trail, she scrambled up the tree as high as she could climb and concealed herself—she hoped—behind a dense cluster of leaves.

The truck growled into the yard, skidding to a stop behind Betsy Bug. The driver's-side door cranked open (RITTER GAS & TOW was printed in faded red paint on the siding) and a man climbed down from the cab. DWIGHT was stitched on his coveralls. Even in the moonlight, Tilly could see the resemblance to his brother. Unmistakable. The Ritters were a memorable-looking family.

Tilly held her breath as Dwight approached Betsy's trunk. He seemed afraid of what he might find inside. The dog was still barking up at the tree. Dwight picked up a rock and tossed it at the dog. "Shaddup!" The rock hit the dog in the ass and it yelped and tucked tail and scuttled back under the porch.

Dwight hesitated outside the trunk. Gave a nervous flick of his mullet. Then he lifted the lid and his worst fears were realized as he saw his dead brother. He unleashed an anguished scream that chilled Tilly to the core.

She was suddenly very glad she hadn't shown herself when he pulled up. This man would not help her; Tilly wasn't sure he was even *human*. She didn't know how it had happened, but somehow she'd fallen out of the frying pan and into the fire.

Dwight turned towards the house and glared at the bulkhead doors. Hingle was still crying out in the cellar. But nothing like he soon would be, Tilly thought. And right then she would not have traded places with Hingle for all the money in the world. She watched as Dwight threw open the bulkhead doors and stomped down to the cellar.

Now was her chance: While Dwight was busy with his brother's killer—

Praying he'd left the keys in his truck, Tilly started scrambling down the tree . . .

And of course, the fucking dog reemerged from under the porch, trotted over lazily, and stood waiting for her at the bottom. *Are you kidding me?* Stopping her descent, she reclaimed her perch on the outstretched branch and glared at the dog. It wagged its tail and lapped its chops, smiling its glistening fangs at her.

Trapped in the tree, Tilly stared with hopeless longing at Dwight's truck. Ten yards away, but it might as well have been the moon. There was nothing she could do but listen to the screams echoing from the cellar.

22.

"What's . . . what's that?" Hingle wheezed. A rope of bloody bile swung from his lips. The hick had finished working his body like a heavy bag. Now he was coming towards him with what looked like a rusted budgerigar cage. A round hole was sawed in the bottom of the cage. A head-sized hole. "Stay the fuck away from me with that!" The hick slugged him again in the guts. Fractured ribs crunched like kindling. Hingle rocked back on his chains, the air punched from his lungs, his shoulder blades creaking like an old rocking chair. Hanging from the chains like a side of raw beef, he bowed his head and sucked for breath. The hick fixed the budgie cage over his head like a crown. He adjusted the cage upon Hingle's shoulders, positioning the little barred door in front of his mouth. Then he opened the door and shuffled back into the gloom of the cellar.

"Wait . . ." Hingle gasped. "Just wait a minute—"

Wrenching the lid off a coal bin, the hick reached down inside it and withdrew a grain sack. Something wriggled inside the sack, writhing and squealing. The hick unknotted the end of the sack. Peered inside it. Gave it a shake and grinned.

He wriggled on a pair of heavy work gloves, and then reached down inside the sack and pulled out a gnarly black timber rat the size of a puppy. The rat squirmed wildly in his grip, thrashing its thick scaly tail. It sank its long yellow incisors into his fingers. The hick hissed in pain and pulled it loose. The rat's teeth tore a strip from the finger of his work glove. The hick held up the rat for Hingle to take a good long look: The beady black eyes and twitching whiskers and the long yellow teeth, spackled with blood where it had bitten him. Hingle's eyes widened with horror as the rat-wielding hick ambled slowly towards him—

And all of a sudden he was ten years old, cuffed to the drainpipe beneath the kitchen sink, surrounded by rats, their fur slick with momma's blood, Little Cyril's skeleton grinning fiendishly, the rats creeping towards Terry Lee in a bristling black tide, the boy's terror reflected in their hungry black eyes.

"Christ, no—" Hingle cried. "*Please!*"

He cowered back as far as his chains would allow.

And that was nowhere near far enough.

The hick raised the rat to the open cage door and relaxed his grip on it. The rat darted from his hand, inside the cage. The hick closed the door and fastened it shut with a piece of wire. The rat squirmed around the circumference of Hingle's head, its greasy fur filthy as a toilet brush. It gave a panicked squeal as it realized it was trapped—

And then its claws were raking his cheeks, tail whipping at his eyes. It sank its incisors into the soft flesh of his earlobe, blood spurting as it ripped it off and gobbled it down. Hingle roared in pain and thrashed his head, the cage rattling wildly about his shoulders. Biting in frenzy, the rat seized his bottom lip and with a jerk of its head, peeled it away like a strip of chicken skin. Hingle screamed and the rat lunged towards his open mouth. His teeth snapped shut like a guillotine upon its neck. Bones splintered and crunched. Hot, bitter-tasting rat blood flooded his mouth. The headless body jerked back, crashing against the cage bars. Blood jetted from the ragged stump of its neck, blinding him. Its whiplashing tail went limp and it keeled onto its side and lay there twitching.

Hingle retched up the head and dry-heaved.

The hick slapped his thigh and roared with laughter.

"Not bad, mister," he nodded. "Not bad at all."

He reached inside the sack and pulled out another huge, wildly thrashing rat.

"But let's see if you can do that again, you kin-killing sonofabitch."

23.

From her perch on the tree branch, Tilly couldn't see what was happening in the cellar. She wasn't sure she wanted to know. Judging by Hingle's screams he wasn't enjoying himself. Couldn't be happening to a nicer guy, she thought.

She looked down at the dog.

It sat patiently below the tree, watching her with its head cocked.

She gazed along the length of the branch she was perched on. The end of the limb overhung the porch. She glanced at the windows above the porch: One boarded over with wooden slats, the other closed. Maybe there was a phone inside to call for help? Or a weapon she could use to fend off the dog and escape to Dwight's truck? She couldn't just stay here. Dwight would find her up here eventually. That would not be good. Not good at all. Maybe he'd blame her for Dwayne's murder? Fetch her down to the cellar for a taste of the same medicine he was dishing out to Hingle.

Forcing herself into action, she began caterpillar crawling along the branch towards the house. The limb started about the thickness of a telegraph pole. At its end, where it overhung the porch, it became broom handle-thin, tapering to a brush of dry withered leaves. As she inched forwards, the limb sagged beneath her weight. She pictured the branch drooping lazily to the ground and the dog plucking her loose like a ripe piece of fruit. And it was old wood; at any time she felt the branch could just shear away from the tree and hurl her to the ground to be savaged. These weren't the most encouraging thoughts. She pushed them firmly from her mind and continued inching along the branch towards the house.

Below the tree the dog tracked her movements, stalking along beneath the branch. It seemed to realize what she was up to and gave a guttural growl. Hanging from the middle of the branch was the tire-swing. Snatching the tire in its jaws, the dog dug its paws in the dirt and pulled on it. The branch bent back like an archer's bow. The wood creaked under the strain. Tilly let out a cry as the dog released the tire and the branch whipped back and forth and nearly catapulted her from her perch. She gripped the branch tightly between her thighs, looped her arms around the limb, a literal tree-hugger holding on for dear life. The tree shuddered violently. Leaves showered down over the yard. The tire-swing yo-yoed beneath the branch. But she managed to hold on.

The dog whined, snatched the tire, started pulling it again.

The branch began to splinter. Feeling it giving way beneath her, Tilly scrambled the last few feet to the end of the limb, and threw herself onto the porch roof, seconds before the branch snapped away from the tree like a twig.

The branch thudded to the ground, the impact rocking the porch beneath her.

"What in the luvva fuck was that?" she heard Dwight exclaim from the cellar.

Peering over the porch roof, Tilly prayed she'd see the dog crushed beneath the branch . . . But, no. The fucker was right as rain and still barking at her.

She teetered to her feet and turned towards the window that wasn't boarded over. There was nowhere else to run. She cleared a porthole in the filthy glass and peered inside. A black blizzard of flies needled the window, pinging off the glass, obscuring her view—yet what she saw was enough to make her lurch back in horror.

Tilly would have said that nothing on this earth could have compelled her to enter the house. But then she heard Dwight's heavy footsteps ascending the cellar stairs, and in a flash of panic, she hauled up the window, gagging at the charnel stench as she crawled inside.

24.

Dwight emerged from the cellar.

"Damn it Roscoe, I don't have time for your shit!"

He saw the broken branch lying down in the yard.

"Now why the hell can't you do that when I put you in the fighting pit?"

He followed the barking dog's gaze. Peered up at the porch roof.

"What is it, boy? A squirrel?" Dwight thought Roscoe had lost his appetite for squirrel once he'd had him a taste of long pig.

Then he saw Momma's window was wide open, haloed by buzzing flies.

Dwight patted the dog's blood-matted head. "Good boy, Roscoe . . ." he murmured, gazing thoughtfully at the open window.

He returned to the cellar.

No two ways about it, the townie was a fucking mess. Bloody tatters of flesh flapped from his face like open doors on a Christmas advent calendar. He upchucked another rat head and croaked, "Please . . . No more—"

Dwight shushed him, said: "Who you got with you, mister?"

25.

Away—

Look away—

But she couldn't.

And oh, there was so much to see.

A naked young woman was chained to the bed in front of her. She wore a bodysuit of bruises, her wrists and ankles rubbed raw and scabbed where the manacles had abraded her flesh. She looked more dead than alive. One of her eyes was swollen shut, the other glazed, gazing up at the cracked plaster ceiling. Blood-matted blonde hair spiked stiffly from the woman's scalp. She wheezed for breath through cracked bleeding lips, her chest hitching raggedly. Clamped to her breasts was a set of alligator clips, their steel teeth biting sharply into her nipples. The jumper cables were attached to an oil-smeared car battery on the nightstand. Reaching out from between the woman's thighs was a disembodied human arm. Near mummified with decay, the withered brown limb was wedged inside the woman shoulder-first, where the rotten flesh had receded around a sallow stump of bone. The hand was clawed—fingers grasping—begging Tilly for release. The knuckles of the hand were hairy; one of the man's fingers wore a high school football ring; on his wrist was a cheap Timex watch with a splintered face.

On the wall above the bed was a framed photo portrait of an unsmiling woman with shark-black eyes, stern as a Victorian governess. Plastered to the wall around the portrait were pages torn from pornographic magazines.

As Tilly's eyes absorbed the full horror of the room—the woman shackled to the bed, the obscene shrine on the wall—Hingle's cries echoed shrilly from the cellar; coupled with the woman's shallow moans, the buzzing flies, the dog barking, and oh Christ, the smell, all Tilly could do was clamp her hands to her ears and clench her teeth for fear of screaming and being unable to stop.

Retching, she lurched towards the open bathroom door to her left—and then stopped in her tracks. Roped above the bathtub was a one-armed man. The body had been bled white, hanging upside down like a butchered hog. The man's ribs were twisted back like broken cage bars, revealing the gaping red hollow of his chest. Below him the bathtub was full to the brim with a rancid soup of blood and entrails, the surface jeweled with glistening maggots.

Tilly backed slowly from the bathroom. Shaking her head to deny what she saw. Unable to look away. She thumped against the bed frame and the woman cried out as the bed was jolted and a black cloud of flies billowed up around her.

The woman rasped " . . . please . . ." her lips barely moving.

The eye that wasn't swollen shut welled with tears.

Tilly crouched beside the bed, fanning flies from the air. She examined the chains shackling the woman to the posters. Padlocked. Searched around the bed for the keys. Not on the nightstand. She yanked open the nightstand drawer and then let out a cry and slammed it shut. Told herself what she'd seen was just a bony white spider clutching a bible.

Wanting to comfort the woman, but not knowing where to start, Tilly softly stroked her forehead. The dried blood in her hair crackled and flaked onto her pillow like red dandruff. As delicately as she could, Tilly removed the alligator clips from the woman's breasts, wincing in sympathy as the steel teeth relaxed their grip on her nipples and the woman mewled in pain. Her breasts were tattooed with bruises and burns, indented with bite marks from the alligator clips, and human teeth. The woman nodded at Tilly with pitiful gratitude. Tilly threw the alligator clips to the floor and wiped away her own tears with the back of her arm. The woman's eye rolled slowly down her ruined body. She saw the withered brown limb jutting from between her thighs, and hacked out a wretched sob. The arm swayed about inside her like an obscene flyswatter. She looked up at Tilly. "Please . . ." she croaked. "Get it out."

Tilly shuddered. "I . . . I don't think I can." In fact, she was sure she couldn't.

"Please!" The woman tried to raise herself up on the bed. Too weak, and her chains allowed little movement. She hissed in pain and flopped back down. A coughing fit wracked her body. Bloody spittle sprayed from lips and spackled her upturned face. She stared at Tilly pleadingly. "Get it out."

Tilly felt herself nod. She approached the foot of the bed like a squeamish midwife, fighting the urge to heave as she gazed down at the arm. The woman's inner thighs were cobwebbed with bruises. Her sex was swollen hideously around the limb, where it had been forced inside her. It looked like the woman was birthing a fully-grown man. Tilly glanced at the woman, who nodded and gripped a hank of her hair between her teeth like a bit. Tilly took a deep breath. The foul stench did little to steel her for the task at hand. No pun intended, she thought. She turned her head and reached out blindly. Groping the air until she grasped the man's arm at the wrist. Her fingers sank into soft rotten flesh. Papery skin sloughed away to the bone. With a cry of disgust, Tilly yanked the arm like a Christmas cracker. It slid free from the woman with a soft sigh of air. The woman bucked and hissed and bit down on her hair like she'd passed a kidney stone. Tilly dropped the arm to the floor and kicked it away from her and then wiped her hand on her waitress uniform.

The woman coughed out her hair-bit, gasping for breath.

Then she jangled the chains on her arms. "Help me . . ."

"I can't find the keys—"

"Help me!"

Tilly choked back a sob, unable to look the woman in the eye.

"I will," she said. "I'll come back for you, I promise."

She moved around the bed, took a step towards the window.

The woman's eye widened in horror. "Wait, no . . . Don't leave me!" She started screaming, flailing on the bed like she was possessed. Her chains rattled and banged against the headboard. "Don't you dare leave me, you fucking bitch!"

Tilly hesitated at the foot of the bed, pleading with the woman to be quiet.

"I'll get help," she promised.

But the woman was too far-gone to hear her, much less heed her.

"Bitch! Fucking bitch! You fucking bitch!"

Leave her, Tilly told herself. *Just leave her!* But she couldn't. Even as she glanced at the window and told herself to run. *Now!* While she still could.

Then she heard something else . . .

Sly footsteps in the house below them—

Stalking slowly upstairs—

The woman continued to curse her: "You fucking bitch!"

Tilly kneeled at her bedside, pleading: "Quiet, be quiet!"

A creak on the upstairs landing—

"Someone's coming," Tilly gasped.

"Bitch!"

Tilly put her hand to the woman's lips. The woman sank her teeth into Tilly's fingers, biting her thumb to the bone. Tilly hissed in pain and clamped her hand over the woman's mouth, muffling her cries. The woman snorted against Tilly's palm. Her eye rolled in her skull like a panicked horse. Her breath whistled through her blood-clogged nostrils. "Please," Tilly said, "please be quiet—"

The footsteps were approaching slowly down the hall. They paused outside the bedroom. A shadow moved underneath the door.

Tilly glanced at the window. No other choice. If she was to survive, she'd have to leave the woman here. "I'll get help," Tilly promised.

But the woman was beyond help.

Tilly snatched her hand from the dead woman's face.

She staggered to her feet and stumbled back from the bed, horrified at the realization of what she had done. She wiped the hand that had smothered the woman on her apron, as if she could absolve herself of the sin.

She thudded back in shock against the bedroom door—

And heard the jangle of keys on the other side.

26.

Strictly speaking, there was no need for Dwight to keep the bedroom door locked. The Jarvis gal wasn't going no place. But Dwight liked the way she'd start hollering when his key hit the lock, like she knew the fun and games were about to start. It was like that Mexican fella Dwayne once told him about, whose dogs would start drooling at the sound of a bell ringing—Pablo's dogs—a bit like Roscoe when he heard the chainsaw and knew there'd be scraps coming his way.

But the Jarvis gal was unusually quiet as Dwight put his ear to the door.

He couldn't hear the other gal, neither. The one the kin-killing sonofabitch in the cellar said was with him. It hadn't been the easiest interrogation, what with the fella having a rat-bit tongue and no lips, but Dwight gleaned the general idea.

Dwight guessed the gal must've heard him coming and fixed to hide herself someplace. *Good luck with that, sweetie pie* . . . He didn't think she'd slipped out the bedroom window or else Roscoe would be raising holy hell.

Dwight dug two shotgun shells from the bib of his coveralls, fed them into his sawed-off, and then snapped the barrels closed with a flick of his wrist. Bracing the shotgun before him, he toed the door open with his boot and then stalked inside, clearing the room with a sweep of the barrels.

Then he saw what'd happened to the Jarvis gal and gave a sickened moan. All the weeks of hard work just to keep her alive . . . only for some other split-tail to come along and snuff her. Worse than that, the body had been looted; the salesman's arm was missing from the Jarvis gal's cooter.

If there was one thing Dwight couldn't abide it was a thief. Slamming the bedroom door shut behind him, he locked it from his hoop of keys and then slipped the keys back in the bib of his coveralls. The bitch wasn't getting past him now. And there weren't many places for her to hide.

He started searching.

She wasn't in the closet—no room among the literal skeletons.

Nor under the bed—just a rubble of bones and mulch-like rotten flesh that had once been a travelling preacher.

Dwight peered out the window and saw Roscoe standing silent watch in the dooryard, not barking to wake the dead like he would've been if the bitch had snuck outside. He glanced to the bathroom to his right. The door was part closed. Dwight always kept it wide open so the Jarvis gal could see the salesman and not get too lonesome when he or Dwayne weren't keeping her company.

He prodded the door open with his shotgun. The shower curtain was pulled across the tub. The salesman's carcass hung in silhouette behind the translucent screen. Or so the split-tail wanted him to believe, Dwight thought, grinning.

Inching inside the bathroom, he reached a slow hand towards the shower curtain . . . and then ripped it down fast from the rail—

The salesman's butchered body was hanging right where he'd left it.

"Well, goddamn it," Dwight muttered.

The bitch *had* to be here someplace.

Where the fuck could she have got to?

Glancing down into the gore-filled bathtub, he saw his shimmering red reflection in the blood and guts. A bubble popped on the surface.

Dwight frowned—

And then she torpedoed up from the stinking sludge, clutching the salesman's arm by the wrist, swinging the limb like a Louisville Slugger and socking Dwight hard in the jaw. His legs buckled. He staggered back, firing off a barrel from the shotgun. The blast was deafening in the enclosed space. Buckshot shredded the salesman's carcass, splattering the bath tiles with maggoty gray meat. The body jangled wildly on its hook. Tore loose. Splashed down into the tub.

Before Dwight could fire off a second shot, Tilly swung the arm again and knocked the shotgun from his hands. It dropped into the tub and sank beneath the viscera. She swung the arm again and landed another crunching blow to his face. Dwight staggered back, skidding on the slop that had overflowed the bathtub. He lost his balance and crashed to the floor, grunting as the back of his head splintered the tiles.

Dripping with gore, Tilly hauled herself from the tub. She loomed over Dwight and raised the arm high above her head. With a hellcat scream, she brought the arm crashing down on his skull, again and again, pulping his face like a pumpkin.

Dwight finally lay still, apart from one twitching foot.

Tilly dropped the arm breathlessly. It thudded to the floor. She crumpled to her knees, gasping for breath and retching as she caught a whiff of herself. She considered stripping off her slime-sodden uniform, then remembered

Hingle had used her panties to gag her when he locked her in Betsy's trunk. She didn't relish the idea of wandering about this slaughterhouse wearing only her bra.

She'd change later . . . after bathing for a year.

As she fished in the bib of Dwight's coveralls for his keys, Tilly realized he was still clinging to life. Barely. She could feel his heart thudding weakly as she snatched the keys from his coveralls. Staggering to her feet, she stumbled for balance against the toilet. Prizing the heavy lid off the cistern, she raised the slab and was about to bring it crashing down upon Dwight's skull . . . when from the corner of her eye she glimpsed a hellish apparition in the mirror above the sink.

With a ragged moan, she let the cistern slab slip loosely from her hands. It broke in two on the floor next to Dwight's head. She limped towards the mirror and clutched the sink to support herself. The mirror glass was splintered. A jagged crack bisected her reflection. The whites of a stranger's eyes peered back at her through a scarlet mask. She ran the faucet and began scrubbing the blood from her face, her hands, her bare legs and arms with scalding water; snatched a filth-stiffened towel from a rack and scourged her flesh with it. But when she looked once again in the mirror she could still barely recognize herself.

Recoiling from her reflection, Tilly stepped over Dwight—who was splayed across the floor like a bearskin rug—and limped into the bedroom. Her ears were ringing from the shotgun blast. She felt numb and cold all over. Her bloody uniform clung to her body like a wetsuit. She paused in the bedroom and looked at the woman she had killed. The dead woman's eye glared at her accusingly. Tilly searched the room for something to shroud the woman with. She found an old moth-eaten blanket in the closet, draped it over the woman, and then turned her back on her, knowing it would not be so easy to turn her back on what she had done.

27.

Tilly unlocked the bedroom door with Dwight's keys, and then limped down the hall to the staircase. She staggered downstairs, clutching the banister for balance, her blood-sticky feet smacking like toffee on the bare wooden steps.

She limped across the hall towards the screen door. The first light of dawn was spilling inside. What a night it had been. One to tell the grandkids.

Outside in the yard she could see Dwight's tow truck. She glanced at the hoop of keys she was holding and was surprised to see that her hand wasn't shaking.

Reaching to open the door, she'd barely grasped the handle when the dog appeared suddenly at the foot of the porch, snarling and barking.

"Oh . . . fuck you," Tilly croaked. "Fuck you!"

There was no more fight left in her; she wasn't sure what *was* left.

She turned and started limping through the house to the kitchen. Maybe the dog's chain wouldn't extend to the back yard? Surely she was due a small break?

She was crossing the kitchen to the rear porch—her vision was tunneled, and the room so cluttered with trash that she didn't even see the phone—when she heard a familiar voice calling weakly from behind the closed cellar door.

Tilly paused, listening to Hingle's cries. The bastard could shout himself hoarse for all she cared. Then she pictured the dead woman's accusing eye and sighed. She dragged the cellar door open, sunlight spilling down the stairs like luminous paint.

When she saw him—stripped to his underwear, hanging by chains from the rafters, with what looked like a birdcage fitted over his head—the sight was so surreal that she couldn't suppress a mad cackle of laughter.

His face was crosshatched with scratches. Ragged flaps of skin that had once been eyelids hung from his brow. His lips were gnawed away to the gums, his mouth carved into a permanent Harlequin grin; he appeared strangely delighted about his predicament. Disembodied rat heads were strewn about the bottom of the birdcage like cigar stubs, their bodies littering the floor about his feet.

His mangled features made it hard for Tilly to read his expression. But she thought he looked relieved to see her. She continued to laugh.

"What the fuck are you laughing at, cunt? Get me out of here!"

His words hit her like a blow. She stopped laughing. Started closing the door.

"Wait, no! I'm sorry! Please!"

She closed the door on his cries—

Revealing Dwight stood behind it.

28.

"Fugging bish!" Dwight's face was a flattened red pulp, his mouth a sunken crater of bloody teeth, his eyes swelling shut like a prizefighter's. A mad dog foam sprayed from his lips. *"Fugging bish, I keeeee ooooo!"* Dwight hurled himself at Tilly, snatching her throat in a two-handed grip and lifting her up off her feet. He slammed her back against the door. The rotten wood splintered. The door crashed off its hinges and they stumbled onto the landing; tumbled down the stairs, end over end; landing hard on the cellar's earthen floor.

They scrabbled in the dirt at Hingle's feet.

Hingle rattled his chains and roared at Tilly, "Kill him! Kill that sonofabitch!"

Slumped on top of Dwight—much as his brother had been slumped over her only hours before—Tilly kneed him in the groin and staggered to her feet. Dwight grunted in pain and clutched at her ankle, unable to get a grip on her blood-slick legs. She kicked his hand away and lurched towards the stairs.

Dwight heaved himself up and bull-rushed her. The top of his skull crunched into her gut, punching the breath from her lungs. He tackled her back against the pegboard wall. Tilly slumped to the floor, sucking for air. Tools dropped from their pegs in a rain of rusted steel, crashing to the ground all around her.

Dwight stooped to pick up a hatchet, gripping it like a favorite toy as he backed up a step, and measured Tilly for the killing blow. He hefted the hatchet high above his head, backhanding the ceiling light. The bulb rocked wildly about its fixture, casting nightmare shadows through the cellar.

That backwards step was the death of Dwight—

Hingle swung himself forwards on his chains like a trapeze artist. Launching his legs from the waist, he coiled them around Dwight's neck in a chokehold. Hacking for breath, Dwight flailed pathetically at Hingle's legs. Hingle tightened his grip. Dwight sank to his knees before Tilly in grudging supplication.

Blindly snatching up tools, she skewered his chest like a matador spearing a bull. Knives, screwdrivers, scissors, the bladed edge of a garden trowel, the tines of a barbecue fork; whatever her hands could find. The hilts of a dozen tools jutted from Dwight like quills. Blood jetted from the wounds in a high-pressure spray. The hatchet slid from Dwight's grip and thudded to the floor. In a flash of crystal-clear clarity, Tilly saw Dwight or Dwayne's initials (D.R.) carved into the hatchet's wooden handle. She snatched it from the dirt and returned it to its owner, burying the blade in Dwight's skull, cleaving his face to the bone, blood and brain matter erupting from the wound and burbling down his front like lava.

Dwight's body slumped lifelessly from the scissors of Hingle's thighs.

Hingle relaxed his grip and let him crumple to the floor.

He lowered his legs and let the chains take his weight, hissing in agony as his shoulders bulged grotesquely, the bones threatening to rend the flesh and wrench his arms from the sockets.

Panting for breath, pale-faced with pain, he looked down at Tilly.

"Now . . ." he said, "how about you get me the fuck down from here, sis?"

The sound of Hingle's voice snapped Tilly back to her senses.

She tore her eyes from Dwight's butchered carcass and gazed up towards the nightmare Christ suspended above her.

"How about I go fetch the law instead?" she said.

"I just saved your ass."

She staggered to her feet and stood in front of him.

"It's because of you I'm even here," she said.

He glanced about the cellar. "This wasn't exactly what I had in mind."

She stared at him coldly. "I *know* what you had in mind."

"Just get me down from here and we'll call it quits."

"Quits?" She shook her head and gave a hollow laugh.

"You have no idea," she said, thinking of the woman upstairs.

"And if I let you go . . . ?" she asked him.

Sensing a glimmer of hope, he said: "You won't see me leave, I'll be gone so fast."

"You promise you won't hurt me?"

"All I want is a doctor."

Not to mention a good plastic surgeon.

Tilly stared at him.

"Damn it—" he whined, "You got my word!"

"And a man's only as good as his word, right?"

He chuckled weakly. Like he couldn't believe she'd hold that against him.

Tilly thought for a moment.

She reversed the pulley suspending him from the rafters.

He crashed to the floor in a tangle of chains.

"Keys," he wheezed. "Gimme the keys."

Tilly hesitated, and then tossed him Dwight's keys. Hingle unlocked his handcuffs, moaning with relief as the steel bracelets slid away from his wrists. He massaged some life back into his hands, his shoulders. His head remained imprisoned within the birdcage, drooping under its weight. He wrenched it from his head like he was removing a helmet, shrieking in pain as the cage bottom raked across the raw wound of his face. In fury, he hurled the cage away from him. The cage clattered across the cellar, headless rats rolling about inside it like furry lotto balls. He reached gingerly towards his face as if to probe his wounds. Then he seemed to think better of it, asked Tilly instead: "How . . . how bad is it?"

Hingle took her grim silence as an answer in itself.

He wrenched the hatchet from Dwight's skull, wiped the blood off it, and then examined his reflection in the blade, sobbing when he saw what the rats had left of his face . . . his pretty face. He let the hatchet fall limply from his hands.

Tilly backed away and slumped down at the foot of the stairs to the kitchen.

She watched as Hingle crawled on hands and knees to the pile of his clothes that Dwight had tossed in the corner of the cellar. Hauling himself to his feet, he dressed with trembling hands, his movements stiff and uncoordinated, as if he were drugged or suffering concussion. He considered the smiley face tee shirt he'd looted from the LOST & FOUND box in Big Bob's office. Unable to see a way of putting on the tee shirt without aggravating his facial wounds, Hingle tossed it aside, and just dragged on the jean jacket and buttoned it up to the throat. He noticed Tilly watching him. Grinning his lipless grin, he gave her a woozy twirl. "How'd I look?" he croaked through his monstrous bared teeth.

Good enough to eat, Tilly hoped.

He glanced towards the bulkhead doors.

"How about giving me a head start before you call Johnny Law?"

She'd expected nothing less.

He nodded at her.

"Adios, sister."

She watched as Hingle limped across the cellar to the bulkhead doors.

He trudged up the steps and threw the doors open, shielding his eyes and recoiling from the sun as he staggered up into the brightness of the yard—

And then Roscoe pounced and yanked him out of sight and Hingle's scream of surprise was abruptly cut short.

Well . . . Tilly thought. *That takes care of the dog.*

29.

Tilly emerged from the house, raising her hand to shield her eyes from the sun's blinding glare. She stepped down from the porch and began limping across the yard like a wind-up toy at the end of its spring. Crickets chirred loudly in the tall grass and weeds.

Roscoe was busily feasting on Hingle and paid her no mind. Hingle's throat was a ragged raw wound. The dog had a paw pressed down on his chest, pinning him to the ground as it gnawed away his face. Bloody strings of flesh dangled like pizza cheese between the dog's glistening chops and the gleaming white bone of Hingle's exposed skull. Hingle's arms were outstretched, and before Tilly looked away and left Roscoe to his meal, she noticed his fingers twitching, as if he was counting off the seconds before God showed mercy and allowed him to die.

She continued limping across the yard towards the battered truck with RITTER GAS & TOW on the side, Dwight's keys in her hand, jangling at her side.

She paused to give Betsy Bug a final lingering look, and saw her haggard reflection in the splintered driver's-side window. *So long, old girl . . .*

Tilly climbed in Dwight's truck and slammed the door shut and was deafened by sudden silence. The truck was a junkyard-on-wheels. It smelled about as bad as she'd expected, like something had died in it, and it probably had, badly. She wiped away the grime caking the dashboard console. The dashboard clock said it was after seven. Uh-oh. Late for work. Big Bob would be pissed. He'd probably found the empty safe by now. Maybe he thought she'd split with the night's takings and had called the cops? The thought struck Tilly as funny. Glancing down at the nametag still pinned to the breast of her blood-spattered uniform, she started rocking with what she thought was hysterical laughter, until she felt the tears streaming down her face, and she crumpled over the steering wheel and wept.

When she had no more tears left to cry, Tilly raised her head, glanced once again at the dashboard clock, and saw that close to an hour had passed. She unpinned the nametag from her breast and tossed it amongst the trash littering the footwell. Then she turned the key in the ignition and gunned the engine.

Before pulling away, she looked back towards the house, glancing up at the bedroom window above the porch. For a moment, she glimpsed the young woman gazing down at her. Then the sun glinted off the window and the apparition was gone. Tilly eased her foot down on the gas pedal, not knowing where she was going as the truck pulled away, and not looking back again.

GATOR BAIT

1

I fled the city: Two fingers short and sworn off dames for life.

The money I stole from the cuckold bought me a bus ticket out of town. When the ticket ran out, I kept running south, riding the rails and the thumb of my intact hand when I could, tramping by foot when I couldn't, which is what I was doing when I came to that lonely swamp crossroads down Louisiana way.

The metaphor wasn't lost on me.

Dense woods choked the crossroads; crickets chirred, frogs croaked and somewhere in the distance a bull gator growled for a mate. The cataract-eye of the moon glowered down through the clouds like a Cyclops swaddled in gauze. Mosquitoes swarmed around the bloody handkerchief bandaging what remained of my left hand. I might've swatted them, but the pain was sleeping and I was afraid to wake it.

I stopped in the middle of the crossroads, looking around at the whole lot of nothing, trying to decide which way I should walk. I fished the cuck's hipflask from my pocket. His wife had inscribed it in ornate script:

To my darling husband
Forever yours
Laura

I could almost hear the irony choking her voice.

As I uncapped the flask, the stumps of my fingers throbbed, and it crossed my mind to wonder what the cuck had done to his wife. I shoved the thought away. Worrying about Laura wasn't going to help. Booze might. I drained the dregs from the flask and then shook it above my upturned mouth trying to magic out a few more drops. I screwed the cap back on, crouched down stiffly in the middle of the crossroads, set the empty flask on its side on the blacktop, and then gave it a spin, leaving my fate to chance. When the flask stopped spinning, fate was pointing me south, and so that's where I walked, without any idea just how far south I was heading.

The heat should've been a dead giveaway.

An hour later, maybe two, about dead on my feet, my cheap cotton suit was soaked through with sweat and clinging to my body like a cheaper suit. I heard an engine approaching. Headlights speared me. I raised my good hand to shield my eyes and saw a rattletrap pickup truck rumbling my way. Hiding my bloody paw inside my jacket, I plastered a grin on my mug and stuck out my thumb.

The truck driver slowed down to take a good look at me before stopping. He had a thatch of carroty hair, prominent yellow teeth like a prairie dog, a shit-eating grin I wasn't crazy about, and no chin. He narrowed his eyes and sized me up, struggling to decide if I was a vagrant. Glancing down at my suit, I could see his dilemma.

"You lost, mister?" Rusty said.

"Damn car crapped out," I said, scuffing the road with my foot like I was still hopping mad about it. "You probably passed the hunk of junk a few miles back?"

Rusty shook his head slowly.

I gave a grunt of surprise he hadn't seen my non-existent car.

"Well," I said, "I'd be grateful for a ride someplace to arrange for a tow."

Rusty jerked his thumb over his shoulder. "Climb in back with the niggers."

I glanced at the crew of Negro workers slumped in the truck bed. Only the whites of their eyes were visible in the darkness. I glanced back at the empty passenger seat next to Rusty. He was smirking. But I wasn't about to complain my way out of a ride, so I said "Obliged to you," and then climbed on the back of the truck.

The coloreds shuffled down the truck bed to make room. As the truck pulled away, I heard Rusty laughing at my expense, and decided I preferred to be riding with the help. I'd never had no beef with coloreds, had even played with one or two in the speaks that allowed that kind of thing, and those boys could play. I noticed the man slumped beside me admiring my bandaged hand. "Cut myself shaving," I told him, with a wry smile, and he just shook his head like I was crazy.

The truck pulled away and I slumped against the slatted sides of the bed and breathed a long sigh. Since leaving the city—less than a week ago, it just felt like forever—I couldn't remember the last time I'd stopped moving, and a wave of exhaustion washed over me. As the truck rattled along the swampy backwoods roads, the rocking motion lulled me down into sleep like a babe in the cradle.

But even in dreams there was no peace for me.

I'd answered the knock at the door of my apartment, wearing a silk robe and a cocky grin, freshly showered and shaved, and stinking of the fancy French cologne Laura had bought me. Get-'em-in-the-mood music was playing on the gramophone in the bedroom. The satin sheets and pillowslips on the bed were scattered with pink rose petals. An ice bucket of champagne sat chilling on the nightstand. Safe to say the last person I expected to see when I opened the door was Laura's husband.

He was a little gray sadsack with bloodhound eyes, a drooping mustache and worry lines corrugating his forehead. He wore a funeral-black suit. Cobwebs of hair were pasted across his sweat-beaded baldpate. He daubed at the sweat with a handkerchief before returning it to the breast pocket of his tailored suit jacket.

He was the kind of guy you don't give a second glance—especially when looming beside him was a rent-a-thug with a mug like a Universal monster.

The cuck sized me up with his sad puppy eyes and then nodded to the bruiser.

The ape popped me with a stiff right to the kisser. I staggered back inside the apartment, blinded by tears and snorting blood. They entered my digs and the cuck closed the door quietly and chained the lock behind them.

I started babbling, "It's not what it looks like, I was gonna end it—"

The cuck waved away my words like a bad smell.

The ape slugged me in the guts.

I hit my knees like a penitent, retching.

The cuck said, "I do apologize for intruding on the romantic evening you had planned with my wife, Mr. Hammond. Unfortunately Laura will not be joining you tonight." A bugsy smile teased his lips. "Or any other night."

I lay crumpled at his feet, gasping for breath.

"Well?" the cuck said. "Aren't you going to ask me how she is? How I've punished her?"

Her, who? Even if I could speak, I'll admit it, all I was thinking about was my own ass. Hell, Laura and me, it wasn't even serious. She was just another floozy. Practically threw herself on me. You play piano as good as me, the dames can't wait to find out if your magic fingers can tickle the ovaries like they tinkle the ivories.

The cuck shook his head in disappointment. "As I suspected . . ."

He glanced around my love nest. Through the open bedroom door he saw the freshly made bed, the rose petals scattered across the sheets and pillows, the bottle of champagne on the nightstand. "Well, Mr. Hammond. You certainly know how to treat a lady." He glanced at his ape. "Charlie—bring Mr. Hammond through to the . . ." His upper lip curled in a sneer, "*Boudoir.*"

Dragging me to my feet, the bruiser wrenched my arms behind my back and then shoved me towards the bedroom, with a kick in the keister to hurry me along. The cuck turned up the music on the gramophone. I braced myself as he reached inside his jacket. But instead of a rod, he produced a cigar and a gold plated cigar cutter. He wafted the cigar under his nose, inhaling deeply to relish the aroma, before feeding the end through the cutter's guillotine and looking me dead in the eye. "My wife was always a music lover," he said, "like so many other silly little girls." He decapitated the cigar. The severed end dropped to the floor and bounced off the toes of his shiny polished shoes. I shuddered.

His lips pursed in a tight, humorless smile. Then he said to Charlie, "The left pinkie, I think." Like he was ordering from a bill of fare. "For starters."

Charlie growled in my ear as I struggled. "Quit wrigglin', lover boy, or I break the arm." He wrenched my arm out in front of me, like a flatfoot fingerprinting a reluctant suspect. The cuck clutched my arm at the wrist, forcing my pinkie inside the cigar cutter, the guillotine blade shaving the hairs off my knuckles.

I cried, "Please!"

The blade crunched through flesh and bone with a sound like a chicken leg being torn from the carcass. My pinkie plopped to the carpet. Blood jetted from the stump. The cuck turned up the music, the crooner muffling my screams.

"Now the ring finger," he said.

And then he took that one too; it landed right next to the pinkie.

The cuck snatched his handkerchief and daubed at his sweaty red face. My screams didn't seem to satisfy him, and that worried the hell out of me; then he slowly teased open my robe, and that worried me even more, because I was naked as a jaybird underneath, I'd never felt *more* naked. He glanced down at me and clucked his tongue in disappointment. Given how scared I was, he must've wondered what his wife had ever seen in me. The good news for the cuck was that now, in my fear-shriveled state, I would fit inside the cigar cutter. Light glinted off the guillotine blade as he took me in his clammy hand.

Now I'm a lover, not a fighter—that's why I was in this mess—but for as long as I was intact, I was all man. With a desperate cry, I slammed the back of my skull into the bruiser's face. Charlie's nose exploded like a blood-filled balloon. He gave a nasal cry but didn't let me go. Bracing myself against him, I lashed out with both feet, kicking the cuck clear across the bedroom. He thudded into the wall, denting the plaster and slumping to the floor. The cigar cutter flew from his hands. He doubled over and sucked for air. I jacked my heels into Charlie's kneecap—the patella popped like a pistol shot—his legs buckled and we crumpled to the floor in a tangle of limbs. Thrashing free from his grip, before he could rise, I snatched the bottle of champagne from the ice bucket on the nightstand. Wielding the bottle by the neck, I clubbed him across the temple like I was launching a ship, and he dropped to the floor, out cold or dead, I didn't care which. Gripping the jagged bottleneck, I turned towards the cuck. He gasped and begged and pleaded as I stalked slowly towards him; with the bottleneck lodged in his throat, he could only gargle blood, his final breath hissing like a punctured tire. I sank to my knees in front of him, watching and waiting for him to bleed out. As his pupils dilated, I studied my reflection in the black mirrors of his eyes. I'd always been a lady-killer. Now here I was murderer. But I didn't look, or even feel, any different. Had this killer been inside me all along?

The stumps of my fingers were leaking like a faucet. Blood spattered the severed digits on the carpet. I considered putting them on ice in the champagne bucket till I could find a quack to patch me back up. Picturing myself fleeing the scene with the ice bucket tucked underarm like an urn, I gave a squawk of panicked laughter that flew about the room like a trapped bird. *Keep it together* . . . I didn't, I'd be leaving my mind here along with my fingers.

I had to get out of there. Fast. At best, the neighbors would've complained to the super about the gramophone playing too loud; at worst, they'd already reported the screaming to the cops. I plucked the handkerchief from the cuck's breast pocket and bandaged my mauled mitt. Then I threw on a change of clothes. Rifling the dead man's pockets, I found a little cash money pinned together with a gold clip—enough to buy me a bus ticket out of town—and his hipflask, a gift from a cheating wife. I slugged from the flask and glanced about the room to see if I was forgetting anything—apart from my fingers. I was about to leave the apartment and hit the road, when the cuck lurched to life with a rattling gasp, his arm snaking towards me, his hand snatching my shoulder—

And I let out a cry and my eyes snapped open and I looked up in terror at the black faces peering down at me. I shrugged off the hand that was shaking my shoulder. "We stopped, suh," said the colored fella who'd been riding in the truck bed beside me.

Blinking the sleep from my eyes, I looked to see where we were.

For a moment, I thought I was still dreaming.

The truck was parked outside a tumbledown tonk that squatted on stilts above a swampy pond. An electric sign towered on a pole over the parking lot. THE GRINNIN' GATOR was branded on the night in red neon, replete with an alligator that snapped his jaws when the lights flashed. Moths haloed the sign. It looked like the alligator was hungrily snapping at them. The sign seemed pretty fancy for these parts. I was surprised they even had electricity way out here.

Rusty sprang from the truck like we'd just arrived at Shangri-La.

"Comin' inside, mister?" he said to me. "Or you headed to dark town with your friends?" He was still laughing at that doozy as he pushed through the doors and went inside the tonk. Before the doors closed behind him, I heard a chorus of wolf whistles I guessed wasn't for Rusty—who had the kind of face only a blind mother could love—and someone murdering a tune on the piano.

A drink sounded good to me. Anything to shake off the nightmare and dull the throbbing pain in my paw. I climbed down stiffly from the truck. The coloreds were already trudging away down the unlit, unpaved road towards dark town. Except for the fella who'd woken me. He'd lingered behind to light a hand-rolled cigarette. Shaking out his match, he glared up hatefully at the red neon gator.

"Something wrong?" I said.

He started, blinking the hate from his eyes. He glanced around the lot as if to make sure he wasn't overhead. Then he said to me, "I was you, suh. Prone to accidents an' all." He nodded at my bandaged hand. "I'd jest keep walkin'."

He tipped me a tired salute and started following his friends.

I watched him ghost away into the night. Then I turned and went inside the bar. When the hell had I ever taken good advice?

2

The place was packed. Liquored-up yokels with red faces and redder eyes slouched on stools around barrel tables, pounding pitchers of beer and shots of hooch that damn near steamed when it spilled. The men corralled a crude crate stage where a dead-eyed burlesque girl was shedding her undergarments. The piano player wasn't making it easy for the doll to kid herself what she was doing was art. I couldn't tell if he was drunk or stone deaf, but his playing—if you could call it that—was throwing off her rhythm. Not that the audience seemed to care, so long as her brassiere and britches came off, and when they did the men raised the roof. I broke into a grin. This was my kind of place, and after everything I'd been through to get here, probably more than I deserved.

Above the heads of the crowd I saw the sign for the washroom. I started clawing my way through a thick wall of cigarette smoke towards it. The bare wooden floorboards were strewn with sawdust and spackled with blood and glistened with chaw spit that'd missed the spittoons. Whoever built this place wasn't much of a carpenter. Through the gaps in the floorboards—and there were plenty—I could see the swampy pond over which the building stood. Not to mention smell it. The owner might've picked a more fragrant spot, like a cesspool.

Snoring on a stool outside the washroom door was a fat man with an empty bottle in his lap. A fly buzzed around his open, largely toothless mouth; drool dangled from his bottom lip like a limp lasso. The brim of his hat was pulled down like an eyeshade. A tin sheriff's star was pinned to the breast of his uniform shirt. Out here in the willywags, the law seemed to take a more tolerant stance on old Amendment 18 than they did in the city.

I crept past the lawman and went inside the washroom. Above the sink was a mirror. I studied my sorry reflection, cleaned up the best I could, took another look at myself and then wondered why the hell I'd bothered. My eyes looked like cigarette holes burned through a wino's rumpled paper bag. I could've used a shave and then the razor to cut my throat and put me out of my misery.

Gritting my teeth at the pain, I gingerly unwrapped the handkerchief from around my hand, choking down my disgust as I examined the scabbed stumps of my pinkie and ring fingers. The wounds didn't look infected, just hurt like a sonofabitch. I rinsed the blood from the handkerchief under the faucet, wrung it damp, re-wrapped my mitt, took a deep breath and returned to the barroom.

The burlesque girl had just finished her routine. Before the crowd could rush the stage, she bundled her clothes to her breasts and fled out back. The piano player had a puss like a redneck Picasso. He played even uglier than he looked. Not that he seemed to know it. Hauling himself drunkenly from his stool, he took a bow as if the crowd was cheering and whistling just for him.

I went to the bar at the back of the room. Rusty was in hushed conference with the barkeep, the two men standing on either side of the long slab of oak. Behind the bar, the walls were adorned with stuffed gators, gator hides, and photos of gator hunters standing proudly with their feet propped on dead gators; the owner might not have known art, but he knew what he liked.

The barkeep cut his eyes my way and smiled around an unlit cigar stub. "Be right with you, hoss," he said, rolling the stub from one corner of his mouth to the other. He poured Rusty a glass of hooch from a mason jar and then clapped him on the shoulder like he was petting a faithful dog. Then he started limping along the length of the bar towards me, his left leg dragging stiffly across the floor in his wake. He seemed unashamed of his infirmity. Even proud, like it was an old war wound. I wondered if I'd ever feel the same about my missing fingers? I doubted it.

I counted the change I had left on the counter and came up short. But the barkeep took pity on me. I smacked my lips as he poured. "Welcome to The Grinnin' Gator, friend." His voice was a rich, folksy drawl. "The name's Horace Croker. The Double G's my place and you are most surely welcome."

Horace Croker was a barrel-chested, no-necked, tree stump of a man. His salt-and-pepper hair was buzzed to the pink of his scalp. His face was more leathery than the gator hides decorating the walls. He wore a butcher's apron over a sweat-soaked collarless shirt, his sleeves rolled up to reveal smudged tattoos on his beefy forearms, a gator on one, a naked girl on the other. Around his neck was a silver chain looped with three gold wedding rings.

He slid my drink across the counter. Grinning around his cigar, flashing gray gums and brown teeth, he said, "Something happen to your paw, pardner?"

I fed him the same line I'd used earlier.

"That a fact?" he said, a knowing gleam in his eyes. "Mister . . . ?"

"Smith," I said.

He arched an eyebrow. "Not John Smith?"

I feigned surprise. "You've heard of me."

He leaned across the bar as if to impart a secret.

"You know," he whispered, "I kinda took you for a Jones."

I shook my head, "Jonesy's my cousin."

We both chuckled politely.

I raised my glass in a toast and then knocked back the hooch. It burned down my gullet and set my guts ablaze. I leaned against the bar and started spluttering. Croker chuckled as I struggled to compose myself.

"Goddamn," I managed to wheeze.

"Amen," he nodded.

"That's good stuff."

It was better than good; I sopped up the dregs with my finger and rubbed it into my gums.

Croker tapped his nose slyly. "Old family recipe."

He poured me another. Knowing now what I was dealing with, I sipped it with respect. No wonder this joint was jumping. This was grade-A firewater.

"So," Croker said, "Mister Smith—"

"John," I insisted.

He gave a thin smile. "Rusty tells me your car broke down?"

I stifled a snort. "His name really Rusty?"

"Fits him, don't it?"

Like a glove, I agreed.

"Then I guess you'll be wanting a tow?" Croker said.

I grimaced apologetically. "I might've told Rusty a little white lie."

"Your car didn't break down?"

"Kinda hard to," I said, "when I don't even have a car."

"How 'bout that."

"Truth is, Horace— Do you mind if I call you Horace?"

"I'll be hurt if you don't."

"Horace," I said. "The truth is, I'm looking for work."

He glanced dubiously at my wounded hand. "What exactly can you do?" Like he struggled to believe I could even wipe my own ass without help. And I'll admit it had become harder recently.

I jerked my head towards the piano player. "I can make that godawful racket stop," I said, wincing as the guy kicked another tune while it was down.

"You play?" Croker said.

I shrugged. "A little." A rare display of modesty.

Croker and Rusty exchanged a glance.

Then Croker fanned his arm towards the piano.

"Well, shoot, son," he said. "Be my guest."

Before the next coochie gal came out on stage, I weaved my way through the crowd to the piano, and told the dope perched on the stool I was cutting in.

He said, "Like hell you are—"

"Lyle!" Croker barked at him.

Lyle sprang from the stool like he'd sat on a tack.

He shuffled back from the piano, glaring daggers at me.

I shot Lyle a wink, slumped down on the cratered piano stool, and helped myself to the cigarette he'd left smoldering in the ashtray on top of the piano. I slotted the cigarette between my lips as the next burlesque girl sauntered onto the stage. She did a double take when she saw my unfamiliar mug behind the piano. She was built for both dairy and beef and I waggled the cigarette between my lips approvingly. I said to her, "Just follow my lead, toots."

And then I broke into a one-handed boogie-woogie that lit up the joint like a firebug's vision of hell, and she started tearing off her clothes like they burned. I hadn't played a note since the cuck took my fingers, and I'd forgotten how good it felt. Music heals all wounds, and I played through the pain, hammering the keys with both hands now, my mangled mitt smearing the ivories with blood as I closed the show and the place erupted.

The coochie gal dragged me up off my stool to take a bow with her. Before tottering backstage, she whispered something in my ear that I might've been agreeable to if I wasn't sworn off dames for life. And now that the music had stopped, my hand was screaming like a banshee. I needed fresh air and somewhere private to cry me a river.

At the back of the room, double doors led outside to a gallery deck.

I started butting through the crowd, yokels slapping my back and offering to buy me drinks, which I'd gladly accept just as soon as I'd composed myself. About the only person unimpressed by my performance was Lyle. He was pacing around the piano like a rider who's been bucked by his horse and is nervous about getting back on. When he finally plucked up the courage and retook his stool, the crowd cursed him and pelted him with bottle tops and beer nuts.

Croker shook his head and said to him, "I reckon that's your lot, Lyle."

Lyle protested, whiningly. "Hell, Mister Croker, I can play that nigger music—"

"You can leave out the front door," Croker said, "or the back."

Lyle's face bled white.

He chose the front door; I continued out back.

3.

The deck ended at a waist-high wooden rail overlooking the pond. The water was tar-black, treacle-thick, the surface patched with duckweed. The pungent odor of stagnation and rotting meat choked the air. Mosquitoes swarmed in a humming cloud above the swampy soup. Corrugated sheet metal formed solid walls around the pond, the walls cratered in places, as if hammered from within by a giant anvil. In the middle of the pond, a cypress tree stump lay on its side like a fallen goliath, gnarled roots snaking up from the depths. A tattered shirttail flapped from the roots like a forlorn white flag of surrender.

Slumping against the deck rail, I unwrapped the blood-sodden handkerchief from around my hand. The scabbed stumps of my fingers wept scarlet tears that spattered my reflection on the inky black water below. The sight of the blood made me queasy. I choked down my gorge and inhaled deep breaths.

I'd thought I was alone outside. Then I heard the crackle of burning tobacco leaves as someone in the shadows dragged on a cigarette. Startled, I dropped my handkerchief, watching as it fluttered down into the pond and floated on the water like a bloody lily pad.

She stood in profile to me, silhouetted against the low full moon like a bust carved from marble. And speaking of busts, she had plenty; straining against a white silk blouse that was maddeningly close to translucent in the moonlight. Flaxen hair cascaded off her shoulders, a golden waterfall that plunged down the graceful arch of her back, before it crashed against the rounded rocks of her rump. Her lips were painted stop sign-red. She exhaled a plume of cigarette smoke that will-o'-wisped into the night . . . and then she cocked her head towards me. Her left eye was blackened, but it was the kind of imperfection that only drew attention to how perfectly put together the rest of her was, and I might have admired her awhile longer if I wasn't sworn off dames for life.

"You play pretty good," said a voice that was sin dipped in honey.

I gave her an aw-shucks grin. "For a fella with a gimp hand," I said, hoping maybe she'd kiss it better.

"Caught raiding someone's cookie jar?" she said.

I was about to feed her my cut-myself-shaving line, when a smile teased those lips, and she said, "Or the honey pot?"

And right away she had me nailed.

To the goddamn cross.

Blushing like a schoolboy, before I could stammer out an answer—the pond seemed to explode, and I was drenched in a spray of stinking swamp water.

Lurching back in shock from the deck rail, I glanced down into the pond and saw a dinosaur devour my bloody handkerchief with a snap of its jaws.

The huge reptilian head submerged again in a seething froth of bubbles.

"What the Christ was that?"

"Oh . . ." drawled a voice behind me. "That's just Big George."

Croker was blocking my way back to the bar.

He'd removed his butcher's apron. His silver neck chain dangled down the front of his bullish chest. The gold wedding rings chinked together like wind chimes. He squinted at the dame and me like a sniper sighting down his rifle.

"See you've met the missus?" he said.

For a moment I thought he meant the monster in the pond.

Then I said, "We haven't been properly introduced."

"Grace," Croker said to his wife, "this here's Mister Johnny Smith."

He tipped me a wink.

"He'll be playing pee-anna for us awhile."

It took me a moment to register what he'd said; now that I knew what was lurking in the pond, I was more than a little keen to get off that rickety wooden deck. I dredged up my voice. "I will?"

Croker said. "Said you was lookin' for work, didn't you?"

I wasn't so sure about that all of a sudden.

"Nice to meet you, Mister Smith," Grace said, icy and flat.

"Call me John," I said, smiling politely and extending my hand.

"You'll call him Mister Smith," Croker warned her, and I took my hand back without her shaking it.

Grace flicked her cigarette off the deck and it sizzled in the pond. Then she brushed past her husband and returned to the bar.

"Damn it, Grace!" Croker bellowed. "How many more times I gotta tell you not to do that? It messes with Big George's digestion!"

He watched as she sashayed across the room. Hell, I watched too. I hated to see her leave, but I loved to watch her go. Grace was just the right name for her.

When she disappeared through a door behind the bar, Croker shook his head in exasperation, fondling the wedding rings adorning his neck chain.

I forced a chuckle. "Dames." Gave a knowing roll of the eyes.

His head cranked towards me and I quickly changed the subject.

"I never knew gators could get that big," I said. "Outside of fairytales." The damn dragon was fifteen feet, easy. "You oughta have him measured for *Ripley's Believe It or Not!*"

A grin slit Croker's face and his chest puffed with pride.

"Yep," he said, "Big George is a legend 'round these parts."

By implication, so was the man who had caught him.

Croker slung a beefy arm around my shoulder and led me back to the deck rail to show off his pet. We stood leaning against the rail, our moonlit reflections rippling on the pond. The gator surfaced like a submarine, bubbles frothing around the huge angular snout, erasing our reflections on the water. The protective film slid back from the gator's eyes. It peered up at me with an ancient hunger. Croker's hand squeezed the meat of my shoulder.

"I was just a young'un," Croker said, "fishing for channel cat with my Pap when this big bastard broadsided us, flipped our boat, flung us both in the swamp. Pap managed to boost me up onto a tree branch—'bout the only kindly thing that ole snake ever done for me—but not before Big George took my leg. Snapped it off right above the knee." Croker rapped his knuckles against his left leg with a sound like a hollow tree.

"The leg," Croker continued, "well, that was just an appetizer. Pap was the main course. Perched above the swamp on that tree branch, I took off my shirt, bound it tight around the stump of my leg, and then the rest of the night, and right the way through till dawn, I watched Big George play with his food till all that was left of my daddy was just ragged red chunks of meat snagged in his teeth.

"That," Croker said, "was the longest night of my life . . .

"A fishing crew found me the next day. They chased off Big George with rifles. Had to prise my fingers off the branch to get me down outta that tree. I was damn near drip-dried of blood, half-crazed from what I'd seen. Doc Culpepper told my momma he wasn't sure I'd pull through. But even then I was a stubborn sonofabitch, and I healed over time. Soon as I could, I went back to the swamp and went a-huntin' for Big George. Wasn't easy. Took me many a year. Me an' George had us a grand ole game of cat and mouse, never sure which of us was bein' the cat and which of us was bein' the mouse. But I caught him in the end . . .

"Didn't I, George?"

Croker gazed down at the gator. The gator gazed back at him. The way they were looking at each other, I wondered if the two of 'em needed a moment alone together.

"In the end," Croker said, "all it took was the right bait."

My mouth went dry. "What bait was that?"

Croker clapped me on the shoulder and laughed. "Aw, you don't have to worry 'bout that, Smitty. Big George is penned in real good here, see. 'Sides, now I know you play pee-anna so good, you'll be giving the place a touch of class."

I forced myself to laugh along with him, but I wasn't really sure what the hell I was laughing about.

"I'm surprised you didn't just kill the damn thing," I said.

Croker looked appalled. "Kill Big George? The hell I'd do that for?"

"For what it did to your . . ." I paused. Unable to detect any grief for his father, I said, "Your leg."

Croker waved his hand dismissively.

"The night I spent up in that tree," Croker said, "slowly bleedin' out, looking down at Big George, Big George sniffin' the air, looking up at me . . ." He shook his head. "I been married four times—God help me—but I've never knowed an understanding like it . . . We're like kin, Big George and me."

As if on cue, the gator submerged, Croker gave another chuckle, and I watched Grace's cigarette bobbing on the chop, the butt ringed red with her lipstick.

4.

Later that night after closing, Croker took me to his office behind the bar.

It was little more than a stockroom furnished with a desk, a leather recliner behind the desk, and a hard wooden chair for visitors that numbed my ass just to look at it. On the wall above the desk was a crudely drawn painting. More *Looney Tunes* than the Louvre, it depicted a jolly old fisherman, bearded and fat as a hillbilly Santa Claus, casting his line into the river. Baited on the hook was a Negro child, caricatured to resemble a monkey. Standing upright in the river was an alligator wearing a dinner napkin around his neck, clutching a knife and fork, salivating as the child sailed towards his cavernous maw. The painting was titled 'Gator Bait.' I shuddered to recall what Croker had said about "the right bait."

Sinking down into his recliner, Croker gestured for me to sit. The wooden chair was positioned on a ratty oval rug. I tried to move it closer to the desk, but it wouldn't budge; seemed to be nailed to the floor, the chair and rug both. Croker was waiting impatiently for me to sit, so I took a pew, and I couldn't help noticing the way the floorboards creaked and sagged beneath my weight.

Croker grinned at me around his cigar stub. He reached behind the desk, his hands disappearing from view. I heard the snap of buckles; leather straps being loosened. Then his hands reappeared and he tossed his wooden leg down onto the desk and gave a grateful moan.

"My dawgs are barkin' today," Croker said, massaging his stump. "Even the dawg Big George took." He nodded at my mauled mitt. "That's something you'll get used to, Smitty. 'Specially when it rains." I hid my hand self-consciously. "I'll have Doc Culpepper take a look at that paw for you, when the ole souse sobers up tomorrow. Speakin' of which . . ."

He fetched a jar of hooch and two grubby glasses, filled them both and then handed me the cleaner of the two, which wasn't saying much. As I leaned forwards to take the glass, the chair creaked beneath me, the floorboards wobbled like a diving board, and I flinched as Big George thrashed excitedly in his pond. Was it just my imagination, or did it sound like the gator was waiting directly below where I sat? The way Croker was smiling, I knew it wasn't my imagination. I gulped down the hooch to try and quiet my nerves.

"What exactly are you running from, Smith?" He emphasized the phony name.

I played dumb. "Who says I'm running from anything?"

"Me," he growled, a flash of fire in his eyes. "Son, do me the courtesy of not mistaking me for one of them fools out there. Any man plays the pee-anna as good as you, oughta be leading a band in the city someplace, not singing for his supper in a swamp tonk. Now I'll ask you again: what are you running from? And more to the point: what kinda trouble can I expect by hiring you on?"

I thought it prudent to stretch the truth.

"Mister Croker—" I said.

"Horace," he reminded me.

"It's nothing that'll come back to you," I assured him. "Just a big misunderstanding about a gambling debt."

I couldn't tell if he bought it or not.

"Just so long as we're clear," he said, "it's a delicate operation I'm running here."

He raised his glass and sloshed the hooch around inside it.

"Any man rocks the boat, he's going overboard."

Or below deck, I thought.

"I understand," I said.

Croker nodded. "Good enough."

He picked up his wooden leg and beat it on the desk like a giant drumstick. "Gracie!" Footsteps scuttled downstairs. Grace skulked inside the office. I found myself sitting up a little straighter in my chair. "Fix up the spare room for Mister Smith," Croker told her, slurring his words. He was gesticulating drunkenly with his wooden leg. She glanced at me, and her gaze must've lingered longer than he liked, because Croker clubbed the limb in his palm, looking like he wanted to paddle her ass with it. Grace flinched at the slapping sound, gave a servile nod.

She started backing from the room—but as she pulled the door closed she shot me another glance that shivered down my spine like footsteps on the grave.

And that right there should've warned me of the trouble to come.

* * *

The room wasn't much, but it was more than I had. A cot that looked like a torture rack, with a wafer-thin mattress and a rock for a pillow; a washbasin and a shaving mirror next to the lamp on the nightstand. The window looked out on the hills, where Croker's whiskey still fires glowered in the night like red devil eyes. He was running a delicate operation, alright. Had to be making money hand over fist.

"Is everything to your liking, Mister Smith?"

I turned towards the voice.

Grace lingered in the doorway, her hourglass figure haloed by the light of the hall like an angel outside the pearly white gates. But there was nothing angelic about the glint in her eye as she asked me, "Will you be wanting anything else?"

I swallowed hard. "Not right now."

She smiled like she knew it wouldn't be long, and then she shut the door behind her, trapping me in the room with the lingering scent of her perfume. I splashed my face with water from the washbasin, reminding myself—in case my missing fingers weren't enough—that I was sworn off dames for life.

* * *

That dead of night, I snapped awake to the sound of booming drums. For a moment I had no idea where I was. Heart pounding to the drumbeat, I bolted upright. The bed was quaking beneath me like the end of the world. Fumbling to light the lamp on the nightstand, my stumps prodded the edge of the cabinet. Pain bolted up my arm and I let out a yelp. Then I realized the drumbeat was the headboard of Croker's bed thumping against the thin wall of our neighboring rooms as he rutted his wife. *Boom, boom, boom.* Croker was snorting like a hog with his snout in the trough; Grace was yipping like a small dog being kicked. *Boom, boom, boom.*

Sinking back down on the bed, I curled my pillow around my head, which succeeded in muffling the noise but didn't stop the bed from bucking like a bull. It felt like Croker was having his way with both Grace and me. Climbing from bed, I went downstairs and salvaged a cigarette from the ashtrays piled at the end of the bar.

Then I went outside to smoke on the gallery deck while I waited for Croker to finish up. He did—eventually—I had to admire the man's stamina. He climaxed with a bellowing cry that roared like thunder. Moments later his snores joined the chorus of frogs croaking in the night. I hoped this wouldn't be a nightly occurrence. (It would be.)

I finished my cigarette and went to ditch the butt. Warily approaching the deck rail, I peered down into the pond. There was no sign of Big George. All I saw was my reflection, shimmering on the inky black surface. I was about to flick away my butt when Grace appeared suddenly in the window behind me, hovering above my shoulder like an angel. An angel? Maybe that was wishful thinking.

She was gazing off into the distance. Her eyes were dewy with tears. Her lips smeared with blood. Her long blonde hair dangled down off her shoulders and veiled her breasts like gossamer. As she stared out over the swamp, I held my breath and watched her—

Until the cigarette butt singed my fingers and I dropped it with a hiss of pain. Grace heard the noise and looked down and saw me looking up at her. A drop of blood dripped from her lip, spattering her breasts as she smiled at me. Then she was gone, and as my cigarette sizzled out in the pond, I wondered if she'd even been there at all.

I turned back towards the pond, perhaps hoping she would reappear.

But this time all I saw was Big George, the moonlight reflecting off his eyes as he grinned at me.

5.

Despite my concerns—about Croker, about Grace, about Grace and me, not to mention Big George—I settled into life at The Grinnin' Gator with remarkable ease. The twenty bucks Croker paid me each week helped. That was no small spuds for a city gig, let alone a backwater tonk in the willywags. It was plenty enough to get me back on my feet, if not buy me new fingers. If I had any sense I would have saved up some scratch and hit the road just as soon as I could.

But I didn't.

Besides, the money wasn't the only reason I stayed.

True to his word, Croker arranged for Doc Culpepper to tend to my hand. He was the Croker family physician, and looked about old enough to have delivered Croker's great-granddaddy, if not the baby Jesus. He'd treated young Horace when the boy lost his leg to Big George, even carved Croker's wooden peg himself, although given the shoddy carpentry, I wasn't sure that was anything to crow about.

The old buzzard gave me some shots, some pain pills, and some stinking salve to slather on my stumps; he checked my progress, changed my bandages every couple few days; even prescribed some advice I was too dumb to take.

We were perched at the bar. Croker was arranging a rum-run to the city, his voice booming through the closed office door as if he didn't trust the telephone to carry his message. Grace was readying the place for opening, humming to herself as she scattered fresh sawdust on the floor. Recognizing the melody as the ragtime I'd been playing the previous night, I made a mental note to play it again, if it pleased her. One pretty gal is all the audience any musician needs.

"Something wrong with your eyes, too?" Doc Culpepper said, as he examined my hand.

I didn't follow.

"There will be," he said, "Croker catches you eyein' his wife like that."

I hadn't been aware I was. "Like what?"

"Like a hungry dog outside a butcher's window."

I laughed and told the old fool I was sworn off dames for life.

Within a month, the stumps of my fingers were healing over nicely.

The scabs had crumbled away to reveal shiny pink layers of new skin. My hand wasn't pretty to look at—it resembled a lobster claw—but lucky for me I could still play. Nowhere near my best, but way better than anything these hicks had ever heard. It amused me to think, if they'd just cast their prejudices aside, they could have gone to any juke joint in dark town, been enjoying music like this for years.

I played a short set every night, and a longer one weekends, when the place would be ram-packed with rowdies. Croker billed me to the crowd as 'Smitty Three Fingers.' The sonofabitch. "From the city," he'd tell folks. Like The Grinnin' Gator was moving up in the world. He told me to keep the nigger music to a minimum, or at least to mix it up with a few Southern standards, but I could tell he dug my sound. I'd often see him tapping his wooden leg, waggling his cigar between his lips like a conductor's baton leading the orchestra.

When she wasn't slaving behind the slab, Grace would sit in the bar and listen to me play. I'd position my glass on top of the piano so I could see her reflection.

There was no harm in looking, I reckoned; no harm at all, had I left it at looking.

People came to The Grinnin' Gator for the liquor and the girls, and sure, once word got around, for the music too; but they kept coming back for Big George.

Croker fed his pet every weekend.

The crowd would gather on the deck like rubes around a carny barker as Croker leaned back against that rickety wooden rail and gave them his spiel.

Clutching some doomed critter by the scruff of the neck, he'd tell the crowd just as he told me, "I was just a young'un, fishing for channel cat with my Pap when this big bastard broadsided us, flipped our boat, flung us both in the swamp . . ."

And after Big George closed the show, Croker would lead the crowd back inside for another round of drinks, and I'd play a jazzy rendition of The Alligator Crawl.

Big George's diet consisted mostly of chickens and rabbits that were housed in the tarp-shrouded hutch on the gallery deck; feral cats and stray dogs, which people would deliver to Croker in exchange for a jar of the good stuff; and once a prize boar hog that Marvin Scruggs lost to Croker in a fiercely contested arm-wrestling match. The way that hog squealed when Big George clamped his jaws around him, I thought that sound would echo in my memory forever. I'd never heard screams like it, not even my own, when the cuck was taking my fingers.

Not until the night Croker threw a man to the gator.

Those screams were worse.

Much worse.

6.

That night started off so quiet, the proverbial calm before the storm.

A few lonely lushes sat around the barroom, muttering and glaring into their glasses of hooch. I'd finished my set, but was killing time till closing, pecking out a tune on the piano I'd overheard Grace humming in the shower that morning. Grace was sweeping the floor. I saw her cheeks flush as she recognized the melody and I wondered if she'd pictured me handing her the soap?

Croker was wet-ragging the bar like a deckhand. He'd seemed preoccupied that night. Distracted. Kept checking the time on the clock on the wall. By now I'd been working at The Double G long enough to know better than to ask.

And I found out what he was waiting for soon enough.

Around midnight, the front door clattered open and a colored man came sliding across the floor like a hockey puck, smearing blood across the floorboards in his wake. He skated to a stop at the foot of the bar, lay there curled in pain and wheezing for breath through broken teeth and busted ribs. His wrists were roped, his hands clasped together as if in prayer, shaking terribly. His face was swollen and glistening with blood like a freshly dipped candy apple. It took me a moment to recognize him as the fella I'd met on the back of Rusty's truck.

Blood trickled from his wounds and dripped down through the gaps in the floorboards, spattering the pond below. Big George gave a hungry growl that rumbled through the bar like a subway car.

Rusty swaggered inside, wiping the blood off his hands on his pants. "Boy's a bleeder!"

"This him?" Croker said to Rusty. "This the nigger been stealin' from my stills?"

Rusty frowned. It clearly hadn't occurred to him that he might have the wrong nigger. Acting on good enough information, he'd rousted the suspect from a juke joint in dark town, crocked him with an axe handle, before roping him to the back of his truck and then dragging his sorry black ass to The Double G. Rusty didn't seem to relish another long ride to dark town. It was late; he was tired and thirsty. Fortunately for him, the colored man was in no fit condition to plead his innocence.

"Yessir, Mister Croker, sir," Rusty assured him, "this is the nigger alright."

Croker poured Rusty his reward, Rusty salivating like one of Pavlov's pooches.

Then Croker raised the hinged end of the bar, stepped through, and let it slam down behind him. His wooden leg raked across the floorboards as he limped towards the colored man. Looming above him, Croker grinned like one of the stuffed gators on his walls. "So *you're* the one, huh?"

The man shook his head. The whites of his terrified eyes peered out through a bloody mask. "Nuh-nuh-no, suh . . ." he rasped, wincing as his shattered ribs stabbed his insides. "Never stole me nunna Mistuh Croker's whiskey, uh-uh."

It had the ring of truth about it, and Croker glanced up at Rusty with his eyebrows raised. Rusty shrugged sheepishly. "You know niggers, Mister Croker, sir," he said, as if voicing an accepted wisdom. "They ain't stealin', they lyin'."

Croker chewed his cigar thoughtfully before returning his attention to the colored man. "What's your name, boy?"

"Juh-Juh-Johnson."

"Well, 'Mistuh' Juh-Juh-Johnson," Croker said, "you done just poked your finger in the wrong man's pie."

He dipped in his pocket for a match, struck it alight with his thumbnail, fired up his cigar and puffed it greedily, the burning coal casting Jack o' Lantern shadows across his face. He shook out the match and cut a glance at Rusty.

"Get this sumbitch out on the deck."

Grinning like an egg-sucking dog, Rusty grabbed Johnson's ankles and started dragging him through the bar to the deck.

Excitement rippled through the drunks in the bar; this was a rare and unexpected treat. The men piled outside.

Grace dropped her broom. It clattered to the floor. She bolted for the door behind the bar. Croker cackled, "You don't wanna watch, honey?"

I was frozen in place behind the piano.

"What's going on here, Horace?" I said.

Croker was just putting a scare into the guy . . . Wasn't he?

"It's 'Mister Croker' tonight, son," Croker said.

Then he said, and he wasn't asking. "You oughta come see this."

I sloped to my feet and followed Croker outside. He was limping eagerly ahead of me, tracking the trail of Johnson's blood, his gimp leg hardly able to keep up with the rest of him. Outside, Rusty hauled Johnson to his feet and slammed him back against the deck rail. Johnson let out a yelp as the wooden boards sagged against his weight. Croker shooed Rusty aside and then sized Johnson up.

"How much d'you weigh, Johnson?"

Johnson's bloody face crumpled into a frown. "Suh?"

"'Bout a buck-ninety?"

Croker turned to the crowd of drunks. "Two minutes tops, I reckon."

"Hell," said one of the drunks. "I'll take me summa that action."

The men started betting, their voices thick with boozy bloodlust.

Johnson glanced around the crowd for a friendly face and found mine. I saw a glimmer of hope in his eyes as he recognized me from Rusty's truck. But there was nothing I could do to help the poor bastard. I ducked my eyes to light a cigarette, shuffling back into the shadows. Johnson gave a wretched sob.

Croker consoled him. "There-there now, boy." He patted Johnson's head and then grimaced in disgust, wiping the blood from his hand on the man's shoulder.

He turned his head to look at me.

"Back when I was a young'un," Croker said, "we used to play us a game called coon-on-a-log—" He gave a burlesque gasp and raised a hand to the shocked 'O' of his mouth, as if he'd spoken out of turn. "Raccoon, that is. Gee whizz, I wouldn't wanna cause no offence." He winked at Johnson chummily.

"How we played it was," Croker continued, "we caught us a coon and then we floated him out on a log on the swamp. Then we set the dawgs on him. Bet on which of the dawgs would fetch him down off the log and how long it'd take."

I glanced down into the pond at the cypress tree stump.

Johnson was bawling now, choking on snot and tears.

Croker smiled at him wistfully.

"I must be getting sentimental in my old age," he said, "'cause I surely do miss the good ole days."

And then he shoved Johnson hard in the chest.

Johnson carted back over the deck rail, hitting the pond with a splash. He exploded to the surface, retching swampy water, wearing a wig of duckweed. The crowd leaned out over the rail, leering like Romans at the Coliseum. I was about to skulk back inside the bar when Croker caught my elbow and dragged me over beside him. "Best seat in the house, Smitty."

Johnson was thrashing his arms and screaming that he couldn't swim.

Croker laughed. "Boy, that's the least of your worries!"

Below the deck came a guttural growl that chilled my blood to ice.

Johnson must've seen Big George emerging from the shadows beneath the building, because the color drained from his face, his eyes bugged wide, the tendons in his neck stood out in cords, and he screamed, *"Sweet merciful Jesus!"*

For a non-swimmer, Johnson sure learned fast. He thrashed across the pond to the cypress tree stump. Clutching at the exposed roots, he tried climbing up onto the stump, the crowd cheering or cursing his efforts, depending on which way they were betting. Scaling the roots like a ladder, he damn near made it.

Then a huge V-shaped ripple knifed through the water towards him.

I heard someone gasp and realized it was me.

Before Johnson could drag his legs from the water he was yanked below the surface so violently that the tree roots he was gripping snapped away from the stump like twigs.

One of the drunks cursed bitterly as he lost his bet.

Big George exploded to the surface with Johnson clamped between his jaws like Croker's cigar. The gator shook its head with spine-shattering force, and then it went into a death roll, churning the water like a leathery ladle as it drowned its prey. Johnson screamed and spewed blood and beat his fists pitifully against the giant angular snout. And then he finally stopped struggling. His arms flailed lifelessly. His head lolled on his shoulders like a ragdoll. The gator submerged with his prize.

Croker nudged my ribs. "See, what he'll do now is, he'll tuck ole Johnson under the tree stump. Let him turn good and ripe before he snacks on him later." He chuckled at the wonder of nature. "Ain't that something?"

I stumbled back from the rail, choking down a geyser of puke.

"Something you ate?" Croker said. "Or something that ate Johnson?"

The crowd howled with laughter.

Grinning ear-to-ear, Croker turned to Rusty and chided him, "Now the next time I tell you to bring me the nigger who's stealin' my whiskey—you *bring me* the nigger who's stealin' my whiskey."

Rusty paled; nodded sheepishly.

"Aw . . ." Croker said. "S'alright, Rusty. No harm, no foul."

Tell that to Johnson, I thought.

Croker ground out his cigar on the deck rail.

Then he started limping back inside.

"Last call at the bar," he said, "a round of drinks on Juh-Juh-Johnson!"

The cheering crowd barged past me in their rush to refill their glasses. I stayed right where I was. Staring down numbly at my reflection on the water's bloody surface, I couldn't help wondering . . . If this was what Croker did to a whiskey thief—what would he do to the man screwing his wife?

7.

The first time it happened, Croker was away on a rum-run.

He liked to make the deliveries himself, sample the sins of the city. His buyers were always keen to show him a good time—and a good time gal—anything to keep their supplier happy and the liquor flowing. Before he left that night, all dolled up in his best suit, reeking of ship-on-the-bottle cologne, Croker asked me to keep my eye on Grace. That was a little like Othello asking Casanova to watch over Desdemona. But I kept a poker face and told him, sure. Even if he hadn't asked, it would've been hard not to.

It was after closing. Grace was clearing the tables, emptying ashtrays and collecting glasses onto a tray, while I escorted the coochie gals to the door. As I locked the door, I was startled by the crash of glass behind me. I turned to find Grace on her hands and knees, doubled over in pain, a rubble of broken glass from the tray she had dropped strewn across the floor. I rushed to help her—

Stopped in my tracks.

Where her blouse had ridden up, I saw her back was hashed with scars, the flesh lacerated by the straps and buckles of Croker's wooden leg, where he must have flogged her with the limb. Some of the scars were faded with age, others more recent, scabbing away to pink tattoos. Stamped on her kidneys was a fist-shaped bruise, black as a thundercloud, where Croker had signed his work like an artist.

Grace glanced up at me, and her face flushed with shame as she realized I'd seen the scars. She pulled down her blouse to cover her back.

I crouched down beside her as she started gathering the broken glass onto the tray. "Let me do that." I touched her arm gently and she stifled a hiss of pain and I wondered how bad the rest of the bruises were. I said, "Grace—" And then I stopped myself. It was the first time I'd said her name aloud outside of dreams from which I woke hot and sweaty and fearful of the day I might act on them.

She must have realized it, too. Her hands were shaking and she cut her finger on a sliver of glass. A drop of blood dripped to the floor; drizzled through the gaps in the floorboards; landed down in Big George's pond with an echoing plink.

She started crying.

"Hey, now . . ." I said. "It's nothing, just a little nick."

I had more experience with finger wounds than I would have liked.

I helped her to her feet and she teetered against me, burying her face in my chest. She clung to me, crying hot tears that soaked through my shirt and scalded my skin. Her breasts were pressed against my chest. Our hearts beat together like tribal drums. I stroked her back to comfort her—only to comfort her—swallowing hard as my shaking hand traced the outline of her brassiere strap. I took a deep breath, inhaling her scent, and I must have made some kind of sound because she looked up at me, and I looked down at her, and I remembered what her husband had told me, how he and Big George had once stared into each other's eyes, that he'd never known an understanding like it.

"Why the hell do you stay, Grace?"

"Why do you?"

Two reasons.

"Money," I said.

I was looking at the other reason.

She smiled at me sadly.

"We're his pets," she said. "Just like that damned monster of his."

I bristled. "I'm nobody's pet." I tried to pull away but she wouldn't let me go and maybe I didn't try very hard. "I can leave anytime I want," I said. "So could you."

"With you?"

That's not what I'd meant—was it?

"He'd find me," she said, with grim certainty. "Wherever I went, he'd find me." She shuddered against me. "I'd become just another ring on his neck chain."

I pictured the three gold rings on Croker's silver neck chain.

"What are you saying?"

"You think his other wives just up and left him?" she said. "You think he'd allow that?" She shook her head gravely. "They ever drain that pond, they'll find a whole boneyard down there."

"That's crazy," I said.

"He's crazy," she said.

And then I did something crazier; I kissed her.

Her head jerked back and she pulled away from me, and for one sinking moment I feared I'd misjudged things, and I was about to stammer an apology when she mashed her lips against mine and swallowed the words, and the next thing I knew we were attacking each other like wild beasts in a sack, biting and clawing, and I pushed her back across the room and sat her down hard on the piano keys, and a thunder of discordant notes boomed through the bar as I tore off her panties and she clawed at my pants, and then I entered her with a savage thrust that made us both cry out.

It was over quick, but it was good while it lasted.

We told ourselves it had to be a one-time deal, that we could never risk doing it again, even as she took me by the hand and led me upstairs to her bedroom.

*   *   *

After that night we awaited Croker's trips to the city like children counting down the days till Christmas morning—starving for each other, sating our hunger with furtive glances and the electric brush of our bodies when we passed one another in the bar—and then unwrapping each other like presents.

The bastard never suspected a thing; I'm convinced of that; not then, he didn't.

Christ, I came to hate the man. Every night I was forced to endure the sound of the headboard pounding against the wall, or the sound of him beating on Grace if he was too soused to screw, often both; it was more than I could bear.

If I was any kind of man I would've put a stop to it then and there. I'd have kicked in their bedroom door and killed him on the spot. Instead I cuckolded the sonofabitch in his own bed, and as I pounded the headboard against the wall I imagined I was cracking Croker's skull.

*   *   *

Grace lay curled like a cat in the crook of my arm, teasing her fingers through my chest hair as I caught my breath. I fumbled for my cigarettes on Croker's nightstand, lighted one, and sighed smoke towards the ceiling.

I started counting the scars on her back and quickly lost count.

"How'd a girl like you ever get mixed up with a guy like—"

"You?" She cradled her chin on my chest, smiling up at me.

"*Him*," I growled, the hatred in my voice surprising me.

"Just lucky, I guess."

She motioned for my cigarette and I held it to her lips and she took a drag and exhaled a plume of smoke.

"In another life," she said, "I used to partner with a fella called Chauncey Clyde."

I cocked an eyebrow.

"Not like that," she said. "This was strictly business."

I cocked the other eyebrow. "Doing what?"

"The short con, mostly."

I tried not to smirk. "You were a grifter?"

"More like a grifter's apprentice," she said. "Chauncey did the talking; I was there to flash a little cleavage and a lotta leg and keep the mark's mind offa business." She gave a bittersweet smile. "Chauncey used to call me his Judas lamb."

She saw the way I was looking at her and clawed my chest rug playfully. "Oh . . . I would've made mincemeat out of you, darling."

I let her think so.

"Chauncey and me, we were working our way through the state when we came to The Grinnin' Gator. The place didn't seem like much, and I didn't like the feel of it all, but Chauncey took one look at the big neon sign and his eyes lit up like Christmas morning. That was that. We went inside to scout out the owner . . .

"Croker played the country rube to perfection. Chauncey mistook him for an easy mark. Thought we'd hit pay dirt. I don't guess the booze helped his judgment; Croker was laying it on thicker than his country bumpkin act. That's the thing about Croker. He like's a damn gator. Pretending he's a log, floating closer and closer, till he shows his teeth and by then it's too late.

"Croker acted real interested in Chauncey's business proposal. Like he could hardly wait to open his safe and fork over the cash. He took us back to the office to talk turkey. There was just the one chair. The wooden chair opposite Croker's desk. Nailed to the floor on a ratty old rug. Croker calls it The Hot Seat."

The hairs on the nape of my neck prickled with unease. I remembered sitting in that very chair; the way the floorboards had creaked and sagged beneath my weight, Croker's ghoulish grin as Big George thrashed in the pool below me.

"There was nowhere else for me to sit," Grace said, "so I just parked my fanny on the edge of Croker's desk, flashing some leg, which Croker seemed to like. He was petting my thigh like a housecat. Telling me what a 'firecracker' I was.

"Chauncey tipped me the wink to keep Croker busy while he finished baiting the hook. He was about to seal the deal with a contract worth about as much as toilet paper. That's when Croker lit his cigar and reached down behind the desk. Just as casual as you like. I thought he was looking for an ashtray. Before I even knew what had happened, Croker pulled some kind of hidden lever and Chauncey dropped through a trapdoor and landed in the pond below.

"Quicker than it took Chauncey to fall through the floor, Croker sprang from his chair and grabbed me by the hair so hard I thought he'd scalp me. He dragged me over to the trapdoor. At first I thought he meant to throw me down there with Chauncey. But no, he just wanted me to watch what happened next . . .

"That was the first time I saw Big George," Grace said, "and the last time I saw Chauncey Clyde. The first bite cut him off clean at the hips. Chauncey, he—he didn't die right away. Better that he had . . ." She shuddered at the memory.

Took a deep breath and continued.

"When the screaming finally stopped," she said, "Croker gave me a choice.

"I could go the same way as Chauncey Clyde—or . . ."

She stared at her wedding ring, bitter tears welling in her eyes.

"Some choice," I said.

"I didn't have to think too long."

She took another drag from my cigarette, blew smoke, and then looked up at me.

I didn't say anything.

"You don't believe me," she said.

I didn't know what to make of her story. Grifters getting dropped through trapdoors and fed to giant gators . . . It all sounded like something from a bad pulp book.

She didn't seem surprised, just nodded to herself.

"You will," she said. "Stay here long enough, you'll see."

And she was right.

What happened to Johnson was all the convincing I needed.

8.

Leaving Croker and his cronies to drunkenly eulogize Johnson, I made my excuses and hurried upstairs to pack a scram bag. I could still hear them downstairs, cackling and chinking glasses.

I didn't hear the door open behind me.

When Grace said, "You're leaving," I just about jumped out of my skin.

"He's crazy!" I said, like it was a secret she'd been keeping from me.

"I tried to tell you."

"You might've tried harder."

She watched as I continued packing my bag. "Where will you go?"

"Anywhere but here," I said over my shoulder.

"What about me?" she said, in a tiny cracked voice.

I paused. Turning towards her, I said, "Come with me, Grace. We'll leave tonight. As soon as he passes out. I've got enough scratch to give us a start somewhere. I'll find another place to play. The big time's out," I said, with a rueful glance at my deformed hand, "but there's always other places to play."

She was shaking her head before I even finished talking.

"He'd find me," she said. "Find *us*. He's got friends everywhere."

"Just how far is his reach?"

"Far enough."

It wasn't just the local law Croker had in his pocket, she told me; as long as he kept the liquor flowing, his gangster pals in the city would do anything to keep him happy.

"Then . . . then I don't know what else to say, Grace." I forced my eyes away from hers. "I'm sorry."

"Please," she said. "Don't go."

She put a hand on my crotch.

I inhaled a sharp breath. "Grace—"

Her hand caressed me through my pants.

"Don't . . ." I said.

Half-heartedly, I'll admit.

And the other guy—he put up no fight at all, he was putty in her hands.

"There's money," Grace said, as she slid down my zipper and took me in hand. I stifled a moan as she pressed her breasts firmly against me. Her breath was hot and heavy in my ear. "He keeps it locked in the safe behind that horrible painting on his office wall." She told me she knew the combination to the safe—the date Croker had caught Big George—she'd just never dared to do anything with what she knew. "I never had good enough reason to—until I met you," she breathed in my ear. "Darling, why run away with nothing when we could be rich?" I struggled to focus on what she was saying but it was hard for me to think about anything else apart from how much I liked her hand being where it was and what she was doing. "How rich?" I said, in a hoarse rasping voice. And then she whispered in my ear what Croker's life was worth. I didn't need telling what we'd have to do to earn it. But as her hand brought me to release, I bit her shoulder and heard myself saying *yes-yes-yes*.

* * *

In the weeks that followed, and while Johnson's carcass was picked clean by Big George, our pillow talk turned to murder. The stakes were high. It had to be perfect. If we could make it look like an accident, we'd get away clean. The seed had been planted, and from that seed grew a tree from which I saw two nooses swinging in the wind if Grace and me got it wrong; hell, considering what happened to Johnson, if we got it wrong, being hanged would be a blessing.

I started to lose my nerve, kept putting it off.

The strain began to tell on Grace; she grew sick with worry. "What are we waiting for?" she pleaded with me one night. She was sporting another fresh black eye, Croker's going-away gift before he left on another rum-run. "You let him keep beating me like this," she sobbed, "he'll kill me!"

"I'll kill him first," I said.

"When?"

"Soon, baby."

"How?"

The way she kept badgering me, I felt like blacking her other eye.

"I'm working on it, damn it!"

And then I finally figured it out.

It was Big George's feeding time, usual crowd, just a regular weekend night.

I was providing accompaniment on the piano while Croker stood out on the deck, leaning with his back against that rickety wooden rail, clutching a whimpering collie pup by the scruff of the neck as he gave the crowd his standard spiel. "I was just a young'un, fishing for channel cat with my Pap when this big bastard broadsided us, flipped our boat, flung us both in the swamp . . ."

As he leaned against the deck rail, I prayed those wooden boards would collapse against his weight, plunging him down into the pond—

That's when it hit me.

The deck rail . . .

I must've played a bum note. Croker looked at me sharply above the heads of the crowd. I grimaced an apology but it was too late, I'd ruined his act.

Without further ceremony, he tossed the pup over his shoulder.

Big George snatched it from the air with a snap of his jaws.

Even the dog-lovers gasped in awe.

Croker hauled himself away from the deck rail and started leading the crowd back inside. "Sharpen up," he warned me as he limped past the piano.

I glanced back at the deck rail, at the rickety wooden boards Croker leaned against during every show. How easy it would be to remove a screw here, a nail there . . . With a crowd of witnesses to see Croker fall to his death, Grace and me would be beyond all suspicion. The perfect murder. Forget about the money in the safe—that was pocket change—we'd be looking at a juicy fat insurance payout, even the deed to the bar. 'Course, we'd want to get rid of Big George and rename the place. 'Smitty's' had a nice ring to it. But we could have it all, live like royalty.

It would work, I told myself.

"It'll work," I told Grace, the next time we were alone.

And it would have, I'm sure of it.

We just never got the chance to put it to the test.

9.

This time, there was no calm before the storm, just another storm that knocked out the power, even the red neon gator looming over the front lot. The regular crowd stayed home to wait it out. The coochie gals got a rare night off. Candles lined the bar slab, and flickered from tables around the room. The guttering flames reflected eerily off the glass eyes of the stuffed gators on the walls. The rain belted down in a white noise roar; flashes of lightning lit up the bar like a welder's torch; thunder crashed and boomed like God was on a drunken rip-and-tear through heaven. The bar was leaking like a sieve, the floor strewn with pots and pans and spittoons to catch the rain as it bucketed down through the cracks in the ceiling. I was slouched at the piano, smoking and drinking and playing a sloppy duet with the rain as it pitter-pattered the high notes.

Since I'd figured out how to fix Croker's wagon—or rather, his deck rail—it felt like a great weight had been lifted off my shoulders. Come the weekend, Croker was due for a big surprise when he fed Big George; when *he* fed Big George.

I smiled to myself, picturing making love to Grace on a big pile of money.

Then a voice behind me said, "Give your stumps a rest, Smitty." I startled at the voice. Hadn't heard Croker emerge from his office. He'd spent most the night back there. I turned around on my stool and found him looming in front of me.

"Come n' drink with me," Croker said, gesturing to a nearby table. He was clutching a jar of hooch and two glasses and looked like he'd started without me.

I joined him at the table. A candle flickered between us, suggesting a séance.

"How's Mrs. Croker feeling?" I asked him, just as cool as you like.

Grace's nerves were still playing on her. This morning, Croker had insisted Doc Culpepper examine her. She hadn't worked the bar that night and I assumed the old quack had confined her to bed. That was fine by me. The squirrely way Grace had been acting lately, I was afraid she'd tip our mitts to Croker.

Croker seemed touched by my concern.

"Nothin' a good long rest won't fix," he said.

He filled our glasses from the mason jar. His hands were shaking. I noticed his knuckles were skinned, but thought little of it. As he poured the hooch, liquor sloshed across the table and splashed dangerously close to the candle flame.

I said, "You want I should pour?"

He wasn't careful, that damn firewater would ignite like gasoline.

But he just waved me off and raised his glass in a toast.

"Here's to you, Smitty."

He chinked my glass like a butting stag.

I knocked back my hooch in a gulp. It really was good stuff. I told him so.

He nodded and refilled our glasses. "Almost a shame, idn't?"

"What's that?"

"The recipe," he said, "that it dies with me."

I had to stifle a smile; the dumb bastard had no idea how right he was.

"I guess it doesn't have to," I said.

"It's a family recipe, Smitty. Passed down from father to son. I'm the end of my line."

"Never thought about having kids?"

"'Course I thought about it." He winked at me. "And it ain't for want of trying."

No kidding, I thought; I'd had the sleepless nights to prove it.

"Nope," he said, "I just can't have 'em. Took me four wives before I realized the problem was with my own plumbing. Looking back on it now, I almost feel a little bad for them three other wives." He raised his glass and drank to absent wives. Then he teetered to his feet, leaned unsteadily across the table to light his cigar from the candle, before collapsing back into his chair.

I suddenly realized just how drunk he was. I tried to recall the last time I'd seen him actually smoke one of his stogies. Must've been . . . the night Johnson came to The Double G.

A flash of lightning flared through the room, followed by what I thought was a rumble of thunder that shook the bar to its foundations; then the *real* thunder rumbled, sounding tiny compared to the sound the gator had made below us.

I nipped from my drink, willing my hands not to shake, telling myself to stay calm, even as my heart started tripping and I broke into an icy sweat.

Smoke wreathed Croker's head as he puffed his cigar and stared at the flickering candle. The flame glinted in his eyes like hellfire. "Not bein' able to sire me a son," he said, "that's God's punishment what I done . . ." Glancing up from the flame, he smiled at me sadly. Then, as if embarrassed by his sentiment, he hawked a great glob of phlegm into the nearest spittoon.

Clearing his throat, he said, "I ever tell you how I caught Big George?"

"Once or twice," I said, not forgetting the other hundred times.

Croker shook his head.

"Not how he took my leg," he said. "How I *caught* him."

Now that I thought about it, I didn't believe he had; nor was I sure I wanted to know.

"Gator bait," he said.

I chuckled uneasily. "Well, I kinda figured that much—"

"That's what the slavers used to call 'em."

"Called who?"

"The nigger chil'ren," he said. "Gator bait."

I pictured the painting on the wall of his office.

The money in the safe was suddenly far from my mind.

"You gotta understand how bad I wanted that gator, Smitty. I'd never wanted nothin' so bad in my life. Leastways, not until I met Grace. It was like Big George had took something from me—not just my leg, nor my daddy—something I could hardly describe, something I feared I might never get back 'less I caught him. I tried every hunting trick my daddy ever taught me, used every kinda bait I could think to use. But it was no damn good. That bastard gator confounded me at every turn. I was gettin' desperate . . .

"She was ten-years old. Kinda cute, I guess. Name of Abby Collins. 'Course I didn't know nunna that then. The fisherman don't care about the worm when he baits his hook. She was fetching home a block of ice from the store in town. That's all the searchers found of her. A length of twine in a puddle of melted block ice on the road between here and dark town where I snatched her.

"I brought her out to a nice quiet spot on the swamp I'd already staked out. No one around to hear her screams. And she was screaming plenty. Begging for her momma. I tied a rope around her waist, attached to a tire-float so she wouldn't sink; carved up her back with a razor and then tossed her on in.

"Now I knew I might have only one shot at this. I had to make her count.

"Careful as could be, I reeled her in, cast her out, in and out, her cut-up back chumming the water good n' red. The way she was kicking and screaming and bleeding, we weren't waiting long before Big George swum along . . .

"And he was real interested.

"Little Abby played her part to a tee. I was almost sorry I couldn't let her go when we got done. 'Cept I knew she'd only tattletale to the law. And well, there really wasn't much left of her. I let Big George take her feet at the ankles—just a nibble—give him a taste for the bait—then I started reeling her slowly to shore.

"Big George followed the bait like a mule being led by a carrot on a stick. When at last I finally landed him, I damn near lost my nerve. The *size* of him, Smitty!

"As he crawled ashore and came towards her—big ole grin, piece of her feet snagged in his teeth like a chunk of gristle—Little Abby's heart just plumb gave out. A mercy, y'ask me. Big George was busy wolfing down the rest of her when I dropped a sheet of tarp over his head, soaked in chloroform. You blindfold a gator, it takes about all the fight right out of him. Between that and the chloroform, I could chain his jaws shut, hogtie his legs and his tail, and then rustle him back to the bar. And *that* was no walk in the picnic, lemme tell you!"

He chuckled at the memory.

Then he looked at me with concern.

"You alright there, Smitty? Lookin' a little green there, son. You wanna refill?"

He poured me another glass. I didn't trust my shaking hands not to spill every drop. I left the glass where it was on the table.

"Over the years," Croker said, "I must've fed Big George every living thing ever walked or crawled—but there ain't *nothing* he likes more than gator bait."

I startled as another flash of lightning flared through the bar.

Managing to dredge up my voice, I started saying: "Horace—"

But he cut in with, "You call me 'Horace' again, you'll be shitting teeth."

He said it genially enough, but the words rocked me like a slap.

"Why are you telling me this?" I said. "What's going on here?"

He fished in his pocket for a fresh cigar and tossed it down on the table.

"Congratulations," he said.

I watched the cigar roll lazily towards me. "I . . . I don't understand."

Croker nodded. "Neither did I," he said, "when ole Doc Culpepper told me Grace was knocked up . . . Smoke up, Smitty. You're gonna be a daddy."

10.

Panic seized me. I glanced at the door and told myself to run. My legs refused to move. For a moment, I thought Croker must have slipped a Mickey Finn in my hooch. But no, I was just frozen in fear. Like a rat mesmerized by a snake.

Then Croker called out, "Bring my whore out here, boys!"

Rusty and Lyle emerged from the office, lugging what looked like a bloody scarecrow between them. I gasped, "Grace—" Her hair was a matted scarlet mane. A thick rope of blood dangled from her chin. Her lips were split. One of her eyes was swollen shut; the other eye was getting there. She must've seen how she looked in my expression, because she hacked out a wretched sob.

They delivered Grace to Croker. Rusty's arm was slung around her waist so she wouldn't collapse. Judging by his leering grin, he was copping a good feel while he could. In his other hand he was clutching a revolver. Lyle's pistol was tucked in the front of his waistband. I hadn't seen Lyle since I stole his job. He was unshaven, bleary-eyed, reeking like a hog; he'd clearly fallen on hard times and looked like he'd been making ends meet as a carny geek. He shouldered past me to the piano and reclaimed his stool with a satisfied sigh. "Ahhhh, it's good to be back," he said. "I always knew you was a wrong'un."

"Lyle," Croker warned him. "You start in on that I-told-you-so shit, you'll be joining him." Lyle grumbled to himself and started pecking out an off-key Funeral Waltz on the piano. Croker winced at the noise Lyle made. "I'm almost gonna miss you, Smitty."

I took a deep breath. "You know what I'm gonna miss, Croker?"

He raised his eyebrows.

"Fucking your wife in your own bed."

Quick as another lightning flash, there was a knife in Croker's hand, a Bowie with a blade the size of a machete. I flinched in my chair—my tough guy act vanishing—as he stabbed the knife down into the table. The hilt quivered to a stop. "You think you can provoke me into killin' you quick, you're wrong."

He rolled his cigar from one side of his mouth to the other. "But I'll make you a deal, Smitty . . . You cut that bait out of my whore's belly and feed it to Big George and I'll have my boys shoot you; you don't, I'll hang you from the deck rail and let him eat you from the toes on up." He shrugged extravagantly. "Can't say fairer than that, now can I?"

Behind him, Grace said: "Horace, please—"

"Whore!" Croker roared. "You'll shut your hole if you know what's good for you!"

I stared at the knife on the table before me.

Glanced up at Grace—couldn't hold her gaze—dropped my eyes to her belly.

She wasn't showing . . . Would that make it any easier?

I tore my eyes away, horrified. Christ, had I even considered it?

I found myself looking at the knife again.

"No . . ." Grace whimpered, seeing what I meant to do before I did.

Croker watched me with ghoulish curiosity. As he puffed his cigar, the coal burned red like the eyes of the devil who would greet me in hell if I did what I was thinking. "That's it," he coaxed me, " you just cut that bait on outta there . . ."

I choked down a cry of shame.

"I'm sorry, Grace . . ."

My trembling hand reached towards the knife.

"Hold her steady now, boys," Croker said to Rusty and Lyle. "She's liable to buck some." He greedily sucked his cigar, the coal glowing red-hot.

My fingers brushed the hilt of the knife—and then I jerked my hand to the side and snatched up my glass and flung the hooch into Croker's face. The coal of his cigar ignited the liquor with a violent woof and he screamed as his head burst into flames. Lurching up from his chair, beating at the flames but seeming only to fan them, Croker staggered back into Rusty and Grace. Rusty stumbled off-balance. Grace grabbed his gun hand and started wrestling him for the revolver.

As they fought for the gun, I wrenched the knife from the table and whirled towards Lyle, slashing the blade across his throat, blood erupting from the wound in a scarlet spray. I kicked him back against the piano and the sound he made when he crashed against the keys was the best he'd ever got from the instrument. The gun fell from his waistband and skittered across the floor.

As I scrambled across the room to help Grace, I saw Croker—screaming and beating at the flames, dripping fire in his wake—crash to his knees at the foot of the bar. He grabbed a spittoon and slopped the contents over his head, anointing himself in slobbery brown spit and dousing the flames. A great cloud of smoke billowed from his cindered skull. He slumped facedown to the floor.

Then a bullet whizzed inches above my head and I turned back towards Grace and Rusty. As they fought for the gun, they looked like winos ballroom dancing.

Rusty fired off wild shots that fizzed through the room. Bullets shattered bottles. Liquor flooded to the floor and ignited in the flames that Croker had dripped in his wake. The rain pissing down through the ceiling might well have been gasoline, the speed with which the fire took hold.

Clutching Rusty's gun hand, Grace raked his wrist with her nails. Rusty howled in pain as she bent back his wrist. He fired his last shot reflexively and his face was shorn away in a brilliant spray of blood and skull and teeth and brains that splattered the ceiling. The faceless man crumpled to the floor at her feet.

I dragged Grace into my arms. Not knowing where to kiss her without causing her more pain, I just held her against me as the room burned around us. I stroked her hair and whispered in her ear that never once had I truly considered cutting the child—our child—from her belly. I prayed she believed my lies.

She raised her head from my chest. "The money?"

"It can wait," I said.

Maybe not for long—the bar was burning fast—but it would have to.

Croker was still alive.

He was crawling through the smoke and fiery ash towards Lyle's gun. I let him lay a paw on the pistol before I stepped on his hand. I ground my heel and his knuckles crunched like gravel and he gave a wheezing cry. I wrenched the gun from his broken fingers and gave it to Grace. Then I kicked Croker onto his back.

His head was a smoldering chunk of barbecued meat, his ears melted nubs, his nose seared flat to his face, carved with slits I guessed were nostrils. His skull was blistered and cracked and tufted with patches of singed hair. His cigar stub was fused to his bottom lip. I guessed he didn't mind that. He was never without a damn stogie in his mouth anyway. The lids of his left eye had melted together like a fleshy pirate patch; his other eye glared at me hatefully. "I'll see you in hell," he said. Not very original, but it clearly pained him to say even that much. The flames must have burned down his gullet as he was screaming; his voice sounded as cooked as his face looked.

I nodded at him. "You be sure to save a seat for me."

Then I grabbed him by the ankles, meaning to drag him outside onto the deck. His wooden leg tore away from his thigh, and I stumbled and fell, landing heavily on my ass, clutching the limb with a look of surprise. Croker gave a bark of throaty laughter. I had to admit it was pretty damn funny. I started laughing too. Even Grace had an uneasy smile on her face. Soon we were all roaring with laughter.

Croker was still cackling—a laughter tinged with madness—even as I clubbed him with his own wooden leg, and the straps and buckles scourged his face and lacerated his hands like a cat-flail; even as I herded him outside, and he crabbed across the deck to the rail; even as I tossed his wooden leg down into the pond and Big George shattered it to sawdust with a snap of his jaws.

Then the laughter stopped and the tears started.

"Please, Smitty—I'm begging you, son—not like this."

I dragged him to his feet—his foot—leaned him back against the deck rail.

And then I gave him a good hard shove.

Croker tumbled back over the rail. The last thing I saw before I turned away was Big George rising from the pond with his maw open wide to catch his old friend. Croker had been wrong; there *was* something Big George liked more than 'gator bait' after all.

11.

The bar was an inferno.

So much for the perfect murder. We'd have to take what money we could and hope it was enough to bury us somewhere Croker's gangster pals wouldn't find us and buried us for real.

Beating back the flames with a wet tablecloth, I charged the office door with my shoulder, knocking it down off its hinges. I stumbled inside the room, catching my balance against Croker's Hot Seat. The floorboards wobbled beneath me and I remembered what Grace had told me about the trapdoor. It had seemed like something from a bad pulp book, but I wasn't taking any chances now; I scuttled off the ratty rug the chair was nailed to. Then, shouting to be heard above the roaring flames, I called to Grace to fetch a bag for the money. I tore that hateful painting off the wall and flung it aside and there was the safe. Praying Croker hadn't changed the combination—the man was arrogant enough, I didn't think he would have—I dialed it into the safe, the lock yielded with a clang, I dragged the heavy steel door open, and there was the money. All of it. And more. Croker clearly hadn't put his faith in banks.

I laughed and called to Grace, "Better make that two bags—"

And then a chain of firecrackers *pop-pop-popped* behind me. The breath was punched from my lungs and I pitched forwards with a grunt of pain. I glanced down to see the front of my shirt blooming with blood. My knees buckled and I clutched the open door of the safe before my legs collapsed beneath me. I turned and saw the smoking gun in Grace's hand. Lyle's gun. The gun I had given her.

Then my sweaty grip slid away from the safe door and I keeled towards Croker's desk and collapsed down into the recliner. Sucking for air in agonizing gasps, I tore open my shirt and tried in vain to staunch the wounds. Blood gushed through my missing fingers. My hands fell away and dropped to my lap.

My eyelids grew heavy, my head started drooping; I could feel the big sleep coming. In my weakening state, I could only watch as Grace emptied the bundles of cash from the safe and stacked them neatly inside a leather Gladstone bag. Barely able to breathe, let alone talk, I tried willing Grace to look at me, but she wouldn't. She was all business—just like her mentor, Chauncey Clyde must have taught her. She clasped the bag shut and then turned to leave the office and me for dead. I gutted down the pain, and managed to croak: "Grace . . ."

She paused at the door, turning around and looking at me with all the warmth of someone checking their shoe for dog dirt, and as we looked in each other's eyes, I'd never known an understanding like it.

"The baby?" I said, knowing the answer already.

She came towards me, resting the bag on the Hot Seat and smiling at me like *I* was the baby. She placed her hand on her belly. "Who says it's yours?"

I gave a grudging snort of admiration; blood spattered my chin.

She'd played me better than I ever played the piano.

As she turned to leave, with the last of my strength I reached down and hauled back the lever under Croker's desk—just where she'd said it was—and Grace dropped through the trapdoor with a falling dream-gasp, and landed with a splash in the pond.

For a moment, I wondered if Big George had lost his appetite.

Then the screaming started.

I sank back into the recliner, watching as tongues of fire began licking inside the office, devouring the painting I'd flung to the floor, and the bag of money Grace had left behind. As I watched the banknotes burn to cinders that swirled in fiery motes about the room, I wondered what would kill me first, the bullets or the flames; or maybe Big George would clamber up through the trapdoor and finish the job? It didn't matter. Where I was going there'd be plenty of everything: fire, teeth and pain. And who cared? Me and Grace and Croker and Big George . . . There could be nothing worse waiting for us all in hell.

STORY NOTES

DIE DOG OR EAT THE HATCHET

Every so often, I'll write something so disturbing it gives me pause. Case in point: The "fisting" scene between Dwight Ritter and the Jarvis gal . . . *Die Dog* was originally conceived as a short story with the working title *Treed*, in which a door-to-door salesman arrives at the Ritter house, where he is attacked by a dog and forced to shelter in a tree. From there his only option is to caterpillar crawl along an overhanging tree branch to the porch roof. Through a bedroom window he spies Dwight . . . shall we say, *tormenting* the Jarvis gal with a disembodied human arm. I had a vague notion that the salesman would become an unlikely hero and attempt to rescue the Jarvis gal while playing cat-and-mouse with the maniac. Little did I know what the salesman would see until he peered through that window. Given the nasty shit I write about, I suspected it would be unpleasant. But the force of the scene stopped me dead. I saw it, I smelled it; I heard the screams. (And now I've rubbed your nose in it—sorry about that . . .) Not knowing how to proceed from there—the scene didn't seem to suit the sleazy salesman hero I'd written—I shut down the computer and for the rest of the day wondered where these fucking ideas come from . . .

I was inspired to return to the story by a beat from the movie *Blue Ruin.* (Good movie, check it out.) Our hero has trapped one of the villains in the trunk of his car. Having left him there for some time, he returns to the car and, not knowing if the man is dead or alive, nervously approaches the trunk and knocks on the trunk lid—And the guy in the trunk goes batshit, starts hollering for help. Nice little jump scare. It's not a big moment in the movie, though it's nicely played. But it gave me the 'What if?' moment which brought me back to *Die Dog.* What if a car trunk captive started hollering for help at an inopportune time for the captor? At a gas station, say. While the attendant is gassing the car. And what if the gas station attendant is an even nastier piece of work than the kidnapper? This became the genesis for the scene between Hingle and Dwayne at the RITTER GAS & TOW filling station, which in turn led me back to the *Treed* setpiece. The Jarvis Gal scene remained (and remains) disturbing, but seemed to work better within the context of the kidnap-thriller involving Tilly and Hingle.

I hope the story kept you entertained. It's a pulp piece, a dark thrill ride in the mould of Richard Laymon and Jack Ketchum. Early readers told me it reads like a survival horror movie, which was the scuzzy feel I was aiming for. Other influences? There's a nod to *Psycho*—Hingle is my Marion Crane; I even attempted a little trick known as "The *Psycho* Switch" midway through the story. I liked the idea of this Ted Bundy-style serial killer finding himself at the mercy of a pair of *Texas Chainsaw*-style brothers. Poor Tilly is the meat in a maniac sandwich and must undergo a *Straw Dogs*-style transformation to survive.

I'm hugely grateful to Champion Mojo Storyteller Joe R. Lansdale for the title. "Die dog or eat the hatchet" is apparently an old nautical expression, meaning "do or die," or "needs must when the devil drives." It's a phrase I'd noticed in a lot of Lansdale's works. When I contacted Joe and asked his permission to use it here, he told me it was a phrase his dad had used—along with many other colourful expressions that have found their way into his work. So thanks, Joe. Chances are the title's better than the story!

GATOR BAIT

For some time, I'd wanted to write about little-known Texan serial killer, Joe "The Alligator Man" Ball, the Prohibition bootlegger turned bar owner who fed a bunch of gals to the pet gators he kept in the pond behind his place. Horror movie fans will be familiar with the Joe Ball story from Tobe Hooper's *Eaten Alive* (known in the UK as *Deathtrap*), the director's follow-up to *Texas Chainsaw.* Back in my screenwriting days I pitched a riff on the Joe Ball story. "*Boardwalk Empire* meets *Jaws*" was what I then had in mind. There was some resistance to a period genre film. This was hard for me to shake when I finally attempted to write a prose version. I kept trying to update the story but it wouldn't pop. I reminded myself I was writing prose fiction, and no longer bound by the same constraints as a screenwriter. So fuck it, I went back to what I had in mind. By now enough time had passed that my initial idea of "*Boardwalk Empire* meets *Jaws*" had changed. Now I saw it as a traditional hardboiled crime piece—my template was *The Postman Always Rings Twice*—with creature-feature horror elements.

What really kicked the story into gear was something I read in one of James Lee Burke's Dave Robicheaux books, a passing mention of the barbaric bayou bloodsport "coon-on-a-log." Innocent that I am, I believed this was something Mr. Burke had surely invented. A quick Google search proved otherwise . . . From this grew the scene in which poor Johnson is fed to Big George for the entertainment of Horace Croker and his cronies. This scene, I knew, would be highly racially charged, though I felt it was in keeping with what we know of the South of the time. But little did I suspect the horrific historical detail I would stumble upon as I keyword-searched my title. (I figured someone must've the title *Gator Bait* before. And sure enough, they have. I figured what the hell and used it anyway.) What I found were archive documents claiming Southern alligator hunters had used slave children as "gator bait." It's difficult to believe this was a widespread practice. That it happened even once is quite horrifying enough. But on consideration, I'm probably just being naïve . . . When I wove this detail into my plot, it gave the narrative an even greater intensity, and in Horace Croker allowed me to create a truly terrifying villain.

DAMN DIRTY APES

The North American Skunk Ape, as any hominologist will tell you, is the redneck cousin to Bigfoot and Sasquatch. Native to the swamps and sticks of the American South, offensively odorous, and aggressive towards humans, the loveable Bigfoot of *Harry and the Hendersons* fame he is not. Little is known about this reclusive hominid. Despite compelling evidence from hominologists, mainstream science would have us believe the creature doesn't even exist. As such, the skunk ape of *Damn Dirty Apes* is largely my own invention.

The inspiration for this story came from an article I read in the *Fortean Times* about legendary skunk ape hunter Gerard Hauser. (For a full account of the problems this would ultimately cause me, see the next chapter entitled: The Damn Dirty Apes Controversy.) I was indebted in my research to an entertaining book by Lyle Blackburn, *The Beast of Boggy Creek: The True Story of the Fouke Monster*. Of course, I put my own lurid spin on things . . .

I had a skit about a group of "amateur filmmakers" making a "nature documentary" in the backwoods— Ah, who am I bullshitting? Okay: They're gonzo pornographers shooting a skin flick involving a guy in a monkey suit banging a gal in a cavewoman costume. Before they get to the money shot, a randy skunk ape crashes the shoot and kidnaps the male porn star (the guy in the monkey suit) as a sex toy. This leads to a misfit posse assembling on a rescue mission to slay the skunk ape and save the porn star . . .

I ran the idea past my partner Suzie, who's the (often unwilling) royal taster for my crazy ideas. To my surprise, she liked this one, so I started writing, thinking maybe it'd make a fun companion piece to the unrelenting grimness of *Die Dog*. I had no idea it'd wind up being the longest story in the book. I envisioned the piece as an offbeat throwback to 80s action/adventure movies. So this one's chockfull of references to *Roadhouse*, *Jaws*, *The Legend of Boggy Creek*, William Friedkin's *Sorcerer*, the Brian Bosworth biker flick, *Stone Cold*—even *Scooby Doo!*

If *Damn Dirty Apes* has you yearning for more stories about humans versus hominids, you're in luck: I've written another one called *"Kid" Cooper & the Blackwood Ape-man*. A Depression era yarn in the Robert E. Howard/Joe R. Lansdale mould, it's an epic slugfest between a hobo boxer (based on the young Jack Dempsey) and the fighting pride of a backwoods lumber camp: A captive Bigfoot. You can read it in *Mythic Delirium Magazine* Issue 1.4. And depending on how readers like *Damn Dirty Apes*, I might have more Reggie Levine fiascos to tell. Like so many of my characters, the poor bastard's a magnet for trouble.

THE DAMN DIRTY APES CONTROVERSY:

ADAM HOWE
VS.
THE SOCIETY FOR THE PRESERVATION
OF THE NORTH AMERICAN SKUNK APE

Writing for the small press, without an advertising budget to promote your work, the best an up-and-coming writer can hope is that an established writer will endorse your work, that you might poach a few of their readers.

I've been very lucky. Early in my writing career, Stephen King chose my short story "Jumper" (written under the pseudonym Garrett Addams) as the winner of his international *On Writing* contest; should you wish to read that story, you can find it at the end of the Kindle edition of King's *On Writing*—but cut me some slack, I was very young when I wrote it. Since then, I've received encouraging praise from other great writers whose work I admire—enough to keep me plugging away at this writing lark.

For *Damn Dirty Apes*, an offbeat throwback to 80s action/adventure movies, I thought it might be fun to request an endorsement from a more unusual source. Little did I imagine the shitstorm that would erupt when I sent the manuscript to Mr. Lambert Pogue, General Secretary of the Society for the Preservation of the North American Skunk Ape.

Here in full is Mr. Pogue's letter to my publisher, dated 3rd September 2015:

> Sir,
>
> This morning I received among my usual correspondence a manuscript entitled *Damn Dirty Apes* by Adam Howe, with a request to provide an endorsement. Now let me say in advance, in my official capacity as General Secretary of the S.P.N.A.S.A, I am not in the habit of reading, much less of reviewing fictional works. Having read enough ill-conceived, ill-researched and illness-inducing titles exploiting the Bigfoot, Sasquatch and Skunk Ape phenomena to last a lifetime, I will politely decline, citing more pressing work commitments. Yet Howe's manuscript is so deeply offensive that I feel I must respond, frankly and fully.
>
> From a research point of view, it is clear that Howe has exerted himself no further than a cursory Google search, spicing his narrative with only the most lurid tidbits. In so doing, he serves the reader a rancid broth of gross distortions, misrepresentations and half-truths, played for shock value and scatological humor. No doubt the small print prefacing the published book will contain the usual disclaimer: *"This is a work of fiction. Any resemblance to characters living or dead is entirely coincidental."* And readers would be well advised to take these words to heart. Unfortunately for me, this advice was more difficult to apply.
>
> As I waded through Howe's nauseating pulp fiction, I became uncomfortably aware that the protagonist named as "Jameson T. Salisbury" was based on a decidedly non-fictional character. And furthermore, someone I regarded as a personal friend. There is no

doubt in my mind that "Salisbury" is a thinly disguised, grotesque caricature of the late Gerard Hauser, author of the seminal work *Among the Skunk Apes of the North American South: One Man's Journey of Self-Discovery* (Pine Marten Press, 1972, sadly long out of print).

I daresay only a handful of people are alive today who remember the hermetic Hauser well enough to take offense at the injustice Howe does to the man. To the best of my knowledge, he left no next-of-kin to defend his reputation, much less to pursue litigation. So it seems that apart from my own modest protest, Howe's slanderous portrayal will remain unchallenged.

For those unaware, it is due to Hauser's lifelong study of the North American Skunk Ape, that the majority of our knowledge about this reclusive hominid derives. Taken as a whole, the decades of self-sacrifice in Hauser's pioneering field research comprises a huge debt to which all of us in the field owe him.

Yes, there were controversies that dogged the man. It hardly bears repeating the allegations made by young female campers who reported Hauser for voyeurism and public indecency; embarrassing episodes Hauser claimed to his dying breath were simple misunderstandings. And yes, the unanswered questions surrounding Hauser's final expedition, in which an amateur cryptozoologist tragically lost his life when he stepped into a hominid-snare, are difficult for even his staunchest supporters to defend. But these are, in the main, anomalies that can be excused as the enthusiasm of a field researcher with no formal training. (In the latter case, it should also be noted that the authorities cleared Hauser of any criminal wrongdoing, a fact many of the man's critics so conveniently forget!) Hauser's shortcomings and eccentricities pale in comparison to the sheer volume of data he left to us—physical evidence, photographs, and compiled eyewitness testimonies; a life's work spanning decades.

Until Hauser's premature death in 1982, he and I exchanged semi-regular correspondence. I met him personally only once, when he was scheduled to lecture at the annual hominology convention in Atlanta, Georgia. I found him to be considerate, courteous, lucid, and well balanced. In Howe's repellent pulp fiction, Hauser is lampooned as an unhinged and callous misfit, who thinks nothing of endangering others in the obsessive pursuit of his cause. He bears little resemblance to the kind and gentle man I felt privileged to call my friend.

I cannot, in all good conscience, endorse this work. Moreover, I call on all hominologists, whether in the Bigfoot, Sasquatch or Skunk Ape fields, to put aside our differences and unite in a boycott of this disgraceful book. Quite apart from Howe's literary shortcomings, which will quickly become apparent to the unsuspecting reader, the author's attack on Hauser's integrity is the action of a cynical coward seeking profit by besmirching the reputation of a man no longer alive to defend himself. Furthermore, I wish it to be known I am prepared to render my fullest assistance to any parties pursuing legal action against Howe and his publisher for the injustice done to Gerard Hauser.

Sincerely,
Lambert Pogue, General Secretary S.P.N.A.S.A.
Clawson, Ohio

This was just the beginning. Mr. Pogue proceeded to make good on his threat to boycott the book. Rallying a small army of hominologists, they besieged the Comet Press Facebook page with angry calls for my head. Such was the furor, I genuinely believed *Damn Dirty Apes* would never see print, and I am enormously grateful to Cheryl Mullenax at Comet Press for weathering the storm and sticking by me.

In my defense, the character of Jameson T. Salisbury was written as an affectionate (if mischievous) tribute to the late Gerard Hauser. What little I know about Hauser—and indeed, very little is known—I gleaned from an article in the *Fortean Times* relating to Hauser's doomed final expedition in the Arkansan backwoods. Hauser struck me as exactly the kind of colorful character I enjoy writing about, a real-life Quint from *Jaws*. *Damn Dirty Apes* was written as a light-hearted romp, no more or less. I had no intention of maligning Hauser's reputation and I deeply regret any offence I may have caused.

Fortunately, I was able to placate Mr. Pogue with an apology, and a modest donation to the S.P.N.A.S.A. He lifted his embargo, and even kindly provided the somewhat terse disclaimer that precedes the story. Mr. Pogue would like me to stress that this should be in no way read as an endorsement, and advises any serious student of hominology that their time would be better served reading S.P.N.A.S.A. approved non-fiction.

Lesson learned, and in future I'll stick to asking other writers for blurb.

ABOUT THE AUTHOR

Adam Howe is a British writer of fiction and screenplays. He lives in Greater London with his partner and their hellhound, Gino. Writing as Garrett Addams, his short story "Jumper"* was chosen by Stephen King as the winner of the *On Writing* contest, and published in the paperback and eBook editions of King's book. His fiction has appeared in places like *Nightmare Magazine, Thuglit, Horror Library 5*, and *Plan B Magazine*. His first book, *Black Cat Mojo,* is available now from Comet Press. He is currently working on his first novel, *One Tough Bastard*. Tweet him @Adam_G_Howe.

* "Raw, punky, and genuinely surprising." —Stephen King on "Jumper"

COMETPRESS
www.cometpress.us
facebook.com/cometpress
twitter.com/cometpress

PUBLISHING THE VERY BEST OF HORROR AND DARK CRIME SINCE 2008

"With sharp writing and a crisp design to match, the anthology makes a strong case for 2009's best . . . the small-press label has distinguished itself as a reliable name brand. Pick it up, if you've got the balls." ***—Bookgasm* (on *The Death Panel*)**

"So if you're looking for something a little different to read in your horror fiction, a book with stories that are edgy and cool as all hell, then pick up *The Death Panel*, and then be prepared to be blown away by some of the best genre short story fiction written in the last few years. Yes, this book is that good." ***—Horror World***

"God Bless Comet Press for giving us great collections of wonderful NEW ideas. What a revelation." ***—Toxic Graveyard***

". . . this novel is every bit a winner. Chandler introduces PI Joe Dall in a slick, atmospheric work that captures the underbelly of the 1950s with a sharp eye for detail and a flair for the sinister. The Deep South, voodoo, bad cops, a depraved movie star, and a glamorous, gun-toting sidekick—all add their share of pulpy ambience in this first-rate debut." ***—Booklist* (on *Dime Detective*)**

"She (Barbie Wilde) has developed a remarkable flair for the perverse and the poetic that echoes her mentor Clive Barker, but offers tales of inner hell and body terror told from a ferociously feminine point of view." **—Chris Alexander, Editor-in-Chief *Fangoria* (on *The Venus Complex*)**

CHECK OUT ALL OUR TITLES AT WWW.COMETPRESS.US

CHECK OUT ALL OUR TITLES AT WWW.COMETPRESS.US

CHECK OUT ALL OUR TITLES AT WWW.COMETPRESS.US

Lightning Source UK Ltd.
Milton Keynes UK
UKHW02f2028260618
324833UK00018B/808/P

9 781936 964253